*Dedicated to the memory of my cousin,*
*Flying Officer Gordon Ernest Malbon Parker RAF,*
*killed in action over Hanover in*
*September 1943, aged 22.*

a&b

# THE GIRL
## *at the*
# FARMHOUSE GATE

## JULIA STONEHAM

Allison & Busby Limited
13 Charlotte Mews
London W1T 4EJ
*www.allisonandbusby.com*

Hardcover published in Great Britain in 2009.
This paperback edition published in 2010.

13-ISBN 978-0-7490-0813-0

Typeset in 11/16.5 pt Sabon by
Allison & Busby Ltd.

The paper used for this Allison & Busby publication
has been produced from trees that have been legally sourced
from well-managed and credibly certified forests.

Printed and bound in the UK by
CPI Bookmarque, Croydon, CR0 4TD

# Chapter One

The small, overworked bathroom was, even on this cold February morning, warm and faintly perfumed by the cheap scents of the soaps and shampoos favoured by the ten land girls who shared its claw-footed bath, washed their smalls and shampooed their hair in its tiny washbasin and sat on the Edwardian wooden seat of the WC whose worn brass chain connected it to a noisy cistern, way overhead.

Alice Todd lay in the hot water, relishing the one event in her crowded day which provided the closest thing to relaxation and even luxury available to her since twelve months ago, when she had become warden of the Land Army hostel that was housed at Lower Post Stone Farm.

During the first, chaotic days following her arrival, Alice had discovered that the early mornings – when the girls were gone and the only sound in the solid old building was a distant clatter from the scullery where Rose Crocker, the cowman's widow, was washing up the breakfast dishes – belonged to her. The empty bathroom was hers as were the contents of the tank of wonderfully hot water.

By late afternoon, when the land girls came roaring back from the fields, hungry, cold, muddy and irritable, the pressure on the bathroom was extreme. The altercations which arose over whose turn it was to use it, how much water was allowed and how long was too long to spend in possession of each meagre tubful, erupted on a regular basis and had been known to come close to violence. Frequently as many as three girls used the same bathwater, climbing in and out, one after the other, while steam drifted and the pipes spluttered and gurgled as the range in the kitchen below struggled and failed to meet the demand for hot water which the girls imposed on it. But in the mornings, when the girls were absent, the plumbing silent and the water hot, Alice would fetch her sponge bag and her towel, make her way from her bed-sitting room, through the empty recreation room, climb one or other of the narrow staircases that led to the upper floor and take possession of the bathroom.

Her mind, while she lay, for the ten minutes or so which she allowed herself, in the warm, soapy water, seldom wandered as far as any contemplation of the situation in which the breakdown of her marriage had placed her. Instead, her responsibilities as hostel warden dominated her thoughts. She would find herself checking, almost unconsciously, the supplies in her pantry, visualising the rows of labelled tins, the bins of dried peas and lentils, sacks of potatoes, turnips or swedes, the packets of porridge oats, pudding rice, flour and sugar. Occasionally her mind would stray towards more personal concerns. Did she, for instance, need to order any items of school uniform for Edward John, her ten-year-old son? Had she replied to her solicitor's most recent letter regarding the divorce proceedings? But, mostly, she pondered on how best to utilise the small amount of fresh meat the butcher would deliver that day. Then she would get to her feet and with the warm water running from her skin, remove the plug, wrap herself in her towel and step down onto a bath mat which was unpleasantly clammy after its heavy use on the previous evening.

Pale sunlight, thin with February cold, was this morning illuminating the bathroom through a low window, frosted by condensation. Alice cleared the steamy mirror above the basin and peered at her reflection.

Sometimes, particularly since her arrival at the farm,

it had seemed strange to Alice that despite the huge changes that had taken place in her life, her reflection so closely resembled the woman she had been before the progress of the war had so radically altered it. Her marriage had failed. Another woman had taken possession of her husband. Her home in Twickenham remained deserted and boarded-up since a German bomb had struck the leafy, suburban street in which it stood. Her son was at boarding school, spending only his weekends and holidays on the farm, where he shared his mother's attention with the diverse group of young women for whom she found herself largely responsible.

Alice contemplated the oval face reflected in the misted mirror. The grey eyes were steady, the brows fine, the mouth good-tempered and the dark blonde hair, piled onto the top of her head, was luxuriant. Despite the loss of home and husband, the months of unremitting hard work, the pressure of responsibility and the various crises that had punctuated her time at the farm, she was still, recognisably – and slightly surprisingly – herself. Somehow she had survived it all, and perhaps by following the predictable but sound advice of the indomitable Rose Crocker – 'Just take things one day at a time, my dear' – she would, she realised, continue to survive for as long as she had to.

At first Alice's task as warden, work for which

she was neither qualified nor temperamentally suited, had overwhelmed her. She struggled to fulfil the huge demands made on her and often came close to giving up and retreating back to the rented room in Exeter which had housed her and Edward John after the London bombing had left them homeless, and where her husband had arrived suddenly, one evening, and told her that their marriage was over. But, needing to provide an income for herself and safety for her son, she had squared her shoulders and struggled on.

It had been obvious to Alice that, initially, her employer Roger Bayliss, the farm's owner, had little or no confidence in her. The Land Army Registrar, too, had doubted her suitability as warden and only appointed her in the absence of anyone more able.

The farmhouse, which had stood empty for years and would, in any other circumstances, have been declared unsuitable for human habitation, was more or less derelict when Roger Bayliss, having lost most of his able-bodied farmhands to the war, had been obliged to utilise it as a billet for the ten young women who were to replace them. A lick of paint and a few partitioned bedrooms on the upper floor had hardly transformed it. Years of neglect and a dozen harsh Devonian winters had left the building so cold and damp that months had passed before constant fires followed by summer weather had made any impression on it.

Although Alice was largely unaware of it, her year as warden at Lower Post Stone Farm had changed her. She had grown stronger and more assertive. No longer simply a submissive, dependent wife, her association with her land girls and her increasing familiarity with their circumstances, some of which had astonished and even shocked her, had broadened her mind and extended her sensitivity. She was protective of them and without being conscious of it, had won their respect and their loyalty. Even her domestic assistant, the sharp-tongued Rose, initially her harshest critic, had been won over and had become a staunch ally.

The lack of confidence, which in her early weeks on the farm had coloured her employer's opinion of her, had developed, without her being aware of it, into an undeclared regard, now bordering on stronger feelings which, possibly, even he did not fully recognise.

Back in her room, Alice had dressed, quickly pulling on the slacks, silk shirt and thick sweater that kept her warm in the draughty farmhouse. She brushed her hair, coiled it onto the nape of her neck and was working a trace of lipstick onto her mouth when Rose's penetrating Devonian voice reached her.

'The boss be 'ere!' she called, 'Rabbits, he's brung. And daffs! Bain't your birthday, be it?' Alice said it wasn't and went to open the door.

Roger Bayliss had ridden down from the higher farm, dismounted, hooked his horse's reigns over the gate post and was approaching the front door of the farmhouse. From one hand three recently snared rabbits swung. In the other he held a bunch of daffodil buds, the tightly furled petals still more green than gold. He stood, his head slightly inclined to avoid contact with the warped oak lintel, a self-conscious smile on his usually grave face.

He was a tall man whose general bearing was slightly at odds with the broad shoulders and well-shaped, leonine head. There was something withdrawn, almost joyless, about him which had always puzzled Alice. She thought his years of widowhood might be its cause, or, more recently, the near-tragedy that had befallen his son.

Christopher, a pilot in Fighter Command, had, a few months after Alice's arrival at the farms, suffered a spectacular breakdown and been discharged from the service. After some time confined in a military psychiatric hospital he had retreated, alone, to manage his father's neglected woodlands, which lay on rising ground between the Post Stone farms and the moor. Roger's reaction to this had baffled Alice, who had expected him to show a fatherly concern for his son's welfare but had instead seen nothing more than a reluctance to involve himself in it.

Alone at Higher Post Stone Farm and preoccupied by the demands the war put on the running of his farms, Roger had possibly been unaware of the depth or extent of his solitude until Alice's arrival. At first he had regarded her as an incompetent liability and considered that her middle-class background contributed to her unsuitability for the role which her unfortunate circumstances had forced on her. After living for so long alone with his own growing son, his contact with women had, for many years, been restricted to giving instructions to his housekeeper and to the aging wives of the few men who remained on the farm and who occupied his labourers' cottages. He was used to being respected and obeyed but had forgotten how charming the company of an attractive, educated woman could be.

'Happy anniversary!' he announced and when Alice smiled blankly, added, 'It's twelve months to the day since you arrived here! And to be honest, Alice, I didn't think you'd last twelve hours!'

'Neither did I! But to everyone's surprise I did!'

'You certainly did!' He held the daffodils out to her. 'Wild ones,' he said, 'from the orchard.' She thanked him, accepted the flowers and invited him into the kitchen where Rose, who had already poured their cups of morning tea, took the rabbits from him, laid them on the marble working surface at one end of the kitchen and prepared to skin them.

During the early months of her presence at Lower Post Stone, Roger and Alice had met only occasionally and usually in connection with the running of the hostel or to deal with some personal problem encountered by one or other of the land girls. These meetings between them had initially been formal and slightly stiff. But, as time passed, their association had developed into an amicable working partnership. Roger began inviting Alice out for an evening drink or to modest social events hosted by neighbouring landowners. Their relationship had, as far as Alice's perception of it went, remained platonic and almost professional – a state of affairs which Rose, her sharp eyes and ears tuned to catch any hint of gossip, could neither comprehend nor accept. Now, on the morning of the anniversary of Alice's arrival at the farms, when Roger asked her to celebrate the occasion by having dinner with him, Alice was amused to catch Rose's sharp eyes on her as she smilingly accepted his invitation.

Later, with Roger gone and Rose sweeping the bedrooms, Alice stood at the scullery sink and began to peel vegetables for the rabbit stew. The familiar, monotonous task freed her mind and she smiled ruefully at the fact that she had been so deeply immersed in her responsibilities as warden that an entire year of her life had slipped by, almost without her being conscious of its passing.

Over those twelve months the inmates of the hostel had come and gone. Some of the girls, whose stay had, for one reason or another, been brief, Alice had forgotten. One had left after a few weeks because her mother had died and she was needed at home to care for her young siblings. Another, a newly-wed, had discovered that she was pregnant and, in accordance with Land Army regulations, had been forced to resign, and one had left the service to become a ferry pilot with the RAF Air Transport Auxiliary. But the others, who had arrived at the farm during the same, freezing February week as Alice, were almost like a family now.

There would, without doubt, be more girls coming and going this year. More squabbling over bathwater and bedrooms. Irritations and jealousies would erupt, often involving the sulky, critical Gwennan Pringle, the oldest of the group, whose spiteful, Welsh tongue and ceaseless, sulky sanctimony provoked regular outbursts from everyone except sweet-natured Hester, whose ability to forgive stemmed from a strictly religious upbringing at the hands of her preacher father. Mousy Hester, who had arrived, dressed in dark colours and black stockings, convinced that the inhabitants of the hostel were conspiring to lead her into temptation but who had, as the months passed, responded to their influence and then fallen in love with a young GI, whose innocence matched her own. Her family had refused to sanction the engagement and had rejected her. But on a snowy January day, only a few weeks previously, Hester, without their blessing, had married her Reuben at the barracks where he was stationed, after which he had been sent off to train for the invasion of France, practising war on a South Devon beach.

'Fancy Mr Bayliss bringin' flowers!' Rose exclaimed when, dustpan in hand, she rejoined Alice in the kitchen.

'Nice of him, wasn't it?' the warden said lightly, dumping potato peelings into the pig bin. 'We'll put them in the recreation room where the girls can enjoy them.'

'They bain't for the girls, Alice!' Rose teased. 'They'm for you and you knows it! A married woman too! Ought to be ashamed!'

Rose missed nothing. She was shrewd, sharp-tongued, inquisitive and, if it suited her, protective. When the two women had been thrown together, Alice as warden and Rose as her domestic help, Rose had at first been spiteful. She saw only the warden's obvious lack of confidence in her ability to carry out her work and resented what she perceived as Alice's unjustified authority. Then she had watched as the warden struggled with her situation, overcoming her initial panic and vulnerability, turning her determination to survive into strengths and then skills. Gradually, as Alice had established respect from the land girls, their employer and the farm hands, she had won Rose's unconditional support. She had flushed with pleasure when, after only a few weeks, the warden had put the relationship on Christian-name terms. 'Alice,' she had breathed to herself. 'I am to call her Alice!'

Alice had put the daffodils into a china jug and set it in the centre of the large, scrubbed pine table where the buds soon responded to the warmth of the kitchen. By five o'clock, when the lorry delivered the land girls back to the hostel, they were already unfurling.

Before the girls were allowed into the building they were expected to remove their boots and, if the weather was wet, their waterproofs. Often these were so caked with mud that Rose would insist on the girls taking them into the yard and sousing them under the pump before they could be hung, in a dripping row, under the porch. Damp dungarees, sweaters and even socks would be hoisted up above the kitchen range, where they would steam and then dry, ready for the next morning.

Today, half an hour after they arrived home, some of them already bathed and all of them at least warm and dry, the girls clustered round the kitchen table where Alice and Rose were doling out stewed rabbit, mashed potato and carrots.

The two close friends, Marion and Winnie, both Northerners, had over the months observed Alice's table manners. To begin with they had dismissed them as 'posh' but after a while they adopted them and now, when they had finished eating, placed their knives next to their forks and no longer pushed away their empty plates.

'Your roots is showin', Marion.' Winnie, with her mouth full, eyed the dark parting through her friend's bleached hair. 'I'll have a go at 'em after, if you want. That's if there's any peroxide left.' Marion did want and was sure there was at least half a bottle of peroxide, which, she said, would be more than enough.

Marion's ambition, when it came to her appearance, was a simple one. She wished to be – in fact she needed to be – glamorous. Her hair must be as blindingly blonde as Jean Harlow's, her lashes as thick and dark as Jane Russell's, her stomach flat, her breasts voluptuous, her fingernails long, curved and crimson. Since joining the Land Army she had been forced to rethink the fingernails but, as a result of an hour or so of hard work, when she was bathed, foundation creamed, eyelashed, powdered, corseted and perfumed and ready to respond to the hooted horn of the army staff car that had arrived at the farm to collect her and Winnie for a night out, Marion would have transformed herself from a plain, scrawny bottle-blonde, with features that were too sharp, eyes that were too small, lips that were too thin and skin that was too coarse, into a being, scented with Californian Poppy, who, in the subdued light of a public bar, a dance hall, or the back row in a cinema, would pass as beautiful. Knowing she had achieved this gave Marion an assurance which captivated and held the male attention she craved. She would be the life and soul of every party, the loudest voice in a sing-song, the leader of the conga. She jitterbugged and Lambeth-Walked longer and faster than anyone, and when she kissed a bloke, he stayed kissed. Winnie, on the other hand, was basically pretty. It required very little time for her to reach the standard of readiness for a night out which it had taken Marion hours to achieve. Her naturally blonde hair may not have been as brilliant as her friend's but it was lustrous and heavy, curling prettily round her winsome face. Men liked her smile. Marion may have been their first choice but with Winnie they could relax. She would happily spend an entire evening with one young man or another without him feeling threatened, as Marion's conquests would often be, by uniformed rivals, who pulled rank and challenged for her favours.

'You'll ruin your 'air, you will!' Gwennan's comment, as usual, was a negative one. 'Girls as carry on like you do, bleachin' and dyeing and that, are bald by forty! I read it in the paper!'

The land girls, their rice pudding bowls scraped clean, were preparing to leave the table when Rose, not to be outdone by her employer's attention to the warden's anniversary, emerged from the pantry bearing a sponge cake, decorated with Devonshire cream dotted with strawberry jam. The girls responded enthusiastically to the treat.

'Is it somebody's birthday?' they chorused.

'Whose?' several demanded.

'Nobody's,' Rose announced. 'But 'tis an anniversary just the same! Alice...Mrs Todd to you...'as been 'ere at Lower Post Stone Farm for a whole year!'

'Never!'

'We all have, Mrs Crocker!'

'True,' Rose grudgingly admitted, 'but 'tis Mrs Todd's cake all the same!'

'Twelve months, already!' someone sighed.

'Time flies when you're enjoying yourself,' Gwennan murmured, dolefully examining the line of new blisters across her palm, caused by three days of hoeing between rows of brassicas.

'Cut the cake, Mrs Todd!'

'Go on!'

'Make a wish, Mrs Todd!' Alice took the knife from Annie, the vivacious young Jewess who was smiling up at her.

'What shall I wish for?' Alice asked them.

'For a week's leave for my Reuben,' Hester suggested, her Devonian accent matching Rose's. 'So us can honeymoon proper!'

'For someone to put a bullet through Adolf Hitler, so we can all go 'ome!'

'For that gorgeous GI I met last Sat'd'y to make an honest woman of me and ship me off to the States!'

Alice expertly divided the cake into eleven equal portions. There were eight girls in residence. Then there was Rose, Alice herself and Edward John who, as usual on a Friday evening, had arrived from his boarding school for the weekend. She did not make a wish except in a general way, for the well-being and happiness of all of them.

It was on the evening of that day that the war, which had brought about the situation in which she and her charges found themselves, intruded in a violent and distressing way upon it. This was something that had happened on several occasions over the past year, when the quiet, pastoral routine of the higher and lower farms had been disrupted by disasters which always seemed to take their occupants unawares.

The Post Stone girls were, of course, always conscious of the war, which was rumbling on, far away, in Italy, Greece, Russia, North Africa, in the skies over England and at sea, where the North Atlantic convoys and their Royal Naval escorts were constantly under attack from German U-boats, but the details of the various theatres of operation and the outcome of specific battles mostly escaped them.

Letters from men on active service were heavily censored and when home on leave, boyfriends and brothers had better things to do than talk about the war.

Alice kept herself informed of the war's progress by listening, when time permitted, to the regular bulletins broadcast by the BBC. She sometimes discussed the news with Roger Bayliss and occasionally with Margery Brewster, who, as village registrar for the Women's Land Army, was responsible for Lower Post Stone and a number of neighbouring hostels. But Alice's girls were, most of them, fully occupied by the struggle to survive their punishing workload, to keep as warm and dry as they could and, on Saturdays, to make themselves as attractive as possible for a weekly outing, when they hitched a ride to Exeter and went to the flicks or a dance, or, if they were lucky, both.

And so it was that on the night of Alice's anniversary, they were again pulled up short and shocked by what happened.

When they recalled it, during the hours, days, even weeks, that followed, no one was ever quite certain who had been the first to hear the weird howling sound as a burning aircraft approached, fast, through the darkness and roared, low, over the farmhouse and its cluster of barns. Trailing smoke and flames, it dropped briefly out of sight before smashing into the stand of elms at the far end of the five-acre paddock, less than a mile from the building in which nine women and one ten-year-old boy listened, transfixed.

Edward John, engrossed in the latest Biggles book, was already in his bed, which stood at one end of the large downstairs room designated as his mother's bed-sitting room. Rose, the scullery tidy after the meal and the kitchen table set ready for breakfast, had crossed the yard to her cottage and was just about to prepare her bedtime cup of Ovaltine when she remembered she had washing on her line. Scolding herself because the night air would have dampened it, she went out into the total darkness of her back garden to fetch it.

It was then that she heard it and almost instantly saw it. What she heard, and what everyone at the farm became simultaneously aware of seconds later, was a sound like an express train approaching at speed – or a hurricane – or a tidal wave. Everyone had subsequently described it differently but all of them agreed that it was the most terrifying sound they had ever heard.

In the hostel bathroom the bottle of peroxide was almost empty and Marion's hair was standing in pungent tufts as Winnie worked the pad of saturated cotton wool, back and forth across her friend's skull. Both girls heard the noise and reached the window as whatever it was skimmed the farmhouse roof, grazing the ridge tiles of the barn and spraying burning fuel into the darkness. Gwennan, clad in flannelette pyjamas, curlers dangling from her thin hair, stood aghast at her bedroom window and later described what she saw as looking like an enormous sky-rocket.

It was Annie, from the small window in her room above the porch, who distinctly saw the dark shape of the plane as it dropped below the outline of the barns. Seconds later, they all heard the shuddering thump and tearing of metal as it ploughed into the trees. Alice and Roger, returning to the lower farm in Roger's car, had simultaneously glimpsed, from the lane, the astonishing sight of a plane just clearing the farm roofs before plunging into the ground.

The Dakota had been on a routine exercise with three others. It had dropped its group of trainee parachutists in the designated area some miles west of Bridgewater and all of them had been safely recovered. It was when the three planes turned and headed away from the drop-site that there had been an explosion in the engine of one of them.

As the stricken aircraft began to lose height, the pilot banked, making for the small airstrip at Dunkerswell. He ordered his crew to bale out, intending to follow them once he was certain that if he failed to reach the airstrip he could put his plane on a course that would ensure a crash-landing in open country.

High ground above the Post Stone farms, known locally as The Tops, loomed ahead of him. The altimeter read six hundred feet and the pilot knew that to deploy his parachute effectively he must jump before he lost any more height. It was at that moment that he saw, between him and the rising ground, the solid outline of a farmhouse and the cluster of barns surrounding it. He forced the stick back, managed to gain fifty feet and then, as he narrowly cleared the buildings, felt the aircraft judder and stall. Seconds later, as it began to drop, he hauled himself away from the controls and leapt clear of the plane, pulling his rip cord as the slipstream took him and spun him, the ground looming rapidly towards him, the useless 'chute barely inflated behind him.

Most of the land girls who were already prepared for bed had pulled sweaters and jackets on over their nightdresses, run down the stairs, shoved their bare feet into the first pair of boots that came to hand, elbowed their way along the cross-passage and pushed out through the porch. Roger, his car lurching from one pothole to the next, wrenched on his handbrake as the girls streamed out of the building, clutching at each other for support as they negotiated the slippery cobbles. Alice, grabbing a pair of rubber boots from the porch, ordered her son, who, his dressing gown over his pyjamas, was heading after the girls, to stop at once and wait for her.

Rounding the barns, the girls emerged into the field that lay between them and the blazing plane and stumbled forward, increasingly dazzled by the glare of the flames. Edward John kept pace with them until his mother grabbed him by the hand and slowed him. Gwennan, her curlers bouncing as she ran, pulled at Alice's sleeve.

'Don't go too near, Mrs Todd!' she gasped breathlessly, stumbling over the uneven ground, her gaunt face lit eerily by the fire, her sing-song Welsh voice thin with alarm. 'They could be Jerries for all we know!'

The impact had split the plane into two. Fire engulfed the fuselage but the cockpit section, several yards from it, was intact and was not burning.

Roger Bayliss had used the yard telephone to summon the air raid warden on duty that night in Ledburton village and then hurried through the stumbling girls. Moving ahead of them, he stopped, spread his arms and forbade them to go closer to the wreckage.

Annie Sorokova, her dark hair loose and streaming, the flames of the burning plane reflected in her wide eyes, was reminded of the nights in the East End before she had been old enough to join the Land Army. The London Blitz had been at its height and every night the area around the docks, where the Sorokova family had lived since their arrival from Poland in the 1920s, had been set ablaze, the air shuddering as warehouses and factories disintegrated, crumpling into gritty dust as the shock waves rolled along the streets.

Each morning there had been more gaps in the reeling rows of terrace houses in Duckett Street, more doors and windows smashed in or blown out. There had been empty desks in the schools, shops that didn't open for business-as-usual because their keepers were dead or dying under piles of rubble. Annie stopped and stood, choking on country air that was now fouled by the stench of aviation fuel and burning rubber.

'There's no one in the cockpit!' Marion's sharp North-Country voice rose above the noise of the fire. The towel had slipped off the bleached corkscrews of her hair, giving her, in the light of the flames, the appearance of Medusa.

'Thank the Lord!' Rose gasped, arriving breathlessly, her apron spattered with mud.

'There were parachutes!' Winnie shouted. Several of the girls had seen the 'chutes drifting silently down and being carried eastwards by a rising westerly breeze.

The ARP warden, his tin hat slightly askew, wobbled across the field on his bicycle, looked round anxiously for something against which to lean it and, finding nothing, laid it carefully on the ground. This was by far the most serious incident he had been called upon to attend. Dry-mouthed, he struggled to remember the procedure he had been taught on the Air Raid Wardens' Induction Course. The sight of half a dozen wide-eyed, scantily dressed young women, clutching at dressing gowns below which flimsy nightdresses were fluttering incongruously in the wind, confused him, but supported by Roger Bayliss, he began moving them back, out of range of possible explosions.

The plane's markings, just visible as the flames blistered the twisted metal, confirmed that it was 'one of ours' and there did not appear to be any casualties scattered on the ground.

'There wasn't no one inside the burning part, Mr Bayliss, sir!' Gwennan informed her boss, irritably shrugging off the ARP warden's hand when he tried to move her further from the wreckage and adding spitefully, 'Don't you pull at me, mister! I've already gone over once on my bad ankle!'

Reassured that no airmen had been visible, trapped and possibly dying inside the shattered fuselage before it was engulfed by flames, and given the fact that parachutes had been seen before the moment of impact, it was assumed that no lives had been lost and the mood of the onlookers lifted. They clustered, shivering with a pleasurable sense of guilty excitement as the heat of the fire began to reach them.

Soon the first of several military vehicles lurched onto the scene and it was confirmed that a training parachute-drop had been successfully completed before the mishap. With this news the atmosphere became positively jovial and when Marion and Winnie recognised several acquaintances amongst the attending servicemen, a robust banter began.

Roger Bayliss suggested to Alice that it was inappropriate for the girls, most of whom were in their nightclothes, to be engaging the servicemen in small talk, in a field, at what was now past ten o'clock at night, so Alice, despite being labelled a spoilsport, rounded up her charges and with Rose beside her, walked behind them as they picked their way across the wet grass towards the farm, stumbling over tussocks and molehills and protesting sulkily at being packed off, back to the hostel, when there was a good time to be had at the scene of the plane crash.

It was Hester who spotted the pale, undulating shape in the far corner of the field. She stopped in her tracks, clutched at Annie and pointed.

'Look, Annie! Be that a ghost?' Annie peered through the darkness.

'More like a parachute!' she said. 'Come on!' and she started to move off towards the white object which, by then, had caught the attention of the rest of the girls, who changed direction and began loping and stumbling towards it, laughing, tripping and staggering as they crossed the uneven ground.

Parachutes were made of silk. You could make them into cami-knickers, nighties and petticoats. Even wedding dresses. This one would probably already be snagged on brambles. Perhaps torn. But yards of it would be salvagable. They would fight over it and argue about who should have the best bits.

They reached an area of the field which had, earlier that day, been ploughed, making the going even more difficult, their boots sinking into the soft loam, slowing their progress. Marion and Winnie thrust their way into the lead and were the first to arrive at the rippling, translucent mass. Squealing with excitement they lunged for it, and were gathering the silky folds into their arms by the time Annie, Hester and Gwennan joined them, Alice close behind them with Rose a few breathless yards in her wake.

The cords, anchoring the billowing 'chute to the ground, ran off, upwind. Alice, who had maintained a firm grip on Edward John's hand, released him and he followed the cords to the place, twelve yards away, where they appeared to be imbedded in the earth. Suddenly he was back at his mother's side, pulling at her sleeve.

'There's someone there!' he shouted shrilly, pointing into the darkness beyond the mound of white silk. 'There's someone in the ground!'

The pilot's body was barely visible. He lay, face down, imbedded in the newly ploughed soil, which had absorbed much of the impact. But as he was lifted out of the earth and laid carefully on his back, it was obvious to the watching land girls that he was dead.

'It'd be comical if it wasn't so awful,' Annie sighed later, looking round at the woeful faces of her fellows. They had returned to the farmhouse. Rose had heated a pan of milk and made cocoa. They had carried their mugs of it into the recreation room where Marion, her bleached hair now dried into stiff ringlets, had thrown some kindling onto the dying fire. They had all been sitting, sipping, watching in a shocked silence the quiet, domesticated flames when Annie had spoken. Gwennan turned on her sharply, her clipped words cutting the air.

'Comical? What d'you mean comical? There's nothing comical about it! An airman's dead! I don't call that funny, Annie Sorokova, and nor should you!'

'I don't mean "funny", Taff. Not him dying. It's just...well, whenever anything awful happens, we always end up in 'ere, don't we? Sittin' like this... round the fire...no one saying nothin'. Drinkin' cocoa. That's all I meant, Taff. Most of the time when there's bad news we just get on with things, don't we? Keep "smiling through" like we're s'posed to. But every so often, something 'orrible 'appens and 'ere we are...

sort of...sort of admitting that the war *is* goin' on out there and people *are* dyin' and...' There was a pause. A log shifted in the hearth and sent a scatter of sparks up the chimney.

'Them RAF blokes reckon it were the pilot we found,' Winnie murmured.

''E should of baled out sooner,' Marion added knowledgeably.

'They said 'e would of bin trying not to hit the farmhouse.' Hester's words were almost inaudible. 'What 'e done prob'ly saved our lives.'

The silence that followed her words was broken by the sound of a vehicle arriving outside the farmhouse gate. They heard the light tap on the front door and then the familiar creak of its hinges as it was pushed open. Footsteps moved along the slate floor of the cross-passage and then Christopher Bayliss was standing in the doorway to the recreation room.

Before his breakdown, their boss's son, whom they had occasionally encountered when he was home on leave, had been a brash RAF fighter pilot, concealing shattered nerves under a facade of swaggering arrogance. His increasing exhaustion had left him pale and hollow-eyed. Now, almost a year after his catastrophic breakdown and many months since he had taken refuge in the forester's cottage, he appeared taller and more robust than the girls remembered. His clothes were the colours of the forest in which he worked. He seemed relaxed. Strenuous exercise, supported by the regular supply of nourishing food that was sent up to him by Eileen, his father's housekeeper, had restored him, building him physically and soothing his damaged nerves. His hair, untouched by a barber for six months, fell, dark and glossy, almost to his broad shoulders.

'Well, I never did!' Rose had exclaimed, coming from the kitchen with her own cup of cocoa in her hand, stopping and staring at their visitor. ''Ere... you take this one, Master Christopher,' she said, offering him the cup and addressing him as she had done when he had been a small child. 'Go on! I'll make meself another in a bit!' But Christopher had interrupted her.

'No, Rose, you have it. I won't stay... But I saw the plane come down and guessed it was close to the farmhouse.' He glanced round at the wide-eyed girls. 'Just wanted to make certain everyone's all right.'

They assured him they were and he listened while they described to him what had happened. He breathed the words 'poor sod' when they told him of the pilot's fate. Then, as the girls stared at him, astonished by his changed appearance, he seemed suddenly to become aware of their attention.

'Well, if everything's OK here,' he smiled self-consciously, 'I'll say goodnight.' He turned and disappeared into the darkened cross-passage, leaving the girls staring at the empty doorway.

Alice followed him out and went with him to the front door.

'How did you get here?' she asked, and he explained that an old farm truck was kept, at his father's insistence, at the woodsman's cottage 'for emergencies'.

'It was very thoughtful of you,' Alice said, and when he hesitated at the doorway she guessed he wanted news of Georgina Webster.

Georgina was one of the initial intake of eight girls who had arrived at Lower Post Stone Farm two days after Alice had begun work there. Unlike most land girls, who came mainly from working class areas and had left school after receiving only a basic education, Georgina, or Georgie, as the girls came to call her, was considered 'privileged'. Her father farmed extensively in West Somerset, where the family lived comfortably in a handsome manor house. They were staunch pacifists who, when war was declared, wanted no part in it. But by 1943, when their only son, Lionel, reached the age of eighteen, he would, unless he declared himself a Conscientious Objector, have been conscripted into one of the armed services had not Georgina, his senior by twelve months, volunteered to enlist, allowing Lionel to remain on the family farm. Of the services available to Georgina, the Land

Army, which was never involved in combat, was her obvious choice.

Her first weeks at Lower Post Stone had exposed Georgina to open hostility from the other girls when they discovered that she was what they called a 'conchie'. The person with whom she had most in common was the warden, whose middle-class background matched her own. She and Alice spoke with similar accents and, until the girls' reaction made them aware of it, used words and phrases which set them apart. The girls had resented it when Roger Bayliss, in view of Georgina's education, her maturity and her natural air of authority, had appointed her as forewoman of the unruly gaggle of young women which had been assigned to him and they noticed, when their boss's son came home on leave, that he ignored them and took a shine to Georgina. Not that they cared. 'Master Christopher', as the farmhands called him, was posh, like she was. And stuck up.

The relationship between Christopher and Georgina started badly. His swaggering, flirtatious approach irritated her and he was dismissive, even spitefully disapproving, of her pacifism. Yet it was she who first picked up on the warning signs of the breakdown which was about to shatter his nerves and end his flying career. Too many missions, insufficient leave, his squadron decimated by the enemy, friends blown out of the sky before his eyes or burnt beyond recognition in runway pile-ups all took their toll on him, eventually pushing him to the edge of sanity and over it. It had been Georgina, not his father, who had visited him in the psychiatric ward.

While Christopher's experience, and various other tragic events that had touched her during her months on the farm, had forced Georgina to question and then reject pacifism, Christopher, as he slowly recovered, had adopted it. Their paths crossed and they moved in opposing directions. When she told him of her changed convictions and that she was going to join the Air Transport Auxiliary, a non-combatative unit of the RAF, he was devastated. Despite this, Alice believed the pair of them still cared for one another and found herself bridging the gap between them.

As he stood hesitating in the doorway, his head, as his father's had been earlier that day, inclined to one side to avoid contact with the low lintel, Alice told Christopher that Georgina had visited the farmhouse a few weeks previously while on a brief leave from the ATA.

'They're working her terribly hard but I think she's enjoying it.' Georgina had been taught to fly by an uncle whom she always referred to as 'the de Havilland uncle' because of his professional connection with that company, and she had achieved her pilot's licence on the day she became old enough. 'She flies all sorts of aircraft, you know, ferrying them between the airfields and the repair workshops.' Alice paused, uncertain how much Christopher wanted to know about Georgina's involvement in a war of which he now disapproved as strongly as she once had. He stood for a moment without speaking. Then he told Alice that he was very out of touch with what was going on in the world.

'I don't get any news where I am,' he said, and then paused. 'But I imagine it won't be long before the Allies invade France?'

'It's what everyone expects,' Alice answered. 'When and where are closely guarded secrets, of course.' After a moment they smiled at each other and shook hands.

''Night, Mrs Todd,' he said. 'And if you see Georgie, would you give her my...' He hesitated.

'Your love?'

'Well...yes.'

'Of course I will,' Alice said.

On the morning a letter arrived from Alice's solicitors informing her of the date of her divorce proceedings in London, two others were delivered to the farmhouse. One was Reuben's regular weekly communication with Hester, his bride of six weeks in which the pair had spent only occasional nights together whenever he managed a few hours of leave.

The third letter, which was addressed to Miss

M Grice, surprised Alice, who could not remember Marion ever having received any mail during the twelve months since she had arrived at the hostel.

Alice had propped the two letters on the dresser and when Hester burst into the kitchen the moment she arrived back from her work, which that day had involved the clearing of a ditch recently blocked by a fallen willow, she reached for her letter, muddy, smiling and blushing with pleasure at the sight of Reuben's handwriting.

'There's a letter there for Marion, Hester,' Alice called to her. 'Take it up to her, would you?' But as Hester took the letter, Gwennan, who always made other people's business her own, snatched it from her hand and examined it closely, her hard features sharpened by curiosity and surprise.

'It's got a US army stamp on it... Bet it's from the bloke as was here Christmas Day when we was snowed in and all those GIs from the camp turned up! You remember him, Mrs Todd? A sergeant, he was. Short and ugly, with a five o'clock shadow. Made a right fool of himself over Marion, he did!' Alice did remember the stocky, vivacious GI sergeant and was irritated, not for the first time, by the Welsh girl's spiteful view of her fellows. She sighed as Gwennan's footsteps thudded up the bare boards of the stairs.

'Letter for Miss Grice!' Gwennan announced, putting her head round the door of the low-ceilinged bedroom which Marion and Winnie shared. 'Reckon it's from that Kinski fellow. Marvin, was it?' She was certain she caught the suggestion of a softening of Marion's sharp features.

'Mind your own business, Taff,' Winnie snapped protectively, 'and give Marion her letter!' Gwennan smirked, skimmed the letter across the room in the general direction of Marion and withdrew.

'What's he writing to me for?' Marion murmured, trying, without success, to appear indifferent to the unexpected attention from a man who, despite falling short of her usual standards, being dark but neither tall nor handsome, had made an undeniable impression on her. It was almost two months since Christmas Day, when Marvin Kinski had breezed into her life and spent an evening jitterbugging with her. He had turned up at the farm a week later in a borrowed staff car, whisked her off for tea and cakes in Exeter, told her he was being posted to a training base in Hampshire, kissed her hand at the farmhouse gate – as he had recently seen Clark Gable kiss Vivienne Leigh's – asked permission to write to her and driven off, beeping the staff·car's horn as he accelerated, slithering dangerously down the muddy lane.

'Well, you told him he could write to you!' Winnie studied her friend's deliberately blank expression.

'I never!' Marion said, avoiding Winnie's eyes.

'You did so! I 'eard you! Well, go on then! Open it! Read it!'

The words were on a single sheet of paper. With it was a photograph of Marvin in his uniform. He was leaning, nonchalantly, against a Sherman tank. His cap was at a rakish angle and the five o'clock shadow was in evidence. Winnie studied the snapshot while Marion read and then re-read the letter. Then she folded it and slid it back into its envelope.

'Well?' Winnie enquired expectantly, and when Marion took her time over lighting a Woodbine, added, 'Oh, come on, Marion! What does 'e say?'

'Just that 'e wants me to write to 'im and send 'im me photo.' She glanced at Winnie's smile. 'I don't know what you're grinning at, Win.'

'Well…'cos it's nice, isn't it, 'im wanting your picture and everything.'

'No, it's not! And anyroad, I haven't got a picture!'

'Yes you have! You could send one of those snaps we took last summer! You remember? That Sunday when it was ever so hot and we all went for a dip in the river!' Winnie searched her friend's face. 'What's up?' she asked.

'Are you daft?' Marion snapped. 'Have you forgot about our plan?'

Their plan, which they had been forced to divulge to Alice Todd at the time of an incident that had

41

taken place some ten months previously, when Winnie, ostensibly as the result of an abdominal strain caused by lifting bags of swedes, had been hospitalised. Rumour had it that Winnie had miscarried and rumour, on that occasion, had been right. Alice herself had been instrumental in giving Winnie a second chance by hushing up the affair, which otherwise would have resulted in the girl's dismissal from the Land Army.

Most of the land girls at Lower Post Stone Farm suspected that both Marion and Winnie were receiving rather more than gifts of make-up, chocolates and silk stockings from the American servicemen they picked up in pubs and at local hops, but only Alice knew that the two girls were doggedly saving their money in order, when the war was over, to purchase the lease of a public house of their own.

Their deprived backgrounds, poor educations and less than perfect looks could have robbed Marion and Winnie of self-assurance and resulted in a passive acceptance of the prospect of a future spent in unrewarding labour or marriages dominated by the poverty that had dogged the lives of their parents. But, lurking in both of these girls, was a spark of ambition, a resistance to what might have been seen as their inevitable fate. Their curtailed education had meant that they were not considered bright enough to qualify for the WRENS or the WRAF, so they had opted for the Land Army because, unlike employment in a munitions factory, it offered an escape from the grimy squalor of the back streets of Leeds in which, until war was declared, they had spent their lives.

They had supported each other through the difficult period of adjustment to the hard work and harsh conditions of their new and alien environment and had quickly established contact with the large, floating population of servicemen who were, at that stage of the war, being trained in southern England for the Allies' invasion of northern France.

When Marion showed Alice Todd the National Savings account she and Winnie had opened together, it had been obvious to the warden that the pounds, shillings and pence it represented amounted to far more than the girls could possibly have accumulated from the meagre wages Roger Bayliss received each week from the Ministry of Agriculture on their behalf. Marion had confessed to the warden that she and Winnie were in the habit of 'selling on' to other land girls the 'presents' they received from the GIs in return for various, undefined favours.

There were some, Rose and Gwennan among them, who suspected the worst where Marion and Winnie were concerned, but Alice, rather than seeing the two girls sacked and probably forced into an even more precarious situation, had, after Winnie's 'miscarriage', procured contraceptives for them and, from the girls themselves, promises of more discreet behaviour. Since then their savings had continued to build and their financial plans, barring mishap, were on course.

'Sometimes you are really daft, Win,' Marion continued, irritably screwing her cigarette stub into a saucer on a dressing table littered with bottles of nail varnish, jars of foundation cream and boxes of face powder. 'If I gives Marvin the old come-on, things could get...well...you know...' Winnie was staring at her, her eyes wide, scanning Marion's sharp features, which, bereft of make-up, were not at their best.

'You fancy him though, don't you?' she whispered, her eyes widening. 'Jeez, Marion, you do! You fancy the little sergeant!'

'You still haven't got it, have you, Win? If I did happen to fancy him and more to the point, if he fancies me...'

'Well?'

'Well...where does that leave our plan?' She watched Winnie's face. 'Penny dropped, 'as it? Got it now, 'ave you? You don't 'ave to worry, though, Win. I won't let you down. Don't look at me like that! I won't! Honest! I want us to 'ave a pub of our own as much as you do.' To demonstrate her intentions she crumpled the envelope and the letter it contained and tossed them into the empty grate of the small fireplace.

'But if you like him, Marion...'

Annie's voice reached them from the corridor

outside their room. 'Bathroom's free, you two!' Marion was on her feet, reaching for her towel and dressing gown.

'Quick, Win!' she said, moving towards the door. 'Or that sodding Taff'll beat us to it and you know how long she takes! Plus she'll nick all the 'ot water!'

'But if you really like him...?'

'The pub wins, love! Hands down! C'mon, girl! Get your skates on!' Marion left their room and catching sight of the Welsh girl making for the steamy bathroom, yelled. 'No you don't, Taff! It's me and Win next!'

From their bedroom Winnie heard the precious hot water running into the tub.

Sergeant Kinski was a complication neither of them had expected or sought. The men they met seldom had ambitions for more than a bit of fun. Their interest lay in discovering how far these two girls would go. What they were 'up for'. Their suggestive behaviour, the revealing clothes and the heavy make-up they wore delivered signals to which the men responded eagerly enough. Mostly they settled for what was on offer and, if Marion or Winnie resisted their fumbling attempts at seduction, behaved decently. Occasionally there was some unpleasantness. Once they had been followed from the village pub by a couple of drunken tommies. The girls had given them the slip by concealing themselves in a thicket until the men, hurling abuse into the night, gave up their search and reeled away down the lane in the direction of their barracks. Marion had fatally damaged the heel of a pair of almost-new slingbacks and both girls arrived at the farm just as Alice was locking up for the night, mortified by the state of their stockings. Gwennan, on her way to bed, guessed what had happened.

'Daft, you two are!' she exclaimed waspishly. 'Expecting to be treated like ladies when you be'ave like tarts!'

Winnie sat staring at the screwed-up letter. Then she retrieved it from the grate, smoothed it out and read it.

# Chapter Two

Lower Post Stone Farm had stood empty for years before being utilised as a Land Army hostel, and during that time had been slowly decaying. Its thatch was mossy. The panes in some of its windows were cracked. Their frames and even the solid oak doors at the front and rear of the building were darkened by mould. The wooden supports of the front porch had warped under the weight of its roof and the nests of generations of swallows and house martins clustered where its exposed slates met the mildewed, pink-washed walls. Smoothed cobbles on the path that ran from the porch to the gate of the rank garden had been bright with cushions of green moss when the land girls had arrived. Now, after twelve months of heavy use, the moss was worn away. Within the farmhouse the slate floors, the treads of the wooden stairs and the bare boards of the upper floor shone again, buffed by a dozen pairs of female feet trekking in and out, up and down, to and fro. Verdigris had vanished from the taps in the peeling bathroom and the chimney breasts in the kitchen and the recreation room gave off a steady warmth, which, initially, had done little more than add to a pervading humidity. Now, after a warm summer and an autumn in which the fires had maintained a low but constant heat, the building was at last tolerable.

Warmth rose from the range in the kitchen and lifted the temperature in the bathroom above it before moving on, up into the attic space.

Here, the warden's son, ten-year-old Edward John Todd, on his weekends and holidays from boarding school, escaped a household dominated by women and played with his Meccano set. He was a methodical boy, storing the dozens of variously shaped pieces of metal in labelled boxes, enlarging his collection on his birthday and at Christmas time when his absent father and his Uncle Richard, unable to think of alternative presents, added to it. If the weekend weather was wet and on Friday and Saturday evenings, when he had eaten his supper, the boy would climb the narrow, upper staircase that led to the attic, light the oil lamp and lose himself in the fascinating construction of bridges and towers, cranes, trucks and challenging industrial machinery, diligently following the printed instructions until his mother's voice called him to bed.

Through the loose floorboards that separated him from the bathroom, a drift of humid air, flavoured with bath salts and various aromatic shampoos, reached Edward John. The girls' voices rose and fell as they took it in turns to soak in the bath, wash their hair and rinse out their smalls, cursing when the supply of hot water ran out and they had to suspend their ablutions until the overworked range in the kitchen reheated it. Then a shout of 'Water's hot!' would be followed by a stampede of bare feet along the corridor.

Edward John, engrossed in his construction work, was only half aware of the girls. To him their chatter, laughter, altercations, the occasional bursts of raucous singing and their constant, noisy movement about the building, had become a background to his life at the farm – a peripheral part of the two days each week when he joined his mother there and pursued his own modest agenda. At midday on Saturdays he would climb onto one or other of the carthorses when they were led along the lane to be turned out into the paddock, where they would graze until Monday. He had ambitions to learn to drive the farm tractor, to sit alone on its metal seat and steer it round the yard of the higher farm. He had soon learnt to milk a cow and how to act as midwife to a sow. He had noticed, before anyone else had, when a valuable calf was sick and had been commended by Roger Bayliss for his sharp eye and the responsible action which had saved the animal's life.

Before the war had split his parents, Edward John's experience of the world had been similar to that of most middle-class English boys. Now, with the family home bomb-damaged and boarded-up and his parents separated – not only by enemy action but by someone whose name was Penelope Fisher, his father's secretary, a tight-lipped, nervous young woman, whom James Todd apparently preferred to Edward John's mother – things were completely changed.

Initially dismayed, Edward John, like many children whose lives where disrupted by the war, had found himself in an unfamiliar environment. Unlike some, who were evacuated from the major cities and billeted with strangers all over the countryside while their homes were threatened and their parents and older siblings struggled to survive German air attacks, Edward John was never far from his mother.

To begin with, his father's absence had merely disconcerted him but no sooner had he grown to accept it, than he was faced with the added complication of the complete breakdown of his parents' marriage. But, with the passing of weeks and then months, he had adjusted to this too and now, occupied by his schooling and relishing the time he spent at Lower Post Stone Farm, he was happy enough.

When Alice had accepted the job as warden, Edward John had been instantly enchanted by the prospect of living on a farm. It had, in fact, been his enthusiasm that had persuaded Alice to take on work of which she was, initially, almost incapable.

The land girls themselves did not interest Edward John. He read the disapproval in Rose Crocker's face when, occasionally, their behaviour was raucous and vulgar and he sensed his mother's concern when he was exposed to language which was considered unsuitable for a young boy's ears.

Had he been a little older or more sexually mature, Edward John might have been intrigued and curious about the land girls and possibly even aroused by their proximity but, that year, when he was ten years old, they seemed to him to not be girls at all but grown-up women and as such he tolerated them, politely taking his cue from his mother when he was uncertain what his own reaction to them should be.

His favourite had been Eleanor, the young runaway, who had absconded from her boarding school and had declared her intention to return to the farm as a legitimate land girl as soon as she was old enough. He had liked the one called Georgina and thought Annie was the prettiest, admiring her lustrous eyes and the cloud of dark hair that framed her face. Sometimes he polished her boots for her while Gwennan, his least favourite, snarled her disapproval.

It was difficult, in the flickering lamplight, to see clearly enough to assemble the Bailey bridge on which he had embarked the previous evening, and when he heard his mother's voice summoning him to bed, he was happy enough to obey her, welcoming the excuse to give up the struggle. Milky cocoa was waiting for him as he clattered down to the warm kitchen, passing the open door of Mabel Hodges' room as he went.

Mabel was sitting reading a comic in the double bedroom she shared with no one, when Gwennan's strident voice reached her.

'Bathroom's free, Mabel!'

There were several things that struck people when they first met Mabel. The first was her shape. She was squat and rotund, a smiling, female Humpty Dumpty, with short, muscular arms and legs, and large breasts, stomach, hips and thighs. Her face, too, was rounded, her deep-set eyes sharp and brown. She had coarse auburn hair, which curled aggressively, and a scatter of freckles across her snubbed nose. Another thing about her, and one which more specifically set her apart from the rest of the Post Stone girls, was that she was what Roger Bayliss described as 'malodorous'. Alice had winced when he first used this word to describe the lumpen girl but had to admit that it was appropriate.

Mabel had brought with her into the hostel on that cold February day twelve months previously, when she had arrived, together with seven others, a curious, thick, sweetish, oily, sweaty female odour which, despite the imposition of regular baths, clean linen and laundered dungarees, clung persistently to her. By popular demand Mabel was the last to use the bathtub each night.

Most of the girls shared the small, double bedrooms but more often than not, as they came and went, Mabel had found herself with a room to herself. No one wanted to hurt her feelings, although Gwennan and occasionally Marion or Winnie would mutter something or other which would have been best left unsaid. But Mabel seemed not to hear them – or, perhaps chose not to – and smiled her guileless smile as she relished her food, always on the lookout for, and never refusing, a second helping of anything.

Alice Todd had been the last to guess that the little boy, whom Mabel referred to as 'me baby bruvver', was, in fact, her illegitimate son. Arthur lived with Mabel's grandmother, who occasionally brought him to visit his 'big sister'. The affection between the chubby child and the girl who had given birth to him and whom he called 'May-May', was as noticeable as his resemblance to her and had not, for long, escaped the sharp eyes of Gwennan Pringle.

'It's obvious, in' it!' she had breathed to Marion and Winnie. 'An' it's disgusting, if you ask me.' Almost all of Gwennan's deliberations ended with the phrase 'if you ask me', and it irritated her considerably that, in fact, almost no one ever did ask her opinion about anything.

'This has nothing to do with us,' Alice had said firmly when Rose's face, as she broached the subject of Arthur's parentage, had also been hard with disapproval. 'If Mabel wants to tell us about it she will. If not, we must respect her privacy.' Rose had muttered darkly and kept her opinions to herself. Gwennan, however, was not to be denied.

'And what about Ferdie Vallance?' she had demanded, self-righteously, her censorious voice sharp with malice.

'What about him?' Alice had asked, as innocently as was possible.

Since her arrival at the farm, Mabel had formed a curious relationship with Ferdie, and in doing so had transformed his life.

Maimed as a teenager in an accident on the Bayliss farm, no girl had ever given Ferdie a second glance, and following the death of his mother, with nobody to cook for him or clean the tiny labourer's cottage that came with his wages, Ferdie Vallance had succumbed to neglect, emerging each morning from the gloom of what was hardly more than a hovel like a wild animal leaving its lair. He was thin because he couldn't cook, and his person, his clothes and his cottage were thick with grime because he couldn't clean. His hair was lank, his teeth stained, his fingernails black and broken. The land girls gave him a wide berth and avoided his leering smile. Expecting no other response from them and with the exception of one, he ignored them. The exception was Mabel.

To begin with he had observed her covertly, on the grounds that although she was not quite like the other girls, even she was unlikely to invite or welcome his attentions. But, from the early morning of the day Mabel had begun work in the Bayliss dairy, Ferdie had been at first fascinated and then distinctly roused by her. The closer he got to her, moving a stool nearer to hers as he taught her how to coax milk from a fidgeting cow, the more the oily, female smell of her inflamed him. He failed to be put off by her unwashed hair, unbrushed teeth and bitten nails, reacting positively to her smile, the brightness of her boot-button eyes, the soft voluptuousness of thighs that spilt over the edges of the milking stool and breasts that seemed barely contained by the straining bib of her khaki dungarees.

'I ain't never done milkin', Mr Vallance,' she smiled engagingly, ''cos where I worked before we was mostly pigs!'

'Doan you fret,' he had soothed. 'Us'll soon 'ave ee

fillin' a pail as fast as anyone – and you can called me Ferdie, if you 'as a mind to.'

That had been the start of it. Soon, and on a regular basis, Mabel was cooking a meal for Ferdie on Saturday nights. While most of the girls went to dances, pubs and cinemas in Exeter, Mabel produced stews, roasts and copious puddings from ingredients which, one way or another, Ferdie had procured during the preceding week.

Salmon and pheasants were poached, rabbits snared and pigeons shot. Once, a lamb, accidentally killed by a fall in a quarry, was inexpertly butchered. Pans of warmed milk were set to cool and then skimmed for Devonshire cream and there were always eggs from the farm hens for custards and even cakes. Strawberries and then raspberries came and went as summer passed and then there were plums, greengages and pears for tarts and later, unlimited apples for pies.

Soon Ferdie had lost the half-starved look with which everyone had become familiar and, while it had to be admitted that Mabel had little effect on the state of the Vallance cottage, she did, from time to time, launder his flannel shirts, his bedding and even his combinations.

Roger Bayliss was in the habit of passing down to Ferdie any clothes for which he no longer had a use. Mabel sorted through the Viyella shirts, tweed jackets and corduroy trousers, replaced a button here and shortened a sleeve or a trouser leg there, until, on Saturday nights, after having a wash-down in the galvanised bathtub in front of his kitchen fire, the Ferdie who sat down with her to guzzle his way through the provisions he had pilfered and she had cooked, was very different from the one she had first encountered on that cold, February morning, twelve months previously.

Mabel's appearance, too, had been changed by her year at Lower Post Stone Farm. Although her particular odour still hung about her and was at its most pungent at the end of a hard-working day, the habits of the other girls had influenced her. She washed her hair once a week, began to relish the feeling of clean clothes against her skin and used a toothbrush and paste in a way which, until she had become a land girl, she had never done. The wartime diet, rich in vegetables and low in the sugary, fatty foods that had been the staples of Mabel's pre-war fare, improved her figure, and although she remained what Gwennan called fat, her body was firmer and her skin less liable to the outbreaks of pimples and pustules that had previously thrived on its greasy surface.

If Ferdie Vallance had ambitions where Mabel was concerned they were, to begin with, focused on her culinary skills. He looked no further ahead than to the meal they would cook on the coming Saturday night. But he also enjoyed her company and appreciated her attention to his laundry.

Life, for Ferdie, had never been so good and he was content, suppressing, for the time being, any desire he might have felt for more than her presence on their regular Saturday evenings together.

Mabel, however, had her own agenda. One that involved the two-year-old Arthur. She wanted him with her in the country. She wanted to stop pretending he was her brother and acknowledge him as her own child. She wanted to raise him herself and she wanted Ferdie to adopt him as his son.

How she would achieve all this was beyond her and she was, to begin with, innocent of any specific plots or plans. It was enough, for now at any rate, to enjoy the changes in herself and those in Ferdie, which had evolved over the months since she came to Lower Post Stone Farm. She respected the short, twisted, limping man and had grown genuinely fond of him. So she let the months and weeks pass in their unremitting routine of heavy labour, in the pleasure of food, both at Alice's sparse but well-ordered table and in Ferdie Vallance's murky kitchen, and her last act each night as she climbed into her narrow bed was to make a wish that little Arthur, probably asleep in the air raid shelter in Deptford, would stay safe until morning.

Mabel shook Vim from the carton and scoured the bath. Being the last to use it each evening, this task always fell to her. She pushed her feet into her slippers and, tying her dressing gown around the part of her body where most girls have a waist, went to the window and opened it. 'To let out the steam,' the warden had said, but Mabel was aware that it was to air the room and clear it of the particular aroma which, she knew, clung to her and which the other girls found offensive.

Most of the lamps in the shared bedrooms were out and their doors were closed as Mabel padded along the corridor to her solitary room.

'...And God bless Ferdie Vallance and Gran and keep little Arfur safe,' she muttered as her cheek met her pillow and she fell, instantly, asleep.

Alice was able, a week or so after the plane crash, to keep her promise to Christopher and give his love to Georgina who, on a 48-hour pass from the Air Transport Service, had ridden over to Lower Post Stone Farm on her brother's motorbike, primarily, she had convinced herself, in order to see the warden whose friendship she had come to value during the ten months she had worked as a land girl.

'Georgie!' Alice had exclaimed, straightening her back after emptying a scuttleful of coke into the kitchen range.

It was early on a Saturday afternoon. Most of the girls were preparing themselves for an evening out or had already left for a trip to the shops in Exeter. Edward John was in one of the barns where a sow was farrowing, while Mabel and Gwennan, on dairy duty, were at the higher farm, driving the cows into their stalls. When the milking was done Gwennan would cycle downhill, back to the lower farm, while Mabel made her way across the yard of Higher Post Stone Farm to Ferdie's cottage, where she would help him cook their weekly feast.

Hester, alone in the hostel's recreation room, was writing her regular letter to Reuben. *Dearest Love*, it began, *This week we've been mostly lifting swedes and carting them out to the cattle. Annie's got a bit of a cold and I daresay I'll catch it, sharing a room with her and everything. Mrs Brewster the Land Army lady came the other day to make sure things was in order here. She comes once a month. She said I was looking very bonny and that married life must suit me. She was red in the face and a bit giggly like she might have been having a drink or two but she wouldn't do that would she? Being a posh lady and everything? Let me know as soon as you can when you'll get your next pass and I'll book our room at the pub. I do love you so much Reuben and think of you all the time. Your wife Hester. Kiss, kiss.*

She sat for a while, chewing the end of her pencil

and occupied by thoughts that were too complex for her to commit to paper. She wondered what it was going to be like when arrangements were made by the US Army to put her on a ship together with dozens of other girls who had married GIs and deliver her to Reuben's folks in Bismarck, North Dakota. If she had the choice she would have preferred to continue to work as a land girl until the war was over and Reuben could come for her and take her home to America with him, but that was not the way it worked and you had to do as the authorities said. It worried her that she had had no contact with her family since they had rejected Reuben as a son-in-law and dismissed her marriage to him as unseemly. 'Forgive us our sins,' the prayer book said but there seemed very little room for forgiveness in the creed of the Pentecostal Brothers, which her father so strictly followed that he was prepared to lose his only daughter because of it. Hester sighed. Then, hearing Alice and Georgina's voices from the kitchen, added to her letter. *PS*, she wrote. *Georgina has come to see Mrs Todd. She's left the hostel now but maybe you remember her from last year. She is the very pretty one with straight dark hair cut short. She talks like Mrs Todd does and we all thought she and Mr Bayliss's son Christopher was in love but he's a pacifist now and they fell out when she joined up in the RAF and he went off to look after the timber. It seems a shame because she was very good to him when he was sick in the mental home.* She thought for a while about Georgina and Christopher. Then she kissed her letter, folded it and slid it into an envelope on which she carefully printed Reuben's address.

In the kitchen, Alice and Georgina were sitting over cups of tea.

'So you haven't seen him since Christmas?' Alice had asked, as they sipped. Georgina had borrowed not only her brother's motorbike but the heavy-duty trousers, jacket and even the flying helmet and goggles that he wore in the winter when he rode it. She looked, Alice thought, as though she had flown, rather than ridden from her parents' house, which lay twenty miles to the east of the Post Stone farms.

Alice, as requested, had given Georgina Christopher's love and caught the resulting look of tension that briefly clouded her open face.

'Nope,' she said lightly, in answer to Alice's question. 'I hardly get any leave and when I do I'm so dog-tired I just go home to my parents and sleep!'

'You could have gone to see him this afternoon,' Alice said, her eyes on the tea leaves in her empty cup. 'The woodsman's cottage is closer to your home than we are.'

'Trying to get rid of me, Mrs Todd?' The implication behind the question was obvious to Alice but she decided, on this occasion, not to mind her own business.

'He misses you, Georgie. You mean a lot to him.'

'I know.' Georgina sighed. 'I know he does. And I know I do and I'm fond of him too, but...'

'"Fond,"' Alice repeated. 'Not a word he'd appreciate, Georgie dear. Not a word lovers use!'

'We're not lovers!' Georgina said firmly. There was a pause.

'Is it still the pacifism thing?' Alice asked.

'Not only. After he got better from his...his...'

'Breakdown?'

'Yes. He got too... I don't know... Too close!'

'Close?'

'I don't mean physically. Although, in a way, I suppose I do mean that. Too...sort of...dependent. He doesn't give me enough space. He's so...there! Waiting for me to... I don't know how to explain it! He's too...'

'Too intense, d'you mean?' Alice asked, trying to remember whether, when she and her husband were courting, he had ever been too intense. She didn't think he had been. Perhaps he had saved his intensity for Penny Fisher...

Hester appeared silently in the kitchen doorway where she hesitated, smiling uncertainly, conscious of having interrupted them.

'Hello, Georgie,' she said, and then, turning to Alice, 'Please can I have a stamp for Reuben's letter, Mrs Todd?'

Margery Brewster's contribution to the war effort had been to accept the role of village registrar for the Women's Land Army and in this voluntary capacity to oversee the hostels in the Ledburton area. She took this task, as she took all her work for the Ministry of Agriculture, very seriously and called, each month, on all nine of the hostels for which she was responsible. She had meetings with the wardens and, when necessary, interviewed one or another of the inmates. Being a committed and diligent woman, she made it her business to know at least a little of each land girl's history and was often instrumental in sorting out various personal problems.

She was sitting, some days after Georgina's visit, across the kitchen table, watching Alice assemble the large apple pie which, that evening and hot from the oven, would be sliced, doused in custard and fed to the land girls after the stew that was already simmering and filling the kitchen with an appetising smell.

Although Margery had not, on this occasion, added a nip of gin to the cup of tea the warden had made for her, there was, Alice had noticed, a telltale hint of peppermint on her visitor's breath, which, together with the slight flush about her face, suggested that at some point that day, Margery had had what she coyly referred to as a 'snifter'.

She sat now, her coat loosened, in the warm kitchen, her scarf and gloves beside her on the scrubbed surface of the table and her folder, containing notes on each of the Lower Post Stone girls, in front of her. But her attention, as her eyes followed the fork which Alice was working round the edge of the pie, was elsewhere.

'I often think,' she murmured vaguely, 'that when we're young and we make the huge decisions which will affect us all our lives...that we are not quite up to it.'

'Up to what?' Alice asked absent-mindedly, brushing egg yolk across the pie crust.

'To making the big decisions. Like who we should marry. Or whether we should marry at all!'

Surprised, Alice glanced at the registrar, whose grey eyes were wide and slightly unfocused.

'I mean,' Margery continued, almost to herself, 'that I sometimes wonder if we sort of drift into things when we are young and make decisions based on what we believe is expected of us rather than what we really want. Don't you think?'

Alice understood that for the second time that week, her opinion was being sought on a serious matter and that a considered response was expected. But before she could produce one Margery pursued her train of thought aloud and with increasing vigour.

'When my Higher School Certificate results were better than expected one of my teachers urged me to persuade my parents to send me to a university. She said I had a sharp brain and that my organising skills were well above average. She felt I had a bright future before me, possibly in the world of commerce or the Civil Service.' Alice, satisfied with her work on the pie, moved it to one side of the table and gave her full attention to the registrar. 'But did I heed her advice? No, I did not! I was expected to marry Gordon, you see. We'd known each other almost all our lives and it was just assumed that when the time came...' Margery paused, gazing into space. 'He was quite attractive then, Gordon. Robust and responsible. Played rugby. Rode to hounds. Had what they called "sound prospects". He was considered a good catch and I felt flattered when he proposed.' She glanced at the small but tasteful diamond ring beside her wedding band. 'Everyone was getting married. It hardly occurred to me not to.' Alice was concerned.

'But you don't regret it, do you? Not seriously, I mean?' Margery pondered, swallowed the last of her tea and set her cup neatly back on its saucer.

'I used not to. My life was very full in those early years. Raising my daughters, running my household and so on. It was after the girls left home and had husbands and families of their own that I...I simply did not know what to do with myself! Gordon had his work, his professional cronies and his golf and I had nothing and no one! I think I would have gone potty if war hadn't been declared and Lady Denham hadn't seized on my offer to help with the Land Army! It was as though I was suddenly alive again! At first I was a bit daunted by all the paperwork and the responsibilities but, to be honest with you, Alice – and I say this in all modesty – it came naturally to me. I found I could delegate and organise and supervise and I love it! I love being in charge and having to make decisions and the awful thing is that I cannot bear the thought of the war ending and everything stopping and having to go back to being plain Mrs Gordon Brewster! I know it's dreadful not to want the war to be over but I'm dreading it, Alice! Absolutely dreading it!' The warden was shocked. Not so much by Margery's outburst but by the intensity and desperation behind her words.

'But when it's over you must find something else to do!' she insisted. 'You have valuable skills and there are always people needing help in various ways! Surely—' But Margery interrupted her.

'No,' she sighed. 'Not in this neck of the woods, Alice dear. Helping with the flowers in the church or raising money for the organ fund is about all that's on offer around here.' Margery drew a deep breath, smiled bravely, straightened her shoulders and patted her notes into a neat pile. 'Rat-catchers,' she announced suddenly, and when Alice reacted in surprise, added, 'They visit once a year and are slightly overdue. They'll be billeted here for three or four weeks while they deal with all the farms in this area. Should arrive sometime within the month. I'll give you as much notice as I can and there'll be extra rations, of course.' Margery had resumed her usual efficient and sometimes slightly brusque manner. She got to her feet, settled her scarf round her neck, thanked Alice for the tea and left. From the kitchen, Alice heard the clash of gears as the registrar reversed her car in the narrow lane.

It was four-thirty and the light, on that overcast February afternoon, was already fading. The girls would return to the hostel in an hour's time, bursting into the old building, filling it with sound, keen to get out of their damp dungarees, fighting over the bathroom, clustering round the fire in the recreation room and relishing the cooking smells that would be reaching them from the warm kitchen.

Alice glanced at the clock, fetched a cabbage from the pantry and began slicing it, her mind occupied by what Margery Brewster had revealed about herself. Here was yet another effect of the war. This time on a middle-class, middle-aged woman who, on the positive side, had realised her potential because of it but, negatively, was almost certainly permanently unsettled by it. Perhaps, Alice deduced, Margery's depression at the prospect of having to resume her pre-war existence was the reason she was resorting, rather more often than she should, to the gin bottle.

Later that night, Ferdie Vallance, blowing on his mittened fingers, had braved the icy, moonless cold and was checking his snares when he heard a sound in the thicket that fringed the four-acre wood. The footfall was too heavy for a rabbit or even a fox. He saw the slight movement, no more than a blurred shape, dark against dark, just as the shot rang out and the flash from a gun barrel was briefly visible in the darkness. This was immediately followed by the heavy sound of human feet trampling through undergrowth.

'Varmints!' Ferdie yelled into the darkness. 'Thievin', trespassin' varmints!'

The shape on the edge of the woodland had dropped to the ground and was motionless but the shooters – at least two, though in the retelling of the incident Ferdie was to increase their number by one hundred per cent – made off, crashing through the saplings, away from Ferdie.Brandishing the stout stick with which he despatched any rabbit that survived his snares, Ferdie continued to hurl righteous abuse in the direction of the retreating poachers, despite the fact that he was, in effect, as guilty as any one of them. 'Murderin', trespassin' varmints! 'Ave the law on you, I will, once I get my 'ands on you!'

The young roe deer lay where it had been felled by the single shot which, Ferdie discovered, had entered its skull below the left eye socket and exited through shattered bones in the base of its neck. It sprawled, quite dead, limp in the long wet grass, a hint of steam rising from its warm pelt.

Ferdie Vallance considered his options. Venison was something he and Mabel had yet to experience in their Saturday night gastronomic indulgences. To forgo the opportunity on moral grounds or because of a degree of squeamishness on Ferdie's part, when it came to the practicalities of butchering the carcass, would be, it seemed to him, a sign of weakness, which he must resist for his own sake as well as Mabel's.

It was the creature's haunches that Ferdie required for his pot. So, gritting his teeth, mustering his strength and with the aid of his hunting knife, he set about the animal, and after a brief and gory struggle, the extent of which, because of the darkness, he was only half aware, he left the remains to marauding foxes, lashed the haunches together and hauled them homewards.

By the time Mabel arrived on the following Saturday his kitchen was already rich with an aroma of roasting flesh that was subtly unfamiliar to her.

Ferdie, basting the meat, turned to greet her and saw her small, bright eyes widen in wonderment.

''Tis venison!' he announced, salivating proudly. It had been difficult keeping his secret from her during the days between the killing and this week's feast. 'What do ee think of that, then?'

'But venison is what posh folk eat!' she gasped. He basked briefly in her approbation until he saw her face cloud. 'You ain't never bin poaching deer, 'ave you, Ferdie Vallance?' Her voice was anxious, for this was dangerous territory and they both knew it. The taking of deer from the herd of the life peer whose land bordered Roger Bayliss's would have been a hazardous departure on Ferdie's part from the small-time poaching he usually indulged in. He shook his head.

''T was poachers what done for 'im, my lover, not I! I caught 'em at it and drove 'em off! But by then t'were too late for this fella,' he indicated the oven door. 'What I reckoned was that, as the damage were done, it seemed a shame to let 'im go to waste. So 'ere 'e be, Mabel my lover! Less than half an hour from our dinner plates!'

They devoured the meat, knifing thick slices from the delicate bones and washing them down with Ferdie's cloudy, home-brewed cider.

When they were done he stood before her, took her greasy, hard-worked hands in his and licked the gravy

71

from her fingers. Then his hands moved down, past the slight indentation of her waist and on, to the parts of Mabel, or indeed of any girl, that Ferdie knew existed but had never before explored. She smiled. Her amiable arms went round his neck and she delivered to Ferdie, for what it was worth to him, a body for which neither she nor anyone else had ever had much respect. Then they lay down on his kitchen floor and relished each other as thoroughly as any pair of lovers in history or out of it. And it was on that night, the first of many joyful, warm and lustful occasions, that Mabel Hodges conceived the child that was to be her second and Ferdie's first.

Over the months that Alice had been working as warden and without her being aware of it, her employer had made it his business to discover all he could of her personal history, while she, lacking his curiosity, still knew very little of his.

The divorce that would end her marriage to James Todd was pending. Roger knew of this and understood that Alice did not expect James to contest it or to waste any time before remarrying. His co-respondent, Penny Fisher, who had been his secretary at the Air Ministry, was, Alice knew, already pregnant with his child.

Roger also observed that one of Alice's concerns was that, following the divorce, Edward John might become estranged from his father and that she was anxious to prevent this.

'I'd like them to have some form of contact,' she confided in Roger over a lunchtime drink where, because the publican produced his own butter and cheese and his wife her own chutneys, a ploughman's lunch was not only possible but equalled pre-war standards. 'I know it'll be difficult for him where his stepmother is concerned but he's almost eleven years old now and I feel he needs to address the situation sooner rather than later.' She bit into a crisp, pickled shallot. 'The longer he leaves it the more complicated it will become. Don't you think?'

Roger Bayliss considered the situation. He liked Alice's son, finding the boy observant, intelligent and polite. Beyond this he had not given him a great deal of thought.

'How does Edward John feel about it?' he asked Alice, and she described to him how, after being predictably disturbed by the upheaval of moving from London to Exeter and then to the farm and making the adjustments to weekly boarding school, her son had settled into the new routine and its contrasting environments with surprising speed and apparent ease.

'He doesn't talk much about his father,' she elaborated. 'He understands the situation with Penny, of course.' Alice paused and sipped the nutty, bitter beer that was brewed on the premises. Roger, watching her, wondered how it was possible for James Todd to prefer any woman to the charming one who was sitting opposite to him across the worn surface of the pub table. 'He was defensive and angry to begin with, but now...' Alice continued. Then she shrugged and smiled. 'He's more interested in your farm than anything else. Says he wants to be a vet when he grows up.'

'Really?' Roger said and sat half smiling, as though the idea pleased him. Then he said he thought it a pity that his own son had failed to show any interest in the land. 'I had Christopher's name down for Seale-Hayne,' he said, and when Alice looked blank, explained that this was the name of a prestigious local agricultural college. 'But with him it was a fireman first and then a train driver! When I bought our first tractor he got Jack to teach him how to drive it – he was still in short trousers – and at twelve I caught him hauling a loaded timber wagon out of the woodland. Soon afterwards he saw his first aeroplane and that was it!'

'I wonder how he would have reacted if you had remarried and perhaps had a second family.' Alice asked and saw Roger's expression change. The slightly wary look, with which she had been familiar during the early months of their acquaintance, once again replaced the more relaxed expression that, as time had passed, she had become used to.

'I never thought about it,' he said quietly.

'Which hadn't you thought about?' Alice persisted. 'Remarrying? Or whether Christopher would have approved?'

'Neither, actually,' Roger smiled.

'You don't talk to each other very much, the pair of you, do you,' she said, making statements of her questions. 'About the serious things, I mean.'

'Serious things?'

'About how you feel.'

'Feel about what, exactly?' He was both mystified and amused but there was also a trace of defensiveness about him which Alice, at that moment, or possibly deliberately, missed.

'About everything!' she plunged on. 'His breakdown! Your reaction to it! His future! Surely you don't want him to spend the rest of his life alone in your woodsman's hut?' She stopped, knowing she had gone too far but disappointed to discover that despite the development of what she still perceived as nothing more that a warm, working relationship between the two of them, Roger was continuing to keep her very much at arm's length, particularly where his relationship with his son was concerned. 'Sorry,' she smiled, cutting into her cheese. 'I shouldn't have pried. None of my business.'

'No, no,' he said, quietly surprised by her words. 'Don't apologise. Please don't apologise. You are very sweet. Very sweet.' He swallowed the last of his beer. 'Better crack on, though. When you're ready, of course... Paperwork piles up a bit at this time of the year.'

As they drove back towards the farms Roger confirmed the imminent arrival of the rat-catchers.

'They've been working in Lincolnshire,' he told her. 'Strange pair. This'll be their third visit to our area. Should arrive around midday tomorrow. They have a terrible little van with their suitcases in the back, along with all their various traps and poisons.'

'Ugh!' Alice shuddered.

'Yes, it is a bit grisly.' He slowed the car, carefully negotiating the approach to a narrow, hump-backed bridge. 'Jack usually digs a pit for the corpses. You'll be amazed at how many there will be.'

'Oh, please!' Alice was repulsed and Roger smiled at her discomfort.

'Has to be done, Alice. Has to be done!'

The rat-catchers, Pat and Connie, worked for the Pest Destruction Division of the Women's Land Army, a speciality that entitled them to a slightly higher wage than the regular land girls earned. They arrived the following day, just as Rose and Alice were about to eat their lunchtime sandwiches. Rose, unimpressed by their timing, found it difficult to produce something to put between the 'couple of slices of bread and marge' which the two girls insisted would 'do them fine'. But she was not one to be found wanting and she located a slice or two of beetroot and a sliver of cheese, set two plates down rather heavily on the kitchen table and did not smile when the rat-catchers reacted enthusiastically to the food and the cups of tea that followed.

They were large, untidy girls with shiny faces and tangled hair. They had driven down from Lincolnshire in their work clothes. Their fingernails, Alice noticed, were dirty. She suppressed the thought that they may not have washed since handling their latest harvest of dead rodents. In Rose's opinion they looked as though the pair of them could do with a good scrubbing and she resented the whiteness and crispness of the sheets and pillowcases on the twin beds she had made up that morning in the spare double room upstairs. The phrase 'pearls before swine' came suddenly into her uncompromising Devonian mind.

On their previous visits to Ledburton and before the hostel had been established, the rat-catchers had been billeted at the village pub and Rose would have preferred it if that had also been the case this year. But the hostel had a vacant room and it made economic sense for them to use it.

'And this be the bathroom,' Rose announced, emphatically, when, after they had eaten, she briskly showed Pat and Connie round the converted farmhouse.

'What's the matter?' Alice asked when, with pursed lips, Rose returned to the kitchen.

'Nothing I can put my finger on,' Rose told her tartly. 'But there's something about the pair of them as puts my teeth on edge.' When Alice laughed, intending to ease the tension, Rose told her that she might well scoff but that time would tell.

# Chapter Three

As often happened when there were changes amongst the inmates of the hostel, the status quo was subtly altered. Sometimes, when one girl arrived or another departed, the impact of the change was minimal. On other occasions it was more evident – usually to Alice, sometimes to Rose and then, to a lesser extent, to the girls themselves. Chrissie, who had arrived on the day the hostel first opened its doors, newly married and brimming with happiness, had been with them for only a few days before she died in an air raid on Plymouth. This tragedy had left its mark and the effect of it was still felt. Eleanor, the young runaway, was remembered with smiles by those who had witnessed the scene when she was hauled off by her irate and embarrassed headmistress, back to the boarding school from which she had briefly absconded. Then there had been Lillian, whose exuberant beauty and instant popularity with the local servicemen had been perceived as a serious and unacceptable threat to Marion and Winnie.

Lillian had looked like a film star. She was glossy and perfect. No curlers were needed to coax her naturally golden hair into the required, luxuriant cascade. The cold wind only brought a charming blush to her cheeks and brightened the incredible blue of her wide eyes. While the other girls huddled against the wind and slouched through their day's work, moaning about the rain, Lillian strode buoyantly through it. Her rich soprano voice echoed round the hostel and when she sang along to the gramophone records playing in the recreation room she sounded very much like her idol, Gracie Fields.

Lillian had auditioned for a job entertaining the troops, been shortlisted and placed in the Land Army on a temporary posting until arrangements could be made for her to join a travelling concert party. Even as she settled noisily and happily into life at Lower Post Stone Farm, strings were being pulled to remove her from it. Had the other girls known this, the tensions that arose during Lilian's brief stint as a land girl would have been less disruptive. As it was, Alice became almost immediately aware of a hostility which, though most obvious in Marion and Winnie's treatment of Lillian, extended beyond them and included Gwennan.

Mabel, awestruck by Lilian's larger-than-life glamour, proved unable to treat her as a normal person. Instead she regarded her as some sort of icon, addressing her as 'she' or 'her', asking 'Shall I hang up her dungarees for her?' instead of 'your dungarees for you?'

''Ave you lost your wits, Mabel?' Marion had hissed in exasperation, overhearing one such conversation, and even the easy-going, tolerant Annie seemed to find Lillian an irritating intrusion into the accepted humdrum of their lives.

In a matter of days and without any deliberate intention on her part, Lillian's presence had disrupted the established routine of life within the familiar, thick walls and under the heavy, damp thatch of Lower Post Stone Farm, and had created what Rose bluntly described as an 'atmosphere'.

Although Alice had done her best to stabilise things, Lillian never did fit in and when, on the day she left the hostel, clutching her belongings and, despite them, elegantly negotiating the cobbled path in her high heels as she headed for the army staff car that had been sent by ENSA to fetch her, she sang to the girls the familiar song that urged them to smile as they waved her goodbye.

'We'll wave you goodbye alright!' Marion had sneered, her jaw clenched in an icy smile.

'And good riddance!' Winnie had echoed. Even Hester had found herself sighing with relief as the car lurched away down the potholed lane, with Lillian bouncing dangerously around on the back seat as she attempted to blow extravagant kisses through its rear window. But most newcomers arriving at the hostel were soon put at ease and made welcome by the girls' basic friendliness. As well as satisfying their innate curiosity it was, after all, only common courtesy to ask the obvious questions about their families, their boyfriends, their backgrounds and their previous experience, if any, of life in the Land Army.

With the rat-catchers it was, from the beginning, different. For one thing, the two girls were established friends as well as colleagues. Consequently they did not depend on, or seek, more than a passing acquaintance with the rest of the Post Stone girls. For another, their specialised work meant that they would not be labouring alongside them during the three or four weeks it would take them to carry out their grisly task, the thought of which made the other girls squirm.

'I don't reckon there's that many rats round 'ere anyroad,' Marion had muttered moodily during the first supper, aiming her comment at Connie and Pat, who sat, side by side, at the crowded table.

'Leastways, I hardly ever see one!'

'We hear 'em though!' Mabel said, enthusiastically mopping up the gravy on her plate with a thick wedge of bread. 'Scuttlin' round under the thatch all night!'

'How many will you catch?' Hester wanted to know and was surprised to learn that the number, on an average farm and including mice as well as rats, ran into hundreds.

'Poor little sods,' Annie murmured. 'All they want is a bit of a nibble of this and that.'

'A bit of a nibble?' Connie was astounded. 'Tons of grain, they get through! Not to mention spuds and swedes and beet!' Her face had flushed with indignation at the suggestion that her work was unnecessary.

'Not much point you lot floggin' yourselves half to death growin' the food to feed the nation if rats is gonna eat 'alf of it!' Pat added, supporting her friend. There was a brief silence, broken only by the clatter of knives and forks.

''Ow d'you kill 'em, then?' Mabel asked with her mouth full. 'One farmer where I worked 'ad little yappy dogs. Used to set 'em loose in the barns where the rats was. Loved it, those doggies did! Killed 'em with one bite! Fast as lightnin', they was, and twice as noisy!'

'We mostly use poison,' Pat said conversationally.

'We bait the runs, you see, and...' She hesitated. Several of the girls were staring balefully at her. Winnie had pushed away her plate, her food only half eaten.

'Shall we talk about something else?' Alice suggested brightly. 'Where do you two come from and how long have you known each other?'

Early next morning the two newcomers drove, in their small van, down the lane, following the truck that had, as usual, collected the girls and would deliver them to the higher farm for their day's work.

The rat-catchers spent their first morning locating the creatures' runs, establishing where their nests were and in which sites poison could safely be laid down.

'We can gas your badgers and foxes for you, too, if required, sir,' they told Roger Bayliss when he briefly interviewed them in the farm office. He declined the offer because, despite the fact that a dog-fox had recently raided his poultry shed, he preferred the use of a bullet from his shotgun to the prospect of gassing, which conjured, for him, an image of troops dying of mustard gas in the trenches of France during what had been called 'the war to end all wars'.

'Is that the poison in them bottles and tins, then?' Gwennan asked, peering short-sightedly into the dim interior of the rat-catchers' van. Connie nodded. The containers and jars were all neatly labelled, the word 'poison' very much in evidence. One large tin even had a skull and crossbones emblazoned on it.

'What about the farm cats, though?' Annie enquired suspiciously.

'And Shep and Bonny, what about them?' Mabel's boot-button eyes were dark with anxiety for the two elderly sheep dogs.

'It's a special poison that only kills rodents,' Pat assured them. 'And anyhow, we don't put it where other animals can get at it.'

'Those bags have got baited grain in 'em, see,' Connie elaborated, indicating the small sacks, slung from hooks on the van's side. 'It's already got the poison in it. Impregnated, it is. We lay it in the rat runs and places where only they can eat it.' Nevertheless, when it was Lower Post Stone's turn to be purged of pests, Rose kept her fat tabby safely indoors.

'I'm takin' no chances!' she told Alice, casting a malicious glance at the rat-catchers. 'Not with them two, I'm not!'

Soon, evidence of the effectiveness of the rat-catchers' skills became obvious as the pile of corpses, heaped in a corner of the yard and which Jack would only bury once the girls' work was completed, increased in size each day.

The sight of the odd rat, moving fast in the

shadowy extremities of a barn or scuttling away from a half-eaten swede, was a familiar and acceptable sight to the land girls, most of whom, though they might give a token squeal when surprised by a mouse in the hostel pantry, were reasonably stoical where rodents were concerned. But the gruesome mound of inert creatures, their scaly tails stiff, their blank eyes still wide with the pain they had suffered, nauseated the girls as they hurried past it.

'Can't you dig your bloomin' hole and get the poor things buried straight off?' Annie beseeched Jack, when the pile had reached several feet in height.

'I casn't do that 'til them rat-catchers be done, my lover!' he said, enjoying her discomfort. 'Then I 'as to put some lime into the pit afore I fills 'e in, see. Youse'll just 'ave to look the other way for a couple more days.'

In common with the few hardened farmhands who were exempt from fighting, Jack enjoyed provoking squeamishness amongst the girls whose presence on the land still seemed to him to be unnatural. Sometimes, although he would not admit it, he was impressed by their fortitude and even, occasionally, by their physical strength, but mostly he felt superior to them and consoled himself with the conviction – unjustified as it was – that it took two of them to equal one of him.

'Oh, they mean well enough,' he was heard to

grumble in the pub to anyone who would listen. 'But they 'asn't got the muscle, see, nor the stayin' power, that's the trouble with 'em.'

Although Alice knew that Rose was harbouring an undefined disapproval of the rat-catchers, it was Gwennan who first voiced hers. She had come down to the kitchen late one evening to refill her hot-water bottle. A recent cold had settled on her chest and she smelt strongly, Alice noticed, of camphorated oil.

'I should of had a day in me bed to get over it proper,' the girl wheezed, casting an accusing glance at the warden. 'But what with there being a war on and everything, I do the best I can.' She was screwing the top into her hot-water bottle and coughing noisily when Connie and Pat, on their way to bed, put their heads round the kitchen door and wished Alice goodnight.

'I don't care for them two,' Gwennan said in her usual aggrieved voice, and then, when Alice failed to react, added, 'What do you make of 'em, Mrs Todd? Like 'em, do you?'

Alice, stoking the range and closing it down for the night, told Gwennan that she had no strong feelings, one way or the other, about the rat-catchers.

'But you must admit they're strange. Always together and—'

'They work together, Gwennan!' Alice interrupted, irritated as she often was by the Welsh girl's spite.

'Of course they're always together!'

'But all that smiling!'

'Smiling?'

'All that "Yes, Connie dear" and "No, Pat love"!'

'Oh, for goodness sake, Gwennan! They're friends! Why shouldn't they call each other "dear"? Take your hot-water bottle and get back to bed. P'raps you'll manage to be a little more tolerant in the morning.' Alice could see that Gwennan was inclined to stay and continue the debate so she smiled, took her firmly by the shoulders, turned her round and pushed her towards the door.

'But you must admit, Mrs Todd—' Gwennan's lilting voice began but Alice interrupted her.

'Bed, Gwennan! Now!'

It was on the next morning that the rat-catchers over-slept, arriving in the kitchen, yawning and frowzy, a good ten minutes after the lorry, taking the other land girls to work, had left Lower Post Stone Farm.

'Ever so sorry, Mrs Todd,' Connie apologised. 'Dead to the world, we was! Don't 'spose there's any porridge left?' Rose was already clattering the breakfast things in the scullery while Alice spooned what was left of the porridge into two bowls and made a fresh pot of tea. The rat-catchers ate quickly, collected their packs of sandwiches from the dresser, reminded Alice that they were working at a farm some miles off and might be late home that evening and – after apologising again for being late for breakfast – hurried out to their van and drove off.

It was laundry day, which meant that Rose would strip the sheets and pillowcases from the beds, leaving clean linen on each. The girls were expected to make up their own beds when they returned from work.

Rose was in the habit of throwing the damp towels and soiled linen down the steep stairs and then bagging it up, ready for Fred to collect and deliver to the laundry in Ledburton.

She went up the stairs and then, to Alice's surprise, came quickly down again. Her face, as she joined Alice in the kitchen, was hard with satisfaction.

'I knew it!' she said. 'I just knew there was something!' Before Alice could enquire further, Rose continued, 'Come with me, Alice! Just you come with me!'

They climbed the narrow stairs, Rose puffing ahead and Alice following. Rose led the way into the rat-catchers' room.

'There!' she said, exuding an unattractive triumphalism. 'Didn't I *say*?' she gasped. 'Didn't I just *know*?'

The two beds stood side by side in the small space. One was a chaos of rumpled sheets, its blankets tossed onto the bare boards of the floor. The other bed was as neatly made as it had been when Rose had swept the room on the previous morning. A winceyette nightdress lay, neatly folded, on its pillow.

Rose, breathing heavily, stood waiting for Alice's reaction.

'You are suggesting that they share the same bed, Rose?'

'It's obvious they do! You only 'as to look!' Rose was quivering with indignation. 'That one's not been touched! Nor the nightie! All this going to bed early and oversleeping – and all that smiling and touching!'

'Touching?' Alice demanded. 'I've never seen them touching.'

'That's because you 'aven't been looking, Alice.' Rose went to the window and threw it wide open, as though intending to rid the room of the corrupted air it contained. 'You've heard about women like them,' she said, turning to confront Alice. 'You must of! There's a name for it. Can't remember what, but there is. Gwennan's noticed. She wanted to tell Mr Bayliss about them, or Mrs Brewster. And she would of done afore now if I 'adn't told 'er not to until we 'ad proof and I'd spoken to you about it. Well, now we 'ave proof and what I want to know – what they'll all want to know – is what you're going to do about it.'

'Do about what, exactly?' Unlike Rose, Alice did know the name for what Connie and Pat were. She felt suddenly concerned for them, perceiving at once the level of hostility and intolerance the two girls were about to be subjected to, not only from Rose but from the other land girls, once the word had got around.

'About them being here!' Rose continued, her voice shrill. 'Living in a hostel with other girls! Normal girls!'

Where Connie and Pat were concerned, Alice had perhaps been less observant than was usual for her. She was certainly unaware of the gossip or of the rising level of suspicion pervading the hostel amongst not only the girls who were most familiar to her but also the three comparative newcomers, Elsie, Eva and Nancy, who, although billeted at Lower Post Stone, were deployed on a neighbouring farm.

Rose claimed emphatically that all the girls were determined that the rat-catchers should be immediately removed from the hostel and billeted elsewhere until their work in the area was completed. Alice protested, asking Rose for evidence of any impropriety in the behaviour of either Connie or Pat where the Post Stone girls were concerned, and although Rose blustered and threatened, she was too honest a woman to invent any. But that evening she intercepted the girls when they arrived back from their work, rather earlier than usual, and ten minutes later she led them into the kitchen where Alice was easing a heavy pan of potatoes onto the stove.

Connie and Pat, working that day ten miles from the hostel, were not expected back for some time, so the Post Stone girls, armed, now, with Rose's evidence of bed-sharing, took this opportunity to confront Alice with their grievances.

They gathered, most sitting at the kitchen table, some hovering round it or lurking in the cross-passage and stated their case. Alice listened.

'But what is it that they have actually done that has offended you?' she asked quietly, when silence fell. There were ten of them, including Rose. Ten pairs of eyes, some openly hostile, some mildly accusative, several of them – Annie, Hester and Mabel amongst these – concerned and uncertain.

Alice allowed her question to hang, unanswered, for a moment. The crowded kitchen was filled with such a solid sense of unease that it was almost tangible. When she sensed that Rose or Gwennan were about to speak, Alice continued.

'Have either of them said anything to any of you? Or embarrassed you in any way?' Another silence. 'Have either of them,' Alice hesitated, 'touched you?' There was a stir amongst the girls and Annie shook her head.

'No, Mrs Todd!' she said. ''Course they haven't

touched us!' At this point several of the girls averted their eyes from Alice's and stared instead at the floor or at the low beams above their heads.

'With respect, Mrs Todd,' Gwennan began firmly. It was a phrase she had once heard used to great effect by a village registrar during a confrontation with a farmer whose provision of food and decent accommodation was consistently falling short of even the Land Army's low standards. Two of the three land girls assigned to him had complained of his treatment and one of the three was Gwennan Pringle. 'With respect, Mrs Todd,' she repeated, impressed by the effect her words had, not only on the warden herself but on her fellow land girls, 'we have discussed this between ourselves and we want something done about it right away, please.' Gwennan, slightly fazed by Alice's look of astonishment, concluded, lamely and slightly uncharacteristically, 'If you don't mind.'

Alice Todd's experience of homosexuality was limited to the basic facts, one of which was that for men, at any rate, it was illegal and punishable by imprisonment. As a young woman she had read a novel called *The Well of Loneliness*, which had moved her and because of which she was, herself, inclined to be tolerant where the rat-catchers were concerned. But, as warden, it was her duty to run a hostel in which her charges felt secure and at ease with themselves and each other. Clearly, this was not now the case.

So, after appealing, to no effect, for tolerance while the rat-catchers completed their remaining few days of work on the Ledburton farms, she agreed to speak, the next day, to both Mr Bayliss and to Mrs Brewster and tell them of the girls' unanimous demand that Connie and Pat should be removed from the hostel. She insisted that the girls agreed to behave courteously to the rat-catchers during the course of what was clearly going to be a difficult evening, and they, aware of Alice's disapproval, sulkily agreed to this.

'I will not tolerate any unpleasantness,' Alice repeated firmly. 'Anyone who feels unable to behave themselves this evening had better go to their rooms now and Rose will bring their suppers up to them.' Gwennan was tempted to accept this offer but curiosity kept her in the kitchen where she intended to observe and enjoy the situation.

Alice was just about to suggest that the girls should get out of their work clothes and set about the ritual of the evening ablutions when they caught the unmistakable sound of the rattling engine of the rat-catchers' van. The girls hesitated and then, before they could disperse, froze, as Connie and Pat entered the kitchen.

For a moment both girls stood, smiling. Pat murmured something about not being as late back as they had expected. She stopped in mid-sentence. The smiles left their faces as their eyes moved round the crowded kitchen, registering the embarrassment, the blank disapproval and the open hostility.

The meal that evening was very different from the normal, rowdy, relaxed, weekday gatherings of hungry girls, warm and dry for the first time that day and with no further demands on their exhausted energy than to eat everything that Alice and Rose put before them and then slump in one or other of the sagging sofas in the recreation room until it was time to drag themselves upstairs to their beds.

Tonight the conversation round the table had failed to flow. Alice made a few attempts at small talk, mostly in an effort to make things easier for the rat-catchers, who, when they entered the kitchen, had instantly picked up on the tension and almost certainly guessed the reason for it.

Hester, who was unsure what the problem was, understood at least that Connie and Pat had in some way strayed from the path of righteousness. Exactly what form the straying had taken or why even the warden seemed to find it such a serious matter altogether escaped Hester. Unlike the other girls, she knew nothing of the slang terms for homosexuality with which most of them were familiar. A 'pansy', to Hester, was nothing more or less than a flower, and a 'fairy' simply something found at the bottom of the garden in a children's storybook that had been read to her in kindergarten. A 'dyke' was a ditch and if something or someone was 'queer' it meant that it, or they, were in some way peculiar. So she chewed her way through the rather tough rissoles, which were the best Rose had been able to do with the lump of stringy brisket that was all the butcher had on offer that day, and watched the expressions on the familiar faces. And on Pat's face. And on Connie's.

Mabel, in her simple way, knew quite a lot about evil. She knew there were things no one talked about. Things that some fathers and some uncles did to their daughters and their nieces. And that sometimes you were expected to close your eyes and your ears and pretend, like everyone else was pretending, that nothing was wrong. Or perhaps it wasn't wrong. Perhaps all fathers did to their daughters what hers had done to her. And all uncles did what her Uncle George had done. But whatever it was that Connie and Pat had done seemed to have upset everyone at Lower Post Stone. Mabel wondered vaguely why the other girls found the rat-catchers' behaviour so offensive. It didn't seem to her that they were doing anybody any harm. Anyhow, it didn't much matter. In a couple of days they would be gone and it would be Saturday again and she and Ferdie would cook another feast and afterwards make love in his lumpy, odorous bed. She did miss little Arthur, though. She wondered how long she must wait before she would dare to ask Ferdie if she could send for him. She saw the scene in her mind's eye. 'Ferdie,' she'd say, 'I want to come and live 'ere in your cottage wiv you and I want to fetch Arfur down from London, 'cos 'e's my baby, see? 'E's not my little brother, Ferdie. I'm 'is mum! 'E's my own boy!' But what would Ferdie say to that? Would he ask her who Arthur's father was? And if he did, what would she say? If, at that time, she knew that she was pregnant with Ferdie's child, she was neither ready nor able to confront the situation, either to herself or to him. So, as month followed month, she would ignore the telltale signs of her condition while the thickening of her girth remained unnoticed beneath the familiar rounded shape.

Connie and Pat had finished their puddings. 'We're tired,' they were saying. 'We're off to bed. Goodnight.' Their chairs scraped back across the floor. The girls watched them go and heard their footsteps on the wooden stairs. Then their door closed quietly overhead.

*Dear Mrs Todd,* the letter began. Rose had found the envelope when, after the other girls had left for work and the rat-catchers had still not appeared in the kitchen for their breakfast, she had gone upstairs to wake them. Both the beds were neatly made in the empty room. A sealed envelope, addressed to Mrs Todd, was propped against the dressing table mirror.

In the kitchen, Rose handed the letter to Alice.

'They've gone,' she said, adding as she peered out of the kitchen window into the half-light of the early morning. 'Van's gone too. Funny, I never heard un go!'

Alice, at some point in the night, had heard something. Some small, unfamiliar sound which had slightly roused her. She had listened, only half awake, to the usual night noises. A rising easterly wind, audible in the tall trees behind the farmhouse, had been moaning round the chimneys and must have masked the sound of the departing van. Unable to identify anything that threatened her slumbering household, the warden had allowed herself to drift back into a deeper sleep.

Alice slit open the envelope, slid out the sheet of paper, unfolded it and, with Rose sitting across the kitchen table from her, read aloud the clumsily composed and largely unpunctuated message.

'*Dear Mrs Todd,*' she read. '*Although you have always been kind to us things you do not know about have been said to us by some of the girls which have been hard to bear. So although our work round Ledburton is not quite finished yet we are moving out of the hostel. We will sleep in the back of our van for a couple of nights and drop our reports and time sheets in to Mr Bayliss on Friday pm and the last load of carcasses from the other farms. We are sorry for any trouble Mrs Todd. We try to keep ourselves to ourselves but its the way we are you see not how we would choose to be. We don't mean to upset things. Thank you for your kindness. Yours faithfully.'*

Alice slid the letter across the table to Rose. It was written in pencil and both Connie and Pat had signed it.

'It's no good you glaring at me, Alice,' Rose said, defensively. 'It weren't only my opinion. You know that. All the girls felt the same as what I did!'

'I'm not sure that's quite true, Rose. You, Gwennan, Marion and Winnie were the ringleaders.'

Rose bristled with indignation. 'Ringleaders?' she repeated. 'Some of us is more outspoken than others, I grant you, but they all agreed. All of 'em, Alice! None of 'em liked what was going on and you can't deny it.'

Without asking each girl for her individual opinion Alice had no proof that what Rose claimed was true, so she wisely let the debate cool. She picked up the letter and silently re-read it.

'I think the girls should see this,' she said. 'I shall pin it on the noticeboard in the recreation room. I think they must be made aware of what they've done.'

'Maybe even proud of it,' Rose countered defiantly, under her breath.

'The fact is, Rose, that the rat-catchers were prevented from carrying out their work – important work – by prejudice and intolerance and our girls must take the responsibility for that.'

'But you won't go telling Mr Bayliss or Mrs Brewster, though?' Rose was beginning to comprehend the wider implications of what had happened.

'Of course I shall! Connie and Pat were in my care while they were here and they should have been here until the end of the week. Now the pair of them are sleeping in their van! I am responsible for what has happened here. I should have been more observant but I chose to ignore a state of affairs which, I can see now, was more serious than I realised.'

In Roger's cold office, Alice watched him read the rat-catchers' letter. The one or two of the Post Stone girls who were working at the higher farm that morning, although unaware of the letter or its contents, guessed the reason for Alice's visit to their boss.

'I'll have to track them down,' Roger said. 'Can't have them sleeping rough in this weather; it's dangerous.' He consulted a worksheet. 'They're due to finish clearing Tom Lucas's place today. I'll send Jack. He can take over from them and as it's clearly pointless trying to re-establish them at the hostel we'll get them on their way by midday. That OK with you?' He glanced at Alice, anxious not to appear to be overriding her authority. She agreed that his plan was sound and apologised for what she considered a failure on her part to manage the situation better.

'It's a tricky call, Alice,' he said. 'Not one you or I or anyone has to make everyday and, with respect to the Post Stone girls, mob rule soon gets ugly. I wonder whether the rat-catchers have encountered this sort of prejudice before.'

'It's possibly to do with the size of our hostel,' Alice said. 'Any larger and the rat-catchers' relationship might well have gone unnoticed. Any smaller and my guess is it would not have been challenged. Our girls just sort of...ganged up on them. It's dangerous, that kind of bullying.'

With the centre of contention removed from the hostel, the atmosphere round the kitchen table that night was heavy with reflection, speculation, justification and, in some cases, with touches of remorse.

Annie Sorokova in particular, felt, in retrospect, that she and her peers had been unduly harsh. 'It was like our first night here,' she said at supper, 'when Georgina told us she was a pacifist and we all let her know what we thought of *them*!'

'And still do!' Winnie stated emphatically. Marion, her mouth full, nodded in agreement.

'Anyroad,' Winnie added, 'Georgie stopped being a conchie soon enough!'

'Saw the error of her ways, she did!' Marion had swallowed her food and was laughing. 'And look at her now! In the RAF, bless her!'

'No, she's not!' Annie corrected. 'She's in the Air Transport Auxiliary. Not involved in combat. Just delivering planes...'

'To airmen who *are* involved in combat! Stop splitting hairs, Annie Sorokova, there's a good lass!'

Annie had the grace to laugh but her point had been made.

'Where's the rat-catchers to tonight, Mrs Todd?' Hester wanted to know.

'Off to their homes for a day or two of leave,' Alice told her. 'Mr Bayliss let them go early as they had finished their work in this area.' The girls all knew that Jack had completed the rat-catchers' tasks at Tom Lucas's farm. They'd seen him arrive back at Higher Post Stone with a sack of dead rats. He had dug a deep hole in the soft ground behind the sow-house, wheelbarrowed the corpses that had accumulated in the yard round to it, tipped them in, sprinkled on the quicklime, shovelled back the earth and packed it down with the flat of his spade.

'It was almost like Jack dumped Connie and Pat in that pit with the dead rats, Mrs Todd!' Annie said reflectively, after one of several long silences round the kitchen table that night. 'Buried them under a sprinkle of quicklime and a load of dirt!' When Gwennan sniggered, Annie added heavily that she wondered if the rat-catchers knew how easy it had been to solve the problem of what you do

102

with people like them. It was an unpleasant image and one which Alice soon had to replace with other concerns.

'Mrs Todd...?' Hester began, in the tone of voice Alice recognised at once as a precursor to a request for advice. She led Hester through the recreation room and into the privacy of her sitting room.

'I think I might be pregnant, Mrs Todd. I've missed my monthly and I've never done that before!'

Where pregnancy was concerned, Land Army protocol was rigid and unequivocal. The girl, whether or not she was married, was required to leave the service immediately. Because of this, some girls, more often than not the unmarried ones, concealed their condition until, for one reason or another, it was discovered. This situation often resulted in health problems such as miscarriage and premature, or even concealed, births.

Hester and Reuben, more concerned with their decision to marry, despite her family's opposition to the union, than with the possibility of an immediate result of it, had taken no precautions. Consequently she, together with other batches of pregnant GI brides, was destined to be shipped across the Atlantic and delivered to her in-laws, where she would await the birth of her child and, it was hoped, a reunion with her husband when the fighting was over.

'Are you sure, Hester?' had been Alice's first question.

'Well, I doesn't get sick in the mornings nor nothin' but I was due to come on las' week and I never.' 'Coming on' was a euphemism Hester had picked up from the other girls who used it when they referred to menstruation.

Hester's reaction to her possible condition was a complex mixture of delight at the prospect of bearing Reuben's child and a confused awareness of the complications of her situation. Her bland, open face first blushed with pleasure and then clouded with concern as she sat on the edge of one of Alice's chairs, nervously seeking the warden's advice. What, she wondered, would it be like to leave her native land behind her for ever? Would Reuben's family welcome her? Or would they resent the intrusion of a total stranger?

'They'll love you, Hes!' Reuben repeatedly assured her during the brief hours they were able to spend together. 'Mom's already put your photo on the dresser and my kid brother, Charley, thinks you look real cute!'

'So you're only ten days late,' Alice had confirmed when Hester first broke the news to her. 'It could be just the excitement of the wedding and everything, you know. I'd give it a few more weeks, if I were you, Hester. If you miss your next period we'll get the doctor to have a look at you.' But Alice, observing Hester closely from then on, saw, or thought she saw, certain other subtle changes in her and was unsurprised, early in May and with no sign of any bleeding, when the doctor who examined Hester confirmed that she was, as the girls put it, 'two months gone'.

At first everyone's reaction was positive, though Gwennan, predictably, voiced her fears about the effect on the baby should Hester become seasick on the voyage to America or, assuming she arrived there safely – what with the German U-boats – that she would most likely become lost in that vast, dangerous country and never be heard of again. Gwennan had, she assured them all, read about such things in the newspapers. The other girls howled her down and hugged Hester until she became quite overcome and needed to sit down quietly with a cup of strong tea.

Reuben was allowed a 48-hour pass on the strength of the news, and he and the girl who was to bear his child went off to the pub in Ledburton for the night.

To Alice the situation was problematic. With the pregnancy confirmed, Hester would be required to leave the Land Army without delay. Clearly her departure for the States was not imminent and her estrangement from her parents meant that, in effect, she had no home to go to while she waited for embarkation.

It was Rose Crocker who offered a practical solution. With her son, Dave, in the army, Rose had a spare bedroom in her cottage across the yard. Hester's allowance as a US army wife would more than cover the cost of her board and lodging.

'But what will I do all day?' Hester asked when, a week later and with the arrangement approved by both Margery Brewster on Hester's behalf and Reuben's adjutant on his, she packed her bags and followed Rose across the yard.

'We'll find enough to keep you busy!' Rose assured her. 'Girls who's in the family way shouldn't sit about. 'Taint good for 'em.'

So Hester spent those early weeks of her official pregnancy helping with the chores at Lower Post Stone. Sometimes she even went to the higher farm and collected the eggs or scattered corn to the hens. Reuben visited her whenever he could and while she slowly moved up the queue for a place on a ship to Hoboken, New York, Rose took the precaution of writing a carefully worded letter to Dave.

*Dear Son,* she wrote. She had asked the warden for a sheet of paper and an envelope, carried them back to her cottage and sharpened her pencil. She began by bringing Dave up to date with events. *As you know, Hester Tucker married her Reuben in Jan. Well, it seems she fell pregnant straight off. Her folks do not want her no more on account of their religion and she has nowhere to go until she gets shipped off to America. So she has come to board with me. The money is useful and I have put her in your room. When you get leave you will have to sleep downstairs on the camp bed. I know what you felt for Hester, son. I saw the way you looked at her when you first set eyes on her. She is a nice girl and would of made a good daughter-in-law and I wish sometimes that things had worked out different but they did not and it was Reuben got her not you. You must remember this if you come home while she is here Dave and treat her as a married lady and not as the girl you fancy. I hope you got the cake I sent. From your loving mother.*

# *Chapter Four*

Hester, seeing the postman cycling down the lane, went to the farmhouse gate to fetch the letters and carried them into the kitchen.

'Nothing from Reuben,' she said, searching through the few envelopes. 'There be one for Taff.'

'Miss Gwennan Pringle, to you!' Rose teased.

'And one for Miss HM Sorokova,' Hester read carefully. 'We never think of her as Hannah Maria any more though, do we, 'cos of calling her Annie all the time! It's official-looking, Annie's one. Like it's from the government or something.' She propped the envelopes on the dresser where the girls would see them when they returned from work.

Gwennan collected her letter and took it upstairs.

She recognised the handwriting. Her sister Olwen was sick. Gwennan would read the letter where, in the privacy of her single room, she could deal with the bad news she feared it contained, while Annie sat at the kitchen table to open hers, drawing the folded sheet from the envelope.

Annie's letter was typed and signed with a flourish that suggested its author was someone used to dealing with a large correspondence. Alice, who was beating eggs for a batter, ready for toad-in-the-hole, saw Annie's eyes widen.

'It's from the War Artists' people!' she said excitedly. 'And it's about Andreis's painting!'

Months had passed since the inhabitants of the Post Stone farms had been shocked by the suicide of the Dutch refugee, who, with Roger Bayliss's support, had lived in a loft above one of the barns at the lower farm. He had been a lonely figure and was only occasionally encountered by the land girls. Having escaped from his native Amsterdam while it was being systematically overrun by the Nazis, Andreis had subsequently become tormented by guilt, accusing himself of cowardice for having abandoned his Jewish friends and those members of his own family who had waited too long to escape or had perhaps simply been unable to believe what was about to happen to them, before attempting to flee from the increasing oppression of the Jewish community to which they belonged.

In an attempt to quieten his conscience, Andreis did the only thing he could do as a protest against events in his homeland. He used his skill as an artist to depict, on the huge pair of double doors that divided one half of the loft above the main barn from the other, his reaction to what he had seen and what he now believed was happening to those he had left behind.

No one had guessed, at the start of the war, what the level of barbarity, meted out by the Gestapo, would be, but as the early years passed, rumours had turned into hard evidence and as his horror and his own sense of guilt deepened, Andreis, in his cold and lonely loft, painted the nightmare of the invasion of his city and the appalling treatment of its inhabitants. He painted the families cowering in their homes, secretly supported by friends who risked their own lives to conceal them. He painted their discovery by SS officers who manhandled them out into the streets and onto trains that carried them God knew where. Horrific evidence was seeping out and the darkest suspicions were slowly becoming accepted as either the hideous truth or something perilously close to it.

It was these facts and those fears that drove Andreis. Day and night he developed his ideas, made sketches and then transferred the images onto the doors, which he had smoothed and primed so that they glowed, luminous and challenging in the lofty space. He added colour. Khakis and browns, grey-greens and black. For the faces of the men he used his own face, reflected in the small looking glass Roger Bayliss had had fixed above the china bowl and jug Andreis used for his ablutions.

For the faces of the women and the girls, Andreis used Annie Sorokova as his model, whose classic Jewish beauty he had first noticed as she crossed the yard one Saturday afternoon. He had approached her, asking her if she could spare a few hours to pose for him. He showed her the early stages of his painting and watched her react to the uncompromising images of pain and terror as the fleeing people were pursued and driven towards the railway tracks, for this much, by then, was recognised as indisputable fact.

'You'll have to ask Mrs Todd,' Annie had told him.

'Pose for you?' Alice had enquired, doubtfully, when Andreis had approached her.

'She will of course be always clothed,' he had said, in his precise English. 'She has the classic look of the Jewess, you see. The long neck, the large and beautiful eyes. And the colouring,' he added. 'The darkness of hair and brows and the pallor of skin. All typical. And the bearing too, you understand? The way the head is held?' He had paused, aware of Alice's concern, as warden of the hostel, for the welfare of her charges. She had crossed the yard to the barn, climbed the ladder and stood at one end of the gloomy space, gazing up at the vague shapes and outlines of the proposed composition, at its spare lines, drawn in charcoal and barely suggesting the solidity of the groups of driven figures that would soon materialise on it. At the other end of the loft was a chair. 'She will be quite safe here, Madam Todd,' Andreis had said. 'I shall be over here, where the painting is, and Hannah Maria will be there, where you are, by the stove.' He stood, waiting for her response, the light falling on his gaunt face and unkempt hair and reminding Alice suddenly of another Dutch painter. Another lonely and tormented man.

'If she wants to,' Alice had said eventually, 'I have no objection. But don't keep her too long, Andreis, and don't let her get cold.'

'My many thank yous, madam!' he had said, and smiled. Alice realised then that she had never before seen any expression on his face other than a familiar brooding tension. He took her hand and kissed it.

'And you agreed to it?' Margery Brewster had asked, when Alice told her of the arrangement.

'We trust him, don't we?' Alice had replied. 'Mr Bayliss has sponsored him as a refugee, so presumably he trusts him too. It's only across the yard, Margery, and Annie is a sensible girl.'

Margery Brewster had shrugged and pulled a face that suggested to Alice that, although she would not go so far as to approve of the arrangement, she did not feel strongly enough opposed to it to voice an objection.

So it was that, through the early spring and most of the summer of 1943, Annie Sorokova, whom Andreis always called Hannah Maria, spent many of her Saturday afternoons and sometimes, as the days lengthened, an hour or so on weekday evenings, standing or sitting, stock still, while Andreis made sketches of her. Sometimes he would drape her in a blanket and ask her to stand, bowed and bent, representing an old woman. Sometimes he rolled the blanket into a shape that resembled an infant, which Annie then cradled in her arms. Her hair could be loose around her small, vulnerable face, or piled on her head, or hidden severely under a scarf. But the face was always recognisably Annie's face, just as the men in the painting always resembled Andreis himself.

'It is the point, you see?' he would tell her. 'Of what I am painting. They are, you understand, the same person. The same woman and the same man, suffering the same outrage whether they are a grandfather or a son or the woman is a young girl, a *mutta*, or a even a grand-*mutta*. They are a race, you see? Not individuals.'

When his work was completed, Andreis had astonished everyone by announcing his intention to return to Holland, join the resistance and fight for his country. Roger Bayliss counselled him against this.

'You are not a fighting man, Andreis. You don't have the temperament or the—'

'Or the courage? That is what you mean, of course. That I am a coward!' Roger tried to interrupt him but Andreis would not be silenced. 'I should not have come here when my country was overrun! I should have stayed and maybe died with my friends! I took the coward's way but that decision has made of me a man I cannot live with! Do not wish any more to be! You have been most kind, Mr Bayliss, sir, to give me shelter here and allow me time to make my painting and I am grateful to you for it. But now that it is complete I can no longer stay. We learn each day more and more of what is happening to Jews in my country and so, whatever may happen to me there, I must go home.'

But Andreis did not go home. When he had first arrived at Lower Post Stone Farm, Roger Bayliss had lent him a shotgun to kill rabbits for the stews he simmered on his stove in the loft. On the morning of the day he was to leave he shot himself, clumsily, in the thigh and lay, undiscovered, while he bled to death in the orchard behind the barns.

Of the land girls, Annie, who had known him best, was the most distressed by what had happened and that evening she led the girls across the yard and up into the loft, where she showed them Andreis's painting. They took flashlights with them and lit the oil lamps that Andreis had used when he worked at night. They stood, all ten girls, together with Alice and Rose Crocker, and stared at the amazing work.

Annie had resolved that night to, in some way, preserve the painting. Georgina, who had not yet left the Land Army, had a godfather who was a museum curator and whose work was connected with the War Artists' Scheme. He had subsequently visited the farm, examined Andreis's painting, and agreed it was impressive. He had passed his opinion on to his contacts. Now, eight months later, someone was being sent to examine the work, assess its importance and decide on the best way to both preserve and exhibit it.

Throughout the autumn and the cold, dank winter, Annie had checked the painting, persuaded Roger Bayliss to repair a leak in the roof where the wind was driving rain into the loft and, on the coldest, dampest days, she lit the stove in the sad, empty space.

She had not only known Andreis better than the other girls and acted as a model for the characters depicted in his painting, but it had been she, together with Georgina, who had persisted with the idea of preserving it, not only because of its importance as a work of art but as a tribute to Andreis himself. Aware of her involvement, Roger Bayliss gave Annie a day off from her work on the farm so that she could meet with the representative from the War Artists' Scheme and introduce him to the painting.

Hector Conway arrived at midday in a mud-spattered bull-nosed Morris. He had lost his way in the lanes and squinting through the thick lenses of his spectacles at Alice, Rose and Annie, he apologised profusely for failing to arrive at the appointed time. His short-sightedness, which explained his lateness, also accounted for his exemption from conscription into the armed services.

Hector was tall and lean. His movements were slightly uncoordinated and the way he peered about him suggested that, for him, the world was slightly out of focus, which, in fact, it was. His hair was unkempt. He wore corduroy trousers and his tweed jacket had well-worn leather patches on its elbows. Only his manner, as he made his apologies and introduced himself to the three women who faced him, his firm handshake and his well modulated voice defined him as educated and middle class. One of his shoelaces had become untied and when Rose, who had answered his knock on the farmhouse door, pointed this out to him, he stooped to re-tie it. As he did so some papers from his half-open file slipped through his hands.

'I'll get them,' Annie said, leaning down to retrieve the loose sheets of notepaper that were scattered across the kitchen floor. As he bent over his shoelaces their heads almost collided and they laughed, looking into each other's eyes and both of them seeing something there which they were to remember. It was, Annie recalled much later, almost as though they had recognised each other, despite the fact that until that moment, they had never met.

Rose provided a cheese sandwich, which Hector devoured with a relish that pleased her.

'It's nice to feel appreciated,' she said later, after Annie had taken Hector across the yard and up into the loft where she watched him make his initial assessment of the painting.

It was a bright day and a clear, bluish light poured in through the glazed section of the roof.

'It's huge,' Hector breathed, intently scanning the sprawling composition. Then he produced a powerful flashlight and, standing close to the painting, moved its beam slowly across it, hesitating from time to time in order to pay closer attention to a particular detail.

Annie watched him, trying to read his reaction. His expression gave no clue. Perhaps the painting was not a good one. Maybe she saw its power because she had known Andreis and understood his passion for its subject.

'His drawings are over there,' she said, indicating the trestle table on which the dozens of charcoal sketches he had made, many of them of Annie herself, were piled haphazardly.

Hector moved over to the table and began leafing through them.

'These are of you, of course,' he murmured. 'Hannah Maria Sorokova.' He read the pencilled notes which identified Annie as the sitter and gave the date of each sketch. 'I wondered what the H and the M stood for.' He turned to Annie and smiled. 'The initials were on the first report which was signed HM Sorokova and G Webster. Who is G Webster?'

'Georgina,' Annie told him. 'Known as Georgie. And I'm known as Annie. It was Georgie and me who decided, when Andreis...' she hesitated, 'when he...died...to try to get his painting preserved. Sort of...in his memory. Because it was so sad.'

'His suicide. Yes. I heard about that. Tragic.' Hector was still sorting through the sketches. 'Some of these are good... Very good.' Annie was becoming concerned that he seemed more interested in the sketches than in the painting itself.

'It wasn't just the suicide that was tragic,' she said emphatically. 'It was everything about him. This painting was very important to him! And now it's important to me. And to Georgie. And all the girls here. And Mrs Todd and Mr Bayliss. Everyone who has seen it!'

'Important, yes,' he said vaguely, 'but technically it is not of a very high standard, you know.' He caught her reaction of acute disappointment and perceived at once what a blow his statement was to her. 'Don't misunderstand me,' he added quickly, 'it is, as you say, important. And significant and powerful. The fact that Andreis van der Loos was, I would guess, self-taught, doesn't detract from that significance, nor from its right to be preserved and exhibited.' He had turned back to face the painting and stood, his eyes narrowed, exploring it, Annie watching him. 'My feeling is that it may be in his native land where it will be most highly valued as a record of what happened there during the Nazi occupation. It may take some time for decisions to be made about its future but in the meantime it must be carefully stored.' Hector's voice was low. He spoke, Annie noticed, as he thought. Slowly and considerately. 'I shall recommend that it's taken from here, where, clearly, there is a risk of it becoming damaged.' He moved slowly backwards, stepping away from the painting, his eyes still on it.

'But how can you take it?' Annie asked quietly, matching her tone to his, the practicalities of his proposal slowly occurring to her.

'We'll have to remove the doors,' he said, as though

pulling barns to pieces was all part of his day's work. 'We'll replace them, of course,' he added. 'For your Mr Bayliss.' He was preoccupied and professional. Annie had never before encountered anyone quite like him.

She watched him carefully gather up the loose, smudged charcoal sketches.

'The first thing our arts department will do is spray these with a fixative or there'll soon be nothing left of them... What's this?' The monochrome sketch was of Annie's head and shoulders. Her hair, on this occasion, was much as the other girls wore theirs, piled high on the crown of her head and then falling in heavy curls down to her shoulders. Her summer frock had short sleeves and the sharp definition of her mouth suggested the deep red lipstick she had been wearing. Andreis had written *Hannah Maria, July 1943* in the corner of the drawing and initialled it, as he had most of the other sketches. Annie examined it and smiled.

'I remember that day! It was a Saturday and I'd been to Exeter with Georgie. Andreis said I looked pretty and he would draw me in my frock instead of the dreary old dungarees we girls always wear for work!'

'Did he flirt with you?' Hector asked vaguely. 'Were you his girl?'

'No,' Annie said, and then paused, adding

thoughtfully, 'No, I wasn't. Andreis never flirted. He wasn't like other blokes, you see. Maybe, before the war, he had been. But, here, we only saw one side of him. It seemed like he'd left that part of himself behind in Holland.'

'I think you should keep this one,' Hector said, holding the drawing out to her. 'To remember him by. This sketch is irrelevant to the project, anyway. It was between you and him.' Annie took the sketch and thanked him.

Later, when he had stowed the loose sketches in a portfolio which he carefully placed on the back seat of his car, he hesitated awkwardly beside it, as though he was reluctant to leave.

'I shan't be involved in the removal of the painting,' he said, 'so I may not see you again. But perhaps... when the authorities have decided what to do with it...' he paused, his eyes on Annie's. 'My guess is that the Dutch government will want to display it in the Hague or possibly Amsterdam. We shan't know for certain until after the war... But when we do... may I write to you and let you know?' She nodded and said yes. 'But will you still be here?' he asked, peering through his thick lenses at the shabby face of the farmhouse.

Annie shrugged. Being fully occupied by the here and now of her life, she had not given much thought to what would become of her when the war ended.

With Georgina's encouragement she was working her way through the series of Ministry of Agriculture exams which, if she succeeded in passing them, would qualify her for a career in farming if she wanted one. A brief but intense flirtation with Georgina's brother Lionel had damaged Annie's self-esteem when, to his sister's disapproval, he had ditched her in favour of a girl more suited to his class.

'No,' she said, 'I don't suppose I will be. I reckon they'll close down the hostels, won't they, once the war is over... I could give you my folks' address, if you like?' He searched his pockets, produced a small leather address book and fumbled through it until he reached the page marked S. Annie gave him the number of the narrow terrace house in Duckett Street, which, despite having its windows smashed and its front door blown in, had survived the Blitz. Hector returned the book to his breast pocket. Then he hesitantly held out his hand to her. As they shook hands, he rather formally thanked her for the part she had played in the preservation of Andreis's work. Then she watched the bull-nosed Morris move off down the lane, its driver avoiding the deepest potholes and glancing repeatedly, via his mirror, at the girl at the farmhouse gate.

'I liked him,' Annie told Alice over a cup of tea, as it was too late for her to go back to work before the midday lunch break. 'He talks posh but he's not a bit stuck up. Not like Lionel la-di-dah Webster!' She smiled at Alice, who knew something – but not everything – about her flirtation with Georgina's brother. 'He lives with his folks in Oxford. His dad works at one of the colleges there. He's something called a don, Hector said. What's a don, Mrs Todd?'

'It's a sort of senior lecturer,' Alice told her vaguely, her mind already occupied by the preparation of the evening meal. 'Give Rose a hand with the carrots, would you, Annie? There's a dear.'

When Marion had failed to do so, her friend Winnie had taken it upon herself to respond to the letter from Sergeant Marvin Kinski, in which he had enclosed a snapshot of himself and requested, in return, one of Marion.

The photograph that Winnie mailed to him had been taken the previous summer on a hot Sunday afternoon when the land girls had been cooling off in the shallows of the River Ledbourne, an insignificant tributary of the Exe, which meandered through Post Stone valley. Marion, wearing a bathing dress, had posed on a boulder, arranging herself so that her legs appeared as long and slender as possible. The concentration required to maintain her position on the boulder, hold in her stomach, thrust out her chest, widen her eyes and show her teeth had resulted in a smile of acute tension as she faced Georgina's Box

Brownie camera. The overall effect was, nevertheless, fetching enough and Marvin had been enchanted. Unknown to Marion or even to Winnie, he carried the snapshot everywhere, next to his heart in the envelope in which it had arrived.

A week after he received it, on April 27th 1944, Sergeant Marvin Kinski was among almost a thousand young servicemen, most of whom were American, who were caught up in one of the major training disasters of the war. It was part of the Allies programme in preparation for the Normandy landings but, for a number of reasons, most of which were avoidable, Exercise Tiger ended in tragedy when German E-boats attacked a convoy of under-protected ships, sinking or severely damaging most of them. More than seven hundred men lost their lives.

Sergeant Kinski, one of the few survivors, was dragged, after six hours and only semi-conscious, from the cold waters of Lyme Bay and removed to an army hospital where, for days, he lay, more dead than alive. The snapshot of Marion, water damaged but still recognisable, was dried out and returned to him along with the pages of an illegible letter from his mother, which had been recovered from the same sodden pocket.

For obvious security reasons, and with the planned invasion of France only weeks away, a total news blackout was imposed on the entire incident. The few survivors, most severely traumatised, were sworn to secrecy and removed to special camps where they were held under strict surveillance. Kinski found himself at a small military establishment in Wales. Still suffering from the effects of exposure and with all the men in his own section dead, he was ordered to assume responsibility for the training of a group of almost raw conscripts. He would be allowed no leave and his correspondence, should there be any, would be scrutinised and heavily censored. Anxious letters from his mother prompted him to write carefully to her. 'All well here, Mom. Am with a great bunch of guys and the grub is fine.'

Although Marvin still carried Marion's photograph in his breast pocket he did not write to her. The odds on his survival of Exercise Tiger had, as it turned out, been overwhelmingly against him, yet he had come through it. He believed he had, that night in Lyme Bay, used up the luck he was going to need on the French beaches. Watching his men drown, almost drowning himself, had damaged him. He had no one to confide in and no one to tell him that it was all right to feel as he did. It was better if Marion didn't know how fond he was of her. No point, he decided, as he drilled his new section through the cool days of a Welsh May, in upsetting her. He thought too much of her for that.

* * *

By mid-May good weather had increased the workload of the land girls on the Post Stone farms and, with Hester on light duties and the newcomers – Elsie, Eva and Nancy – working for Roger Bayliss's neighbours, he was reluctant, when Gwennan asked for leave to visit her sister in hospital, to grant the necessary permission. Gwennan took her request to Mrs Brewster, who advised him to reconsider.

'She makes a good case, Roger,' the registrar told him. 'The sister had an operation last year. Cancer, poor woman. She appeared to have recovered but has recently become ill again and is not expected to live. Gwennan is convinced that if she isn't allowed to go and see her now, she will be too late.'

Gwennan, in her Land Army uniform, a bulging carpet bag beside her, sat at the kitchen table, waiting for the arrival of Fred, who was to drive her in the farm truck to Ledburton Halt, where she would board the Bristol train.

'It was just a small lump,' she told the warden, 'but they took away her whole breast.' Alice nodded sympathetically and wished that she had not been so sharp on the many occasions when Gwennan had whined and grumbled and tried to make trouble amongst the other girls. 'They said she'd most prob'ly be all right. But that's what they said to my Auntie Rhiannon and she died, see. And now Olwen's got poorly again.'

'I'm so sorry,' Alice said. And she did sympathise with this difficult girl whom no one liked and who appeared, even when faced with the tragedy she was now confronting, no less gaunt and tense and angry than usual. 'Perhaps the news will be better by the time you get home.' Gwennan did not reply and sat quietly, her eyes blank and almost expressionless, until they both heard the rattle of the truck. Then Gwennan got to her feet and lifted up her bag.

'Thank you, Mrs Todd,' she said tightly. 'I'll not be away no longer than I have to be.'

'Looks like them artist people 'as come,' Rose announced when, towards the end of May, a pantechnicon drew up at the farmhouse gate. Alice had been told to expect the men who were to remove Andreis's painting from the barn loft and transport it to a warehouse in Swindon, where it could be safely stored. She had not been expecting Hector Conway but there was his car, parked behind the pantechnicon, and here was he, standing nervously at the door, saying good morning to her and to Rose, who was hovering behind her in the cross-passage.

'You weren't expecting me,' he said. 'Nor was I. I mean, I wasn't expecting to come – but as I was in the area and as the removal of the doors – I mean the doors with the painting on them – is, well, might be, a bit tricky, I thought I'd come... Just to... You see?' Alice said she did see. Hector swallowed heavily and came straight to the point. 'Is...is Miss Sorokova about at all?' Alice heard Rose's suppressed laugh and thought she heard her say, under her breath, that no, Miss Sorokova was not about at all.

'She's working, Mr Conway,' Alice said, seeing his anxious face fall and experiencing that gentle surge of empathy that tender-hearted women feel when faced with evidence of the onset of young love. 'She might be at the other farm,' she indicated the distant huddle of granite buildings that was Higher Post Stone Farm. 'But they are haymaking this week and the hay fields are on the far side of the hill.'

Annie saw Hector's car as he drove cautiously in, through the gate of a meadow where the girls were turning hay that had been cut the day before and was now drying nicely in the warm sun.

He brought his car to a stop and sat with the Morris's engine ticking over, his eyes on Annie as she approached him and stood, smiling. He noticed that a few stray stalks of hay were caught in the dark mass of her hair and that her usually pale skin was flushed by exertion in the midday heat.

Hector was, Annie realised, looking nervously past her at the eight land girls of assorted shapes and sizes, some with their dungarees cut off at the thigh, others wearing shorts and thin shirts, their limbs and faces sunburnt and shining with sweat, who had stopped swinging pitchforks loaded with hay up onto the wagon and were standing, staring at him. Transfixed with shyness, he blushed and gulped.

'Have you come to collect the painting?' Annie asked him. The question seemed to restore his composure. He smiled and answered her. Then he suggested he might take her for a spin. This experience was something his older brothers were in the habit of offering to their own girlfriends.

'I can't, Hector. I'm s'posed to be working!'

'Go on, Annie!' Marion's sharp voice pierced the heavy air. 'Jack won't be back for half an hour! We'll cover for you! Go on! 'Op it!'

'We'll tell him it were a call of nature!' Winnie bellowed. The other girls shrieked with raucous laughter at the double entendre and Mabel was so overcome that she tripped, lost her balance and sprawled onto a pile of hay where she lay, giggling helplessly.

So Annie got into the little car and Hector, having recovered from his shyness, beeped his horn, let out his clutch, waved to the cheering girls and drove Annie through the gate, out into the lane and along it. He turned onto the main road and they sped towards Ledburton, made a neat circuit of the village pond and headed back again, through open country.

The bull-nosed Morris coped heroically, if noisily,

with the steep inclines. Its canvas roof was folded down and the slipstream lifted Annie's hair and whipped Hector's back from his smooth, high forehead, making him look, Annie thought, almost handsome. He would have driven further but, as he explained to her, his petrol allowance from the War Artists' Scheme had to be precisely accounted for.

'She was taken short!' The girls had told Jack as Annie, who had asked Hector to drop her in the lane, entered the field on foot. To corroborate their story, she pulled a face at the wily old man and rubbed her abdomen.

'Pain under your pinny, were it?' he called to her, rolling his eyes and muttering about 'bloomin' women! Alus got a pain somewhere, they 'as!' He turned to the other girls and bawled, 'Thought you lot'd 'ave got this meadow done by now! I dunno... Turn me back for five minutes...'

Had Gwennan been there she would have pointed out to Jack that his absence had, in fact, been for thirty minutes, not five, and that, as he'd taken the tractor, it was obvious to all of them that he had made a foray down the valley for a quick pint at the Maltster's. Then she would have wondered, aloud, what their boss would have made of that. But Gwennan was not there. She was in Wales at her sister's bedside, reading aloud to her.

* * *

Olwen's pallid face bore traces of pain. It was as though she was braced for the onset of the next spasm, knowing it would come, taking away her breath and her awareness of everything around her while she endured it, her fingers biting into the mattress of her sickbed.

'Go on, Gwennie,' she said. 'Read it to me.' Gwennan was marking her place on the page with her forefinger. She cleared her throat and began to read.

'"I caught at his arm…"'

'Louder, Gwennie,' said her sister. Gwennan raised her voice and continued.

'"And tried to speak to him and failed as I had failed when I tried before. He went on, following the footsteps down and down to where the rocks and the sand joined."'

Olwen's eyes were closed and she was breathing evenly.

'"The South Spit was just awash with the flowing tide; the waters heaved over the hidden face of the Shivering Sand."' Gwennan paused, her eyes on the face that was being slowly and subtly changed by illness.

'Go on then, Gwennie,' Olwen murmured. 'Go on.'

'But you know it,' Gwennan said quietly. 'You've heard it all before. You know what happens to poor Rosanna Spearman.'

'Yes, I do. But I like to hear it again. I like the bit about the Shivering Sand...'

Gwennan returned to the farm after five days and when, several weeks later, Olwen died, she refused to travel to Wales for the funeral.

'I don't believe in the Bible no more,' she told Alice, her pale face hard with anger. '"God in his mercy," it says, but there's nothing merciful about letting our Olwen die like that, is there? Nor our Aunt Rhiannon, either! So I don't want to hear what the preacher has to say, standing there, trying to look sorry and most likely not even properly remembering her name!'

At Lower Post Stone, Rose's washing had dried quickly in the warm May breeze, and it had been barely midday when she sent Hester from the farmhouse to fetch it from the line. Hester had carried the heaped basket of aprons, cotton dresses and undergarments that Rose had soaked, pummelled and mangled earlier that morning, back into the Crocker cottage.

The interior of Rose's kitchen was a dark contrast to the brilliant sunlight of the yard outside it, so, for a moment, Hester failed to see the figure at the kitchen table.

Corporal Dave Crocker sat sweating. The walk from the bus stop in Ledburton had overheated him and patches of sweat darkened his khaki shirt. He had pulled off his heavy boots and was enjoying, through his damp socks, the cool of his mother's slate floor. He laughed at Hester's surprise at seeing him there and then apologised for scaring her.

'You didn't scare me, Dave! Why would I be scared of you? It were just that at first I didn't see you there, sittin' in the shadow – and we wasn't expectin' you, was we! I'll go tell your mum you'm here, but first I'll put on the kettle. She's sure to want to make you a cuppa tea!'

Both of them were remembering Boxing Day, when the farm had been deep in snow. Reuben had hitched a ride back to his barracks, leaving Hester with his grandmother's ruby ring on the third finger of her left hand, the warmth of his kisses on her mouth and the promise that the two of them were going to live happily ever after fresh in her mind.

But by mid-morning Dave had fixed the broken toboggan that was a relic of his childhood and, with Hester securely held between his warm thighs, they had skimmed down the long slope of the hill. As he guided the sledge and protected her from harm when they inevitably overturned, he couldn't believe how much he loved her or how hopeless his situation was. But with the low, winter sunlight glittering on pristine snow and the perfect blue of the sky arcing over them, Hester Tucker was, for that moment at least, his. They had ended up, she helpless with innocent laughter, pitched into a pile of loose hay near the ricks.

Hester remembered how prettily the tiny diamonds on Reuben's ring, which, by that time, had already been on her finger for more than twelve hours, twinkled in the sunlight, and how safe she had felt as she and Dave hurtled down the slope, flying through a fine spray of snow which sparkled in the freezing air and prickled when it struck their cold cheeks. She had been the luckiest and happiest girl in the world that day. And she still was. Of course she was. Despite the letters from her father. Letters that had struck into her like a cold fist, telling her that in the eyes of the Lord she was damned. She was happy because she had married the boy she loved. And she was happy to be carrying his child. Of course she was happy. Why would she not be? She was conscious of Dave's eyes on her as she set his mother's kettle on the hob.

'You'm a married lady now, then, Hes.' Dave was saying as he watched her unhook the teacups from the dresser and arrange them on the table. His rounded accent exactly matched hers. 'Mrs Reuben Westerfelt, eh! With a baby on the way an' all.'

'How d'you know all that?' Hester asked him, blushing. She glanced at him and then, disconcerted by the way his eyes engaged hers and seemed to make it impossible for her to look away, turned her back on him and searched, although she knew where it was, for the tea caddy.

'From me ma, o' course!' Dave told her but did not add the fact that his mother had also told him to forget his earlier attraction to Hester and treat her with the respect her newly acquired status demanded.

'I best go tell 'er you'm 'ere!' she said. 'She'll kill me, else!' For a moment she was a dark silhouette in the doorway and then, lit by brilliant sunlight, she was crossing the yard and he could hear her calling out to his mother, 'Mrs Crocker! Where are you? Come quick! Guess 'o's 'ere!'

That night Dave slept on the camp bed in his mother's tiny front parlour. Every so often he heard the familiar twang of the bedsprings directly above him, where Hester was sleeping in the room that had always been his. The camp bed was uncomfortable. His feet protruded beyond the blanket and the thin patchwork quilt slipped off him as he tossed and turned.

Hester should have been his. None of the Ledburton girls he'd known before the war or the crimped and painted ones that hung round the barracks where he was stationed were a patch on her. But it had been Reuben she was watching for on Christmas night, when Dave had danced every dance with her. She was shy with him but it was not the artificial coquettishness he so often encountered, which, although it roused him, left him unmoved. Hester amazed him. As he had guided her protectively round the crowded floor of the hostel's recreation room the other dancers had dissolved until it was just the two of them, alone in the warm, smoky, darkened space. And then Reuben, determined to keep his promise to Hester, had at last arrived, almost exhausted by hours of trudging through the snow. And Hester had cried out, left Dave and run into Reuben's arms. His mother had warned him. She had observed her son's reaction to Hester and told him that the girl was already spoken for.

Dave did not, for one moment, blame Hester for his disappointment. She had neither encouraged nor misled him. Yet this did nothing to diminish his feelings for her or his conviction that, if there was any sense in anything, Hester was destined to be his.

Day was breaking and the farmyard rooster was crowing by the time Dave slept. Next day he travelled back to his barracks although his leave had another twenty-four hours to run.

Winnie had watched, as unobtrusively as she could, to see whether any mail arrived for Marion from Sergeant Kinski. It was over a month now since she had slipped the snapshot of her friend into an envelope and posted it to the US army address he had printed on the letter he had sent to Marion, but when week succeeded week and no response arrived, Winnie had assumed that the sergeant had found some other girl to fancy.

In fact, Marvin Kinski, together with most of the young men who were being mustered for an assault on the beaches of northern France, sensed the approach of the moment when they would be ordered to board the thousands of landing craft that were concealed along England's south coast, be transported across the pitching waters of the English Channel and delivered into whatever sort of hell the German army was preparing for their arrival.

The cloak of secrecy that shrouded every aspect of the preparations for the Allies' coming assault on France fooled no one. Exactly where the troops would be landed and precisely when remained unknown, but the more intelligent and observant of them were aware that the midsummer solstice was not many weeks away. The nights were short, the sea, at almost midsummer, should be relatively smooth and warm, so they were, even if only subconsciously, aware of what was about to happen to them, of what was going to be asked of them and that many of them would not survive it. So they drank as much as they were able to and went as far as they could with as many girls as possible. They wrote home, thanked their mums for the tin of cookies or the batch of blueberry muffins, sent their best to their brothers and sisters, uncles and aunts, told their girls how much they loved them and promised to write again soon.

## Chapter Five

The morning of June 6th 1944 began, on both the Bayliss farms, much as any other. The weather was quiet after several stormy days and the dairy herd had already been turned out into one of the water meadows and was hungrily pulling at the succulent grass. Mabel was hosing out the milking stalls and Winnie and Marion were in the yard, shovelling dung onto a cart.

As usual, the old wireless set, donated by Margery Brewster and plugged into a power point just inside the door to the milking shed, was broadcasting a programme of popular music transmitted by the BBC to boost morale amongst war workers. The same upbeat tunes and soulful ballads echoed across munitions factory floors, along aircraft assembly lines, through the laundries of hospitals, in the kitchens of schools and around government offices up and down the nation. Anywhere and everywhere where workers were working.

At Higher Post Stone Farm, Winnie and Marion, breathless as they were from exertion, joined in lustily with the choruses while Ferdie Vallance, an accomplished whistler, extemporised, his efforts encouraged and appreciated by Mabel.

'Lovely whistler you are, Ferdie,' she told him, looping up the hose and hanging it on its hook.

'An' that's not all I'm good for, is it, my lover!' They leered at each other, sharing their secret.

Roger Bayliss, like many civilians at that time, had been keeping an ear open for news. He had brought his own wireless set from the farmhouse and, as he worked his way through a stack of paperwork, the same music that was blaring across the yard was faintly audible in his office. Rose, too, in the kitchen at Lower Post Stone Farm, carefully selecting ten large potatoes which she would later bake in the oven for the girls' dinner, heard the familiar tunes and sang snatches of the words. Then, as the programme was interrupted, she froze.

'This is the BBC Home Service,' a familiar voice announced. 'Here is a special bulletin read by John Snagge.'

In his office, Roger Bayliss reached for the volume control on his receiver.

Ferdie Vallance, passing the barn door, caught the words and shouted to Mabel. 'Quick, Mabel!' he called. 'There's a special bulletin comin' through!' Marion and Winnie heard him and hurried across the yard, and Gwennan came rapidly out of the poultry shed, where she had been sorting eggs, and joined them as they clustered round the wireless. The reception was poor, distorting the words as the girls and Ferdie tried to catch them.

'D-Day has come...' the broadcaster's voice continued. 'Early this morning the Allies began the assault on the north-western face of Hitler's European fortress.' It was an announcement that no one who heard it would ever forget, wherever or whoever they were. Old, young, rich or poor, sick and injured or safe and well, the words imprinted themselves on the minds and in the hearts of everyone. At Lower Post Stone Farm, Rose ran out of the kitchen shouting.

'Alice! Come quick!' she yelled. 'It's D-Day! The man says D-Day has come!' Hester, who had been upstairs sweeping bedrooms, ran down the steep stairs, colliding with Alice as she came quickly through from her sitting room. The three women burst into the kitchen and stood, motionless, round the wireless set, open-mouthed, as John Snagge's words reached them, his level delivery of the facts helping them to absorb and understand the news that everyone had been waiting for.

'Knew it!' At Higher Post Stone Farm, Marion's sharp Northern voice rang triumphantly round the farmyard. 'Didn't I say?' she yelled, 'I knew it! I did!'

'How could *you* 'ave knowed *that*?' Jack growled, his scorn palpable.

''Cos where's all the fellas bin these last few days then, eh? Gone off, ready for the invasion, that's where! There's not a uniform in sight no more!' She moved close to the aging man, her flushed face inches from his sulky, weathered one, and she tapped the side of her nose with a grimy forefinger. 'Some of us 'as put two and two together, Mr Jack!'

'And made five, most like!' The altercation would have continued if Gwennan, who was trying to concentrate on the bulletin, picking up on the time of the invasion, where it had taken place, which forces were involved and who their commanders were, hadn't told them to shut up.

'Montgomery!' she shouted triumphantly, 'Good old Monty! And Eisenhower! Listen will you... The man says as King George is going to be on the wireless tonight, talking to the nation... And they've dropped paratroopers! Normandy, they landed! Well I never,' she breathed, suddenly unable to take in any more information. 'Well I never! D-Day! At last!'

In the kitchen at Lower Post Stone Farm, Alice

saw Hester's face blanch. She clutched at the edge of the table and breathed the name of her husband, repeating it, over and over. As her knees began to buckle, Alice took her by her elbows and set her down on a chair.

'Head between your knees, Hester, there's a good girl, and Rose...put the kettle on, will you?' But Rose, too, was ashen faced.

'My Dave,' she said, looking accusingly at Alice, as though she was in some way to blame. 'On'y las' week he said as the balloon was gonna go up! Any minute, he said. "I can't say no more'n that, Ma, but take it from me, any day now, the balloon..."' Rose's throat closed on the words but she did as Alice had asked and filled the kettle, then stood it on the hob.

That evening Roger Bayliss arrived at the lower farm with two bottles of a good Burgundy. He was possibly a little disappointed by the girls' lack of appreciation of the gesture. They sipped and smiled politely enough but, as Alice told him when they carried their own glasses through to her sitting room, 'They would probably have preferred beer! But it's the thought that counts and it was a very kind one. Thank you, Roger – on their behalf.' They sat in the half-light and toasted the day's good news. 'How d'you think it's going?' she asked him, meaning the invasion.

'Hard to say,' Roger answered, and then paused. 'It can't have been a complete disaster. Certainly not another Dunkirk. We'd know by now if it had been. But my guess is that they won't tell us much until a few goals are achieved. Caen will be the first major objective. Until we secure Caen there's the risk that we could be outflanked and if we can't maintain dependable supply lines across the Channel and well into Normandy, our people are going to be in trouble.' He sipped thoughtfully and added, 'No casualty figures yet, of course. But it must have been carnage on those beaches.'

'Hester is already asking how soon she can expect to hear whether Reuben is all right,' Alice said. 'And Rose is worried sick about her Dave.' Roger drained his glass and got to his feet.

'Thought I'd drive up to the forest,' he said. 'Christopher probably doesn't know about the invasion.'

'D'you think he wants to know? I mean, he is a pacifist.' Roger thought about this for a moment.

'I believe he's lost too many good friends in this scrap not to want to celebrate the fact that the end of it is in sight at last.' He hesitated, and then invited Alice to go with him. She declined, explaining that she had promised to listen, with the girls, to the King's broadcast and that she felt she should be on hand just in case any bad news came through for anyone. Roger nodded.

'I'll be on my way, then,' he said.

The track up through the lower slopes of his woodland was too step and uneven for the suspension of his Riley, so Roger drove the farm truck along the valley floor and then turned left, up into the trees, noticing as he climbed that the plantations of spruces which interspersed stands of beech, oak, ash and bat-willow, were already benefiting from Christopher's attention over the eight months since he had assumed responsibility for them. Dead wood was piled in organised heaps and recently planted saplings stood, securely staked, in the open spaces where trees had been felled during late summer and early autumn.

If Roger had questioned what it was that had motivated this visit to Christopher, he would have found it difficult to find an answer. While it was true that he felt a natural desire to communicate the news to his son, he was also experiencing, although he was only half aware of it, a growing concern that, even now, almost a year since the boy's RAF career had ended in a humiliating discharge, he still chose to live in total isolation and in primitive conditions only four miles from the comparatively luxurious farmhouse in which he had been born and comfortably – and presumably happily – raised.

Roger was, by his own standards, an honourable man. He had never, as far as he knew, been dishonest or cruel. He had adopted the middle-class principles laid down for him by his parents and when there were difficulties he had followed their advice and, as much as was possible, survived them. Like many of his generation, he was disinclined to analyse his feelings. To do so was, he believed, a sign of introspection and self-indulgence. Instead, he repressed his anxieties by applying his mind to the task in hand, whatever that might be at the time of the difficulty. The second occasion on which he had employed this method it had helped him through the loss of his wife. He had buried himself in work in much the same way as he had buried her in Ledburton churchyard. Believing that Christopher, who at that time had been hardly more than a child, was too young to dwell on such things as illness and death, he had discouraged the little boy from talking about his mother.

'There's nothing more to be said, old chap,' he gently told the solemn child, who, only hours before, had watched earth being thrown into his mother's grave and heard it thud onto the lid of her coffin.

The sound of the labouring engine had reached Christopher through the quiet evening air several minutes before the truck heaved into sight. He saw that the driver was not, as he at first assumed, Jack or Fred, delivering food and provisions prepared and cooked by Eileen, his father's housekeeper. Instead he recognised his father. Watching him climb down from the cab, he sauntered forward to greet him.

'Pa!' he said. 'How are you?' When they had exchanged greetings Christopher suggested that as it was such a pleasant evening they might sit outside. 'Whiskey and a splash?' he offered, and when his father accepted, went into the cottage to prepare the drinks.

Roger sat down on a rustic seat that he guessed his son had knocked together, using odd lengths of timber from the quantities of it that lay, neatly stacked, around the cottage and its outbuildings. Through an open window he could hear Christopher moving about inside the small, simple structure, setting heavy glass tumblers on bare wood, opening a cupboard, closing it.

The air was still. A blackbird, from the cottage roof, broke the silence and somewhere, further into the trees, a thrush was under-singing. A robin landed boldly almost at Roger's feet and stared hard at him, the head slightly turned, the eye, unblinking, dark and imperious. It retreated in a flutter of indignation when Christopher emerged from the cottage and, after putting one tumbler into his father's hand, carried the other to a nearby tree stump where he sat, raised his glass and said, 'Cheers, Pa.' Roger reciprocated, they sipped and the silence spooled out.

'It's hard to believe it on an evening as peaceful as this one,' Roger said, and then hesitated, 'but this morning the Allies landed in northern France. I thought you probably didn't know about it and it occurred to me that you might like to. I mean, I'm aware of how you feel about it all but at least now the end is in sight, which, I imagine, pleases you as much as everyone else, whatever their viewpoint. Except for our enemies, of course...'

'Yes,' Christopher said quietly, 'except for them.' There was a pause. Somewhere below them, down the steep slope of the hillside, a pheasant's alarm call shattered the silence.

Roger experienced a surge of something close to anger at his son's detached, even cool reaction to the certainty that hundreds, if not thousands, of men had died that day, and as darkness fell, were continuing to die in a chaos of ear-splitting noise and flying metal, tossed, like gory rag dolls, by exploding shells and bombs. All of this solidified in Roger's mind until he saw it in monochrome, a series of still photographs, like the newspaper images of the First World War, of which, as a schoolboy, he had been so significantly aware.

Christopher, reading his father's reaction, at once understood how offensive his response had been and apologised for it.

'I don't mean I'm not glad it's going to be over

soon. And I know the invasion had to happen. I didn't mean to sound ungrateful or unconcerned.' He scanned his father's face. 'I know my attitude offends you, Pa. And I'm sorry. Believe me.'

Roger swallowed his drink and nodded. Christopher asked for details of the invasion and this seemed to make the conversation easier for Roger. He cleared his throat and gave his son a concise account of the news of the landings. He followed this with his own assessment of the probable strategies of the Allied commanders and of what they would be hoping to achieve over the next few days.

'Of course the losses on the beaches must have been horrendous but if things hadn't gone reasonably to plan I imagine we would have been told by now and the news bulletin tonight was mostly positive.' He had finished his drink, refused a second and was getting to his feet. 'Anyway...just thought you should know, old chap.'

'Stay and have some grub?' Christopher offered. 'I could rustle up something, if you...?'

But his father declined politely and was moving towards the truck.

When he reached it he pulled open its door and, almost as though the vehicle was a lifeline he could use to haul himself back to the safety of his own thoughts and emotions, climbed inside. Then, with one hand on the gear lever and the fingers of the other reaching for the key he had left in the ignition, he turned to his son.

'You're doing a bloody good job up here, Chris,' he said. 'Your hard work is really paying off.' Christopher was warmed by the rare compliment. 'I could probably spare Jack for, say, one day a fortnight, to give you a hand, if that would suit you?' Christopher welcomed the prospect of Jack's labour. He had lit a cigarette and stood with it burning between his fingers while his father hesitated.

'Things are not going to be the same, you know, on the land, I mean, when this caper's over.' Roger spoke quietly. 'Changes are always inevitable, of course. More mechanisation and so on... But wars make things happen fast and before we have time to consider them.' He was thinking of the hundreds of acres which, since 1939, in order to meet the demand for home-grown food, had been put under the plough at the expense of heathland, drained at the expense of wetlands or cleared at the expense of woodland. Christopher's smile, as he flicked ash from his cigarette, was, Roger thought, slightly patronising.

'Well, there's always change, Pa, isn't there?'

'Of course. But rarely before has it been so sudden or so drastic or so irreversible as we have experienced over the last few years. It's an ongoing process, of course. Machines making horses and men redundant and so on. But believe me, Chris, we've seen nothing yet!'

'Not all bad, though? Workers will benefit, surely? Mechanisation will reduce the amount of back-breaking labour, won't it?'

'Of course. But more mechanism means less jobs. Milking machines instead of dairy workers, automatic feeders making stockmen redundant and so on. Arable crops won't be sown or harvested by hand any more. The corn will be cut, baled and threshed by one man operating a massive piece of machinery, instead of reaped by a dozen workers, stooked by their wives and kids and threshed in a byre. These monsters are on the drawing boards as we speak but, believe me, it won't be long before they're in our fields.'

Christopher nodded and, to please his father, managed a rueful smile. He had stepped back from the truck and prepared to raise a hand in a farewell salute when his father, the ignition key between his fingers, spoke again.

'Don't suppose you'd consider coming home, would you?' Christopher was surprised by this and stood for some seconds without answering. 'Only it seems a bit odd for you to be on your own up here, putting up with…well…this…' His father indicted the near derelict building, shrouded by brooding trees, 'while I'm rattling around in a comfortable farmhouse only five miles down the valley. I understood, when you were…unwell…that you wanted…what was it? Privacy? In which to recover? But now?' There was a pause. 'You're looking incredibly fit, I'm pleased to say.' There was another, longer pause before he continued. 'Anyway…just wanted you to know that if and when you feel like coming home you'll be welcome. Right?' Christopher nodded and said thank you.

'The thing is, Pa, I really like it up here, you know. I've got everything I need and I'm not lonely. Too busy for that!' He noticed a change in his father's expression. He looked suddenly tired, even irritated. He switched on the ignition and the truck's engine turned over, shattering the peace of the woodland.

'It makes a lot of extra work for Eileen, you see.' Roger had raised his voice, pitching it over the clamour of the engine. 'Having to think about keeping you supplied with food up here and so on. Bear that in mind, will you?' Then he was reversing the truck away from his son, turning it and moving off, carefully negotiating the steep track.

Christopher finished his cigarette, collected the whiskey tumblers, went into the cottage and lit two of his oil lamps. He poured himself a second whiskey and sat in the comfortable silence that seemed suddenly less comfortable.

He was approaching the first anniversary of his crack-up. It was almost ten months since he had retreated from a world he could no longer tolerate and allowed the solitude of the woodland to heal him. Now he was fit and strong. His mind was clear and the nightmares that had plagued his sleep over the first months of his withdrawal to the cottage no longer troubled him. When he had been sick and even while he was recovering, he had not been conscious of the future. Now he was beginning to sense it, stretching away before him and needing to be furnished with projects and ambitions. He would go and see Alec Neale, a man who, as his housemaster at public school, had been a father figure to him when, after his mother's death, his own father, dealing in his own way with his own grief, had been little help to the son who was, alone, trying to cope with his.

Neale, now a widower, lived in Exeter with his sister and was surprised to hear, after many years of silence, from a student who had been, although he was too professional for his interest to have been detectable during Christopher's education, a favourite of his.

Neale was, without giving any sign of it, surprised by Christopher's appearance, for although Christopher had done the best he could, his clothes, boots and shaggy hair suggested the life he was living, which appeared to be rather different to the life most of Neale's other ex-students were leading, who, if not officers serving in the armed forces, were mostly professional men, wearing suits and ties and polished shoes.

Over tea and biscuits, Christopher gave Neale a brief history of his flying record, his breakdown and his recuperation as a woodsman in his father's forest. He went on to describe the ambition that had, over recent weeks, caught his imagination, and he asked for advice from his housemaster on how to pursue it. Alec Neale made some notes, suggested that since it was impossible for him to make contact by telephone or even, without difficulty, by post, Christopher should call on him again in a month's time. By then, he told him, he would have put together some options for him to consider.

Days and then weeks had passed since the Normandy landings and no news of either Reuben Westerfelt or Dave Crocker had reached the Post Stone farms. Rose and Hester were thrown together not only by this situation but by the fact that Hester was spending her time helping Rose with the domestic work at Lower Post Stone Farm and lodging in her cottage. They supported one another more or less silently, waiting for news, hoping, and in Hester's case praying, that when it came it would be good.

'"Let us all beseech the blessing of Almighty God," the man on the wireless said,' Hester told Rose one evening when the two of them were sitting in Rose's kitchen, waiting for bedtime. She remembered the words of the radio bulletin on the day everyone now called D-Day, and each morning and night she knelt beside her bed and beseeched that blessing. The child she was carrying had begun to move. Small, fluttering sensations that surprised her.

''Tis quickening, Hester. That's what that feelin' be. 'Tis the baby quickening, my dear.'

On June 12th Mabel stumbled into the kitchen, her usually ruddy face, pale. She had heard in a BBC news bulletin about a new weapon the Germans were deploying. An unmanned plane, carrying explosives, which had crashed in London, causing widespread damage.

'I know, Mabel, I heard about it too,' Alice said. The V1, which was to become known colloquially as the buzz bomb or doodlebug, was a small, pilotless flying bomb, fired randomly into southern Britain from enemy launching sites in northern France. When it reached its target area its engine was designed to cut out and it would plunge down, exploding on impact and causing indiscriminate devastation.

'You can 'ear 'em comin', my gran says,' Mabel told Alice, her lower lip trembling, when some days later she received a letter from home. 'They gets nearer and nearer and then they stop and it goes dead quiet,

Gran says, but there's no time to take cover! They're worse than the Blitz, Mrs Todd! At least when the bombers came over we had the siren and Gran could take little Arfur to the shelter!'

Mabel told Ferdie of her fears for Arthur's survival in the face of this new threat.

'Reckon he'll be OK,' Ferdie said with his mouth full of the rabbit pie Mabel had cooked that Saturday night. 'If you can 'ear 'em comin' like you say, then your gran can pop Arfur under that special table she's got, can't she?' Mabel had told Ferdie about the Morrison shelter, which, since the Blitz, had dominated the Deptford kitchen.

'I've a good mind to go up to London and fetch 'im down 'ere, Ferdie! Where 'e'd be safe!' she announced, challenging him.

'Best not do that, my lover,' Ferdie answered evenly, ''cos who would take care of 'im 'ere, eh? The boss be short-'anded enough as 'tis without 'avin' you gallivanting around after your baby brother!'

Mabel knew he was right. Too young for school and too old to be confined to a pram, Arthur was at precisely the age when a young child is most at risk on a farm. But she refused a second helping of spotted dick and instead of spending the evening in Ferdie's bed, returned to the hostel on the borrowed bike and stomped tearfully up the stairs to her room.

'What's up, Mabe?' Annie enquired. 'Fallen out with your bloke, 'ave you?'

'All I want is my baby safe here with me,' Mabel gulped. She had long since given up any attempt at denial, to the Post Stone girls at any rate, of her true relationship with the little boy. 'And that Ferdie Vallance! 'E won't hear of it!'

'But does he know?' Annie asked. 'About Arfur being yours? 'Ave you told 'im? No! You 'avn't, 'ave you? 'Ow's 'e s'posed to know, Mabel?'

'Everyone else seems to!' Mabel mumbled.

'You gotta tell 'im, love! Why don't you? What you got to lose, eh?'

'I can't, Annie!'

'Why?'

''Cos 'e's goin' to ask, isn't 'e!'

'Ask what?'

'Who Arfur's dad is, of course!'

'And you don't want to tell 'im?'

'I can't, Annie! I can't ever tell 'im that! And don't you go askin' me why, 'cos I can't tell you, neither! I can't never tell no one. Not ever!'


'You won't even know I'm gone,' Alice assured Edward John when, a few days after the V1 attacks began, she told him she was due in London that week for the hearing of her divorce case. 'I shall travel up on Tuesday, go to court on Wednesday and come back here on Thursday. When you arrive from school for the weekend on Friday, I'll be here as usual. Couldn't be simpler!'

'But who will feed the girls?' he asked, and she laughed at the way he had adopted her priorities.

'Rose will,' she told him. 'Hester will help her and Mrs Brewster is going to call in on the Wednesday to make sure everything's in order. So you needn't worry about the girls, Edward John.'

'Will my father be there?' he asked, after a pause. 'In court, I mean.' He had taken, Alice noticed, to referring to James as his 'father', rather than the more familiar 'daddy' he had always used before.

'No, he won't be.'

'Why? It's his fault you're getting divorced.'

'Well... Yes, it is. But you see, he isn't defending the case. So I have to be there and he doesn't.'

'It ought to be the other way around,' Edward John said sulkily. 'It's not fair!' The same thought had occurred to Alice.

'I know. But it's the law, darling.' There was another pause.

'But what about these V1 things?' he asked.

'Oh, you mean the buzz bombs!' Alice answered dismissively, attempting to turn the new threat into an inconsequential joke. 'The doodlebugs! I shall be staying in Highgate with your Aunt Ruth. Well out of harm's way.'

Ruth was, in fact, not Edward John's aunt but his godmother. She and Alice had met at high school and remained friends, despite the very different paths their lives had taken, she being an academic, currently working at the British Museum, while Alice had become a wife and mother.

Highgate was not 'out of harm's way', but Ruth's flat had, so far, escaped damage and from its elevated position she had watched the bombing of the city of London, standing in her darkened room with the curtains open, a glass of wine in her hand. *I stand and curse*, she had written to Alice at the height of the Blitz, *at these bloody Germans! Sometimes I can actually see the bombs falling, silhouetted against the fires blazing around St Paul's. How that building is surviving is amazing. It almost makes one believe in miracles. Long may it continue – the miracle, of course, not the bombing!*

One of Alice's early achievements at Lower Post Stone Farm had been the redesigning of the kitchen. It had been immediately apparent to her that the preparation and serving of breakfast, packed lunches and a satisfying evening meal for ten ravenous land girls was virtually impossible in the cramped space, initially devoid of working surfaces, cupboards or shelving for pots, pans, sieves, colanders, graters, crockery or cutlery. She had eased some pages of graph paper from one of Edward John's school exercise books, considered carefully where, in order for herself and Rose to work efficiently, everything needed to be, and then drawn up her plans. She discovered, in a disused dairy, a dozen slabs of marble together with the heavy timber framing that had once supported them, and devised a new layout, incorporating her ideas.

Roger Bayliss had, at first, been reluctant to spend any more money on Lower Post Stone Farm, but as Alice defined her scheme he soon understood not only how impossible the old kitchen had been but how cleverly Alice planned to use the space and how practical was her application of the materials she proposed to utilise. Within two weeks the streamlined kitchen was in operation. With everything now in its logical place, the preparation and cooking of the food, its speedy transference to the girls' plates, the stacking of dirty dishes near the scullery door and of the clean ones where the pudding was being dished up, transformed the ritual of mealtimes. There was suddenly more space around the long pine table and Alice and Rose no longer got in each other's way as they worked and as a result were visibly less harassed and exhausted.

'I would never of believed it could make such a difference!' Rose exclaimed, finishing the washing-up half an hour earlier than usual for the third time in a week. 'Everything's sorted and put away and supper was bang on time again! I reckon you'm a clever woman, Alice Todd! That's what you are!'

Roger Bayliss had brought a neighbour to admire Alice's achievement and he requested Alice's advice on the layout of his own staff kitchen. As her reputation grew she was requested by the adjutant of a nearby Fleet Air Arm establishment to design the catering area of a new canteen and this was followed a few months later by a commission to suggest a plan for the kitchens of a local nursing home.

'Next thing you'll be too busy for the likes of us!' Rose had once exclaimed, and it was at this point that it occurred to Alice that she might possess a skill that could possibly provide her with interesting and even lucrative employment when the war was over. She had confided these aspirations in letters to Ruth, whose attention had immediately been caught by the prospect of Alice finding a rewarding direction for her life as a single mother.

'Here's to having you here after all this time!' Ruth said, saluting Alice. The rims of their wineglasses chimed delicately as the two well-acquainted women smiled and sipped. 'So... Tell me how your kitchen design project is developing.' Ruth intended to keep the evening's conversation as positive as possible and to avoid the painful subject of the reason for Alice's visit to London.

She had settled herself in one of the pair of armchairs she had recently purchased from Liberty's and listened attentively while Alice gave a brief and characteristically modest account of the various commissions she had recently undertaken, redesigning the catering facilities of several more hostels, a private hotel and two military establishments in the Ledburton area.

'I always told you there was more to life than domesticity,' Ruth teased, lighting her cigarette and exhaling the smoke carefully into the air above Alice's head. 'But seriously, Allie, a year is quite long enough to be up to your waist in mud. Come to London! Move in with me! There's bags of room here! I've been working on a list of contacts for you... Hoteliers, restaurateurs, people who run clinics and venues for large corporation events, that sort of thing. The list is endless once you start thinking about it. And they've all got kitchens, Allie! And most of them are dismal, time-consuming, unhygienic holes! Very like the one on your farm used to be!'

'I doubt that!' Alice laughed, and then became serious. 'It has been an amazing year, Ruth,' she said reflectively. 'It may have scared me and exhausted me but it got me through a really bad time.'

'It's changed you, you know. You've gained confidence.' Ruth smiled and drew on her cigarette.

'I reckon that, when roused, you could be quite formidable, Alice Todd!'

'I shall take that as a compliment!' Alice smiled, letting Ruth refill her glass. 'Life has been – and is – surprisingly good at Lower Post Stone. And your godson absolutely adores it there.'

'Ah!' Ruth said, identifying the problem. 'I hope you're not proposing to put his needs first and sacrifice an opportunity to make a career for yourself on his account?' A glance at Alice's face confirmed her fears. 'You can't be serious, darling! Kids are resilient! And Edward John won't thank you for it, you know. In a few years' time he'll fly the coop without a backward glance!'

'He's had a very disruptive time, Ruth. He loves the farm and he's settled at his school. I don't want to—'

'Great God, woman,' Ruth interrupted good-naturedly, 'you must think of your future now! I absolutely insist on it! In the long run, it'll be bad for both of you if you don't. You'll resent the fact that you gave up an opportunity – should one present itself – and he'll feel guilty that he let you. We all have to adjust to the mess this war is making of our lives and your little boy is no exception.'

The war, Alice noticed, did not appear to have had a detrimental effect on Ruth's life or on her flourishing career, which had, in fact, benefited from the fact that some of her male rivals had been removed from the promotion ladder and diverted into the armed services.

'Of course he'll adjust when the time comes,' Alice said. 'But, for the moment...'

Ruth glanced at her wristwatch. 'For the moment,' she said, stubbing out her cigarette and getting to her feet 'You should be using this precious time in London to meet people! Come on!'

'What? Where to?' Alice was reluctant. She had been looking forward to spending a quiet evening with her old friend.

'Charlie Maitland,' Ruth said. 'He lives down the road, which couldn't be handier and he's just about the most useful man in London! You'll adore him. More importantly, he'll adore you!'

Alice was not certain whether the meeting with Charles Maitland was to be a job interview or a social occasion but by the end of it she had made a good impression on him and he had suggested bearing her in mind when a suitable project, involving a catering complex, came his way.

'Don't be alarmed,' he told her. 'I'll ease you in gently and take into account your areas of expertise as well as the things you've less experience of. Throwing you in at the deep end wouldn't be beneficial to anyone but you've obviously developed a very basic and practical approach, Alice, while a lot of the designers I'm expected to work with exist in cloud cuckoo land when it comes to the logical flow of work through a kitchen and are incapable of visualising one from the point of view of those who will be actually working in it. That's where your skill lies and that's precisely what I'm after! It's a specialist area and a uniquely important one!' He asked Alice to assemble a portfolio of her design projects together with photographs of the completed work. 'A few references from the people who've hired you would be useful, too. We'll keep in close touch and hope to meet again before long.' Then he had smiled, got to his feet and extended his hand. The interview, for that was what it obviously was, had ended.

'What did you think of him?' Ruth asked Alice as the two of them sauntered the short distance back to her flat. Alice shrugged and said that Charles Maitland was clearly a man who knew what he wanted.

'So...will you accept the job?'

'He hasn't offered me a job!'

'But he will, darling! I'd put money on it!'

The air was filled with the scent of the lilac tree they were passing. It reminded Alice sharply of the garden in Twickenham where, until the onset of the war, she had lived with her husband and her young son. Tomorrow's appointment in the courts of law loomed suddenly and depressingly.

Then, through the distant hum of traffic, a foreign

sound asserted itself high above them. It was the burbling, whining stutter of an approaching engine. Ruth, identifying it at once, hesitated. When the noise above them spluttered suddenly into silence she caught Alice by the wrist and hauled her through a gate and into a front garden. Alice was conscious of being forced violently down onto hard, gritty earth, of her cheek connecting painfully with musty bricks, and of Ruth on the ground beside her. The seconds between the cutting-out of the engine and the impact, as the device struck the road two hundred yards from them, seemed eerily silent and impossibly long. Then they were enveloped in the concussion as the explosion fractured the air around them and rocked the earth beneath them. Instinctively they both protected their heads, pressing their faces against the ground while the air thickened with choking dust and debris thudded down around them. Various sounds began to erupt at the scene of the impact. A fire engine's bell was already approaching from the distance. People were shouting.

'You all right?' Ruth asked, without moving. They both sat up. There were dead leaves in their hair. The back of Alice's left hand was bleeding and her frock was torn where the thorns of an unpruned rose tree had snagged it.

'Fine,' she said. 'You?' Ruth nodded and they got shakily to their feet.

'That was our first big adventure together in a very long time!' Ruth said. And for a moment and partly because of the shock, they stood, holding on to one another and giggling like the two schoolgirls they had once been.

# Chapter Six

Roger Bayliss was at Ledburton Halt when the train from London arrived, almost an hour late, and Alice stepped down onto the platform.

'Did Rose manage supper?' she asked anxiously. The delayed train meant that Rose had been single-handed for a third night.

'She certainly did,' Roger assured her, handing her into the passenger seat of his car. 'She and young Hester make a good team.'

'So I am to be made redundant, am I?' Alice smiled, adding, when Roger turned off the Ledburton road, 'Where are we going?'

He drove her to a village pub where the best on offer in the way of food was a thick vegetable soup and slices of homemade bread, which, Alice assured Roger, was exactly what she wanted.

He, without appearing to pry, was keen to know how she had coped with the past three days and whether the divorce hearing had depressed her. Then he noticed the sticking plaster on her hand and the purplish bruise that was discolouring the skin around it. Concerned, he took her by the wrist and examined what he could see of the wound.

'What's this?' he asked. She described to him what had happened to her and Ruth on the evening before last.

'We were both terribly lucky,' she concluded. 'If Ruth hadn't known exactly what to do and shoved us down behind somebody's garden wall, we might have been killed!'

'On the other hand,' Roger said tightly, 'if it hadn't been for this Ruth person, you wouldn't have been there in the first place.'

'True,' Alice said, accepting a second helping of the soup. 'But neither would I have met a man who will possibly be very useful to me when I pursue my ambition to design kitchens. Ever heard of a Charles Maitland?' Roger shook his head. 'He's a design consultant for Woodrow and Bradshaw's,' Alice announced, glancing at Roger and expecting him to be impressed by this information. The company was well known as a major player in the construction industry and Roger had heard of it.

At any other time his concern might have been a vague anxiety that Alice's proposed career was going to threaten his own half formed – and possibly also only half admitted – plans for the future, but now it was focused on her well-being. In the space of three days she had been summoned to a court of law, her marriage had been officially ended, she had narrowly escaped an horrendous death and she had a wounded hand.

'I think we should go,' he said firmly. 'I wouldn't have brought you here if I had known what you've been through. You need rest. Come on. Let's get you back to the farm!' He got to his feet and was holding her coat, ready for her to slip her arms into it, when he realised that she was laughing at him.

'You are very sweet!' she said, 'but I'm absolutely fine! Honestly! Apart from being ravenously hungry. I want to finish my soup. Sit down, Roger, and don't fuss!'

He sat down and watched as she bit into a slice of the bread. 'All I need is food!' she said with her mouth full. He was smiling at her now, relieved to see that she was, as she insisted, absolutely fine.

One of the number of things that Roger admired about Alice was her directness and the fact that she knew what she wanted and, increasingly, was not afraid to try to get it. He was more used to women who followed his lead. His wife, who had been considerably younger than he, had been submissive. His female servants took his instructions and obeyed them without argument. Even the formidable Margery Brewster knew her place in the pecking order and although she sometimes made it clear with a lift of her eyebrows that she did not personally agree with one or other of his decisions, she rarely opposed them.

Although initially insecure and lacking in confidence in her ability to run his hostel for him, Alice, he had soon sensed, always knew her own mind. As her skills developed and her self-assurance had grown, she had, when necessary, been robust in defence of her decisions where the girls in her care were concerned. It had been she who questioned Roger's refusal to let Chrissie go to Plymouth to meet with her sailor husband. She who had refused to divulge the identity of the girl who had alibied Chrissie when, with tragic results, she broke the hostel rules and went anyway. She had defended Mabel when she smuggled her young soldier brother into a hayloft for the night. It was she who persuaded Roger to be generous when one girl or another needed leave in order to sort out a personal problem. And it had been Alice who tried – and was continuing to try – to create a reconciliation between him and his son, whose dismissal from the RAF and subsequent adoption of pacifism seemed to have become an insurmountable difficulty between them.

Roger did not always concur with Alice's actions and some of them, such as her solution to the problem of Winnie's pregnancy and abortion, he knew nothing whatsoever about, but he always respected her views, even when he opposed them. Sometimes, waking in the small hours of the long winter nights, he would wonder whether, after all, her judgement, on one occasion or another, might have been the right one.

'One thing,' Alice said, laying down her soup spoon. 'I'd rather Edward John didn't know the details of the doodlebug incident. It would only worry him.' Roger agreed not to say anything. 'I might tell him a bit about it,' she added, 'mainly because I'm so hopeless at keeping anything from him. But not the details. And certainly not how close it was.'

There was a short, companionable silence in which Roger enjoyed the way Alice's hair, slightly loosened by her protracted train journey, was framing her face.

'When it was happening,' she continued, 'all I could think of was how awful it would be for Edward John if I got killed. I suppose he'd have to go to James and his new wife if I died. I don't think he would be happy, do you? Living with a stepmother and half-brother or -sister?'

'What about godparents?' Roger enquired. 'Up to scratch, are they?'

Alice smiled. 'My brother-in-law, Richard, is one,' she said. 'But he's turned out to be the archetypal bachelor. Postal orders and Meccano pieces for birthdays. You know the sort of thing. Sweet man but hardly a father figure. I was hoping he'd marry some nice girl and provide Edward John with lots of cousins, but there you go, the "best-laid plans" again. And Ruth is his godmother. She's my greatest friend but she wouldn't get many marks for maternal instincts, bless her. You are the one, of course.' She was almost thinking aloud, relaxing in the sympathetic attention of a man she respected and trusted, more, possibly, than she was aware of.

'Me?' Roger asked, taken by surprise. 'I'm what one?'

'The one he admires. You are everything he aspires to be!'

'Me?' Roger repeated incredulously.

'Of course, you!' Alice was laughing at his astonishment. 'He's mad about farming! You're a successful farmer. You're good to your stock. You treat your employees well.'

'Oh, come on, Alice! You make me sound like the patron saint of agriculture!'

'Well that's more or less what Edward John thinks you are! Did you know he wants to farm when he grows up – or possibly be a vet – until I told him how long and complicated the training for that would be. He admires you enormously, Roger. So, watch your step! I don't want him disillusioned or led astray!' She saw his face cloud. 'What?' she asked.

'Nothing, really... I was just thinking about Christopher,' he said. 'He's never shown any interest in the farm. It was always machinery and engines with him. Bikes and then cars and then planes. Things with wheels and wings.'

'He's running your woodland now. That's almost farming, don't you think?' Roger obviously did not. 'Anyway, he was a brilliant pilot,' Alice continued, surprised, not for the first time, by Roger's apparent lack of pride in his son's achievements. 'His record was formidable.'

'Yes,' Roger said. 'It was. Impressive by any standards.' Alice saw his expression become a blank mask of...what was it? Resignation? 'But then he cracked up,' he added, heavily, staring past her, across the empty bar.

'You said that as though he was somehow to blame for it!' When he failed to respond, she continued, 'Surely you don't—'

'He deserted, Alice,' he said, as though suddenly aware of her question and forced to address it. 'He went absent without leave. He ran. They found him cowering in my sheep shed.'

Alice had always suspected that Roger was, for some reason, ashamed of Christopher's breakdown.

This was the first time in the ten months since it had happened that he had admitted it. It was, she sensed, some kind of breakthrough. A crack in his ice. The barrier, which had seemed impenetrable, and behind which Roger concealed his feelings about his son, was, perhaps, about to be breached. She sensed that she must tread carefully.

'He cracked up, Roger,' she said gently. 'It was a complete physical and mental breakdown. Something that happened to lots of pilots. Especially when, like Christopher, they'd flown more missions than they should have done!'

'They call it LMF, Alice. It means "lacking moral fortitude". That's what it said on his discharge papers.' Roger told her, in a low voice. Alice already knew this. She remembered the day when, having been to visit Christopher in the psychiatric ward in which he was slowly recovering, Georgina had told her how Christopher had shown her the official news, a typewritten message on a sheet of buff paper, which his father had, that morning, delivered to him.

Georgina had been outraged, not only by the callous treatment meted out by Christopher's superiors in Fighter Command but by Roger's attitude to his son. Neither she nor Alice had been able to comprehend it, although, unlike Georgina, Alice was convinced that there had to be some explanation for it. She sat now, across the table

175

from Roger, her empty soup bowl in front of her.

'Yes, I know,' she said eventually, and when he looked at her in surprise, added, 'Georgina told me.' Roger remembered the occasion, soon after Christopher had been captured by the military police and after a brief interment in a military prison before being transferred to hospital, when Georgina Webster, the most highly educated and articulate of his land girls, had burst into his office and demanded to know when he intended to visit his son. Faced with his prevarication she had told him that if he would not go, she would. Then she had stormed out, shutting his office door with an emphasis that had left him in no doubt about the level of her disapproval.

'It was none of Miss Webster's business,' Roger said almost reproachfully, his expression suggesting to Alice that he did not consider it to be any of her business, either.

'She was a bit in love with him, Roger,' Alice said. 'And that made her feel...' She searched for the right word. 'Protective,' she finished.

'You're using the past tense. Doesn't she care for him any more?'

'I'm not sure how she feels about him now. I don't think she knows herself.'

Alice considered that the conversation had gone far enough. She also felt, quite suddenly, exhausted by the events of the last few days. This must have been evident to Roger because he got to his feet.

'You are tired,' he said, reading her. 'Don't deny it, my dear. Come on. I'll drive you home.'

It was just after ten o'clock when they arrived at Lower Post Stone Farm and Rose Crocker was either in the act of locking the door for the night, or of going out into the porch, not for the first time that evening, to search the darkness for a glimmer of light from the dimmed headlights of her employer's approaching car.

Most of the girls had delayed going to bed until the warden was safely home. They had felt, although some of them would not have admitted it, oddly bereft during her absence. Now they gathered, smiling, in the door to the recreation room to say hello to Alice and ask if she was all right.

'We're ever so glad you're home, Mrs Todd!' Mabel was glowing with pleasure. 'We 'aven't 'alf missed you!'

'It felt that peculiar with you not here, didn't it, Marion?' Winnie said, and Marion nodded in agreement. Rose Crocker was, however, already bristling.

'Come along, young lady!' she called to Hester, who, having insisted on staying in the farmhouse until Alice had returned to it, was now required to cross the yard with her landlady. 'Time you was in your bed... And I reckon I knows when I'm not wanted!' Rose felt unappreciated and showed it, pursing her lips, lowering her head and making for the door. There were repressed sniggers from one or two of the girls.

'Mr Bayliss tells me you managed splendidly, Rose!' Alice announced loudly, adding, 'Say thank you to Rose, everyone, for looking after you all so well!'

'Thank you, Rose!' they chorused, some more enthusiastically than others.

'Mrs Crocker to you!' Rose said firmly, gratified, despite herself, for the acknowledgment of her efficiency as a stand-in for the warden. Turning to Alice, she told her there was some supper on the kitchen table, 'If you 'as a mind to eat and I reckon you should. Bain't healthy going to bed on an empty stomach.'

More to please Rose than anything, Alice ate the ham sandwich and spooned up the junket that Rose had left out for her. The girls, except for Annie, who was making cocoa for herself and for Alice, trailed off to their beds.

'All done and dusted now, then, is it? The divorce, I mean.' Annie asked, spooning cocoa powder into their cups. A year ago Alice would have declined to discuss her personal life with an uneducated girl from the East End of London and might even have considered Annie impertinent but, as she looked into the wide, dark eyes, she understood that the question was not asked out of idle curiosity but from a genuine concern for her feelings.

'Not quite,' she answered. 'You get something called a decree nisi first and then, later, a decree absolute. But, in effect, yes, it's all done and dusted now.'

'But has it upset you, though?'

'Not too much, Annie. I'd got used to the fact that it was going to happen. And now...now I'm glad it's over. Or soon will be.'

'And then you can start looking round for—'

Alice interrupted her with a dismissive laugh. 'A new husband? I don't think so!'

'Once bitten, twice shy, you mean?'

'That might have a bearing on it, if the occasion arose...which it probably won't!' Alice gazed into space for a moment and then said, almost to herself, 'No. Somehow I don't see myself being someone's wife a second time.' Then she turned, smiling, to Annie, 'Now that I find myself with a sort of second chance in life, I rather fancy trying a career.'

'With your kitchen design business, you mean?'

'Possibly.'

'Well, you're ever so good at it!' Annie looked approvingly round at the well-organised and functional layout of the farmhouse kitchen. 'Look what you've done with this place! It was a cross between a coal-hole and a dungeon when we first come 'ere!' They smiled, remembering the struggle it had been to persuade first Margery Brewster and then Roger Bayliss himself that Alice's proposed alterations to the kitchen would be not only cost-effective but relatively inexpensive.

'I'm a bit tired, Annie,' Alice said, getting to her feet. 'I'm off to bed.' Annie picked up the junket bowl and the two cocoa cups and as she carried them into the scullery she wished Alice goodnight.

'We did miss you, Mrs Todd. All of us.' She raised her voice, calling after Alice. 'And I still reckon you'll get married again one day, so there!'

Roger Bayliss, driving the familiar mile up the hill to Higher Post Stone Farm, considered the various subjects that he and his warden had touched on that night. Was he ashamed of his son? Not ashamed, surely. But obviously this was the impression he had given, not only to the Webster girl but to Alice herself. And she thought badly of him because of it. They both did. He nosed his car in under the covered space, where, in the old days, the horse-drawn carriage had been kept, switched off the engine and sat for a while in the silent darkness.

So the Webster girl – Georgie, they all called her – had had feelings for Christopher, had she? Had perhaps been a little in love with him. But no longer was. He wondered, vaguely, what had changed her mind. He refused to examine the subject of his presumed embarrassment when Christopher had cracked up because he dared not let his mind explore it. Instead, and as usual, he had shut that issue, together with another that also had to be excluded from his mind, into a familiar, dark place, closed the door on it and locked it. He did this almost without being aware of it and turned his mind to the other subjects of that evening's conversation.

The incident of the flying bomb was the first to capture his attention. Then the injury to Alice's hand and her concern for her son, should she die. The boy's ambitions to farm interested him. Then they had spoken of Alice's increasing interest in a career. As his mind moved from one set of facts to another, his tension gradually left him. These things he could relate to, speculate upon. But not the subject of Christopher's breakdown or of his own, apparently unacceptable, reaction to it. The clues to this lay, where they had lain for more than half of his life, buried in the past. Classified information which, at the time, his parents had banned from discussion or exploration. And more or less without question, he had obeyed them. It was, they said, for his own good. The unease he felt when, on the rare occasions he had allowed his mind to stray in that direction, only confirmed the logic of their decision and he would retreat, excluding the intrusive, unsettling thoughts.

* * *

'Tell them that no news is good news,' had been Roger's advice when the warden spoke to him of the anxieties of Rose and Hester.

Rose was uncertain whether or not Dave was in France. Being in the Catering Corps meant, she knew, that he would not be as much at risk as those men fighting on the front line, nevertheless she shuddered whenever she heard on the BBC news bulletins, or read in the paper, reports of hand-to-hand fighting on the outskirts of Caen.

Ever since the Post Stone girls had celebrated the news of the invasion, Hester had existed in a world of her own.

'Come on, Hes!' the other girls had implored, trying to cheer her. 'It won't be long now and your Reuben will come marching home! Our boys 'as got Jerry prop'ly on the run!'

The casualty figures were almost ignored in the general mood of euphoria that pervaded the hostel but Alice and Roger were well aware of the huge loss of life the invasion had already caused, especially during the landings on the fiercely defended beaches of Normandy.

'Omaha was the worst,' he told Alice. They were sitting, one evening, in deckchairs on the terrace at the higher farm. The night was warm as they watched the daylight fade. Swallows and house martins were making their final sweeps across the face of the old building, feeding their young before leaving the garden to the bats. 'And, unfortunately, that is where Hester's Reuben would have been put ashore. It goes without saying that neither the American nor the British military authorities will give out information regarding the welfare or whereabouts of an entire unit, let alone an individual man, involved in this sort of offensive. Your women will have to be patient, along with all the other mothers, sweethearts and wives.'

'So you see,' Alice said, passing Roger's comment on to Rose and Hester, who were sitting, the next morning, mute, at the kitchen table, 'as I said to you before, and Mr Bayliss agrees with me, no news is good news. Now, let's get on with the vegetables for tonight, shall we?'

'She says 'e's in the sea!' Rose whispered to Alice when Hester was out of earshot.

'In the sea?' Alice was confused. 'Why would he be in the sea?'

'Don't ask me,' Rose shrugged, 'but she do keep on about it. She started just after D-Day and I told 'er not to be so daft, but every so often she sits there, starin' into space, and she says, "He's in the sea, Rose. I jus' knows it. Reuben be in the sea." I don't know what to make of her, Alice.'

It was the day after the Allied troops took Caen that the telegram was delivered to Lower Post Stone Farm and shortly after it the chaplain, who in January had married Private Reuben Westerfelt to Hester Tucker, arrived. They took her into Alice's sitting room and sat her in a chair.

'Missing?' Hester repeated, when they told her. 'What d'you mean, missing?' It was explained to her that Reuben had not been accounted for since his unit had left the landing craft and waded ashore on the beach codenamed Omaha. Few of the men in his section had reached the dry sand above the tideline, and even fewer, the dunes behind it. They had lain, dead and dying, waiting to be transported first to a field hospital and then, if they survived that, back across the channel, where the wounds of the lucky ones could be treated and healed. But Reuben had not been amongst them. Nor had his dog-tag been recovered from any of the mangled corpses that were scattered across the sand. So he was posted as 'missing, believed killed in action on 6th June 1944'.

'Missing?' Hester asked again, when no one answered her. 'So they don't think 'e's dead, then. It's just that they can't find 'im?' They watched her helplessly. There was nothing they could say to her. She walked to the door where she hesitated and then turned to face them, 'Tell 'em to look in the sea,' she said. 'Reuben be in the sea. I knows that. I've known it since that first day. That's where they'll find 'im. In the sea.' She went through the door and Rose got to her feet and followed, walking just behind Hester as she crossed the yard and went into the cottage.

'Jeez! What's up with you, George? Look like you've lost a dollar and found a dime!'

Georgina's name, shortened by the land girls to Georgie, had been contracted further by her colleagues in the Air Transport Auxiliary, who, despite her obvious femininity, or perhaps because of it, referred to her as George.

Georgina had, on the previous evening, delivered a Beaufighter to Little Rissington and hitched a ride back to White Waltham in an Anson piloted by Lucinda Frobisher, her closest friend amongst the women ferry pilots. Lu, as she was known, was catching up on some much-needed sleep while, in the makeshift canteen, Georgina sat over a cooling cup of coffee and waited for news of the Mustang she was to deliver to Duxford as soon as the repair workshop had finished with it.

Neil Fitzsimmonds, known as Fitzy, was a Canadian and an experienced ferry pilot. He and Georgina had encountered one another frequently and with increasing pleasure over the five months she had been flying. Evenings spent in pubs, in shared overnight digs and at occasional social events, such as dances and group visits to local cinemas, had thrown them together and for some time they had been aware of an attraction between them, which both of them sensed was mutual. Seeing him standing there beside her, with a plate overloaded with fried sausages and baked beans in one hand and in the other, a second plate, piled with buttered toast, made her smile.

'You hungry, Fitzy?'

'I'll have you know that not a bite has passed my lips since midday yesterday! I am ravenous! May I join you?' She nodded and as he settled himself across the table from her he asked again why she was looking so down.

'It's this wretched Leigh-Mallory person!' she said. 'Apparently he's the one who won't allow women ATA pilots to volunteer for overseas ops.'

'Meaning into France.' Neil Fitzsimmonds was eating fast and with relish.

'Of course,' Georgina said curtly. 'And it's too absurd! Lots of the ATA's women fliers have more experience and better qualifications than some of the blokes who'll be going.'

'This is true,' Neil said with his mouth full. 'But the guy has command of the Second Tactical Air Force as well as the Ninth USAF, so it's a case of "Yes, sir, Air Chief-Marshall, Sir Trafford Leigh-Mallory, sir!" Jeez, by the time we've got to the end of that mouthful, the war'll be over!' Georgina was not amused. 'Oh come on, George! Smile for Fitzy, there's a girl!'

'You've volunteered, I suppose?'

'You bet! Done my dingy drill. Had my inoculations. Sorry. Not gloating. Give 'em a few more months, George. They'll come around. There'll be more and more call for flights into France, then into Belgium and the Netherlands as the Allies push across. I reckon you girls'll be over there in a few weeks' time. Be patient. Want some of my toast?'

They sat for a while, eating in a companionable silence.

'If it wasn't for this war I'd make the most colossal pass at you, Miss Webster!' he said heavily.

Georgina studied his face, uncertain of his mood. She had been at the receiving end of many passes since she quit the Land Army. Some had been charming, others less so.

'What has the war got to do with it?' she asked eventually.

'Oh, I don't know… It's given people an excuse to trivialise things,' he said, and she understood precisely what he meant. 'Which is OK, if all that's wanted is a bit of fun, and God knows that's justified, the way things are…' She watched him follow the lift of a Dakota that was at that moment taking off from the 'strip. 'People flying away and not coming back…' He said and paused again, watching her face and trying to read her. 'I'd like to get to know you, Georgina. Slowly and in great detail. How does that strike you?'

She was smiling as she helped herself to a second slice of his toast.

'As being impossible,' she said. 'We run into each other, what, once a week? Twice a fortnight? Always with a bunch of fliers. Never alone. We don't know where we'll be or when. We can't plan anything. I see no hope for us!' She was laughing as she reached for her coffee cup and drank. He smiled ruefully, offering her a cigarette, lighting hers while he held his own between his lips. Then, his eyes still on her, he exhaled smoke in a long, thoughtful sigh.

'What about leave?' he asked her. 'Got any due?'

She had completed less than six months' service with the ATA and, apart from a 48-hour pass in May, had neither been offered nor requested anything more than a brief visit to her home. 'You should be due for seventy-two hours by now.'

'Yes, I suppose I must be.'

'I've got a mate who'd lend me his car.' He deliberately made his invitation into a light-hearted suggestion so that it would be easier for her to refuse it if the idea didn't please her. 'I could wangle some gasoline and you could give me a tour of your England. So far I've only seen it from the air!'

Neil Fitzsimmonds had arrived in England six months before the outbreak of war. Following his graduation as an engineer and as part of his grooming to prepare him to take on an executive position in his family's aero-engineering company in Vancouver, he was to spend a year or so gaining experience in their London office. Despite family opposition, he became determined, as the war progressed, to play his part in it and was frustrated to discover that his civilian flying qualifications, gained in his native Canada, where he had worked for some time as an instructor, did not, without extensive military training, qualify him for a commission in the RAF or its Canadian equivalent. He was, however, eligible to join the ATA without further training and this he did. The organisation seized on his skills both as a flier and as an instructor and he was, to use his own words, 'having a bloody good war'.

'We wouldn't be able to cover much ground in seventy-two hours!' Georgina had said, keeping her tone as light-hearted as his. She looked at him quizzically and saw his expression become suddenly less confident and more serious.

'I reckon we could cover a lot of ground, George. You and I. One way or another. But I guess you're not the sort of girl who—'

'Who what?' she challenged 'Who would want to spend some time alone with you? Or who, if she really liked you and perhaps even fell a bit in love with you, would…'

'Stop it!' he said laughing. 'You hold it right there, lady!' He leant back in his chair, smiling and drawing heavily on his cigarette, his eyes squinting against exhaled smoke. 'Let's think about it though, shall we?' She was looking past him now, at the mechanic who was making his way through the tables and chairs of the empty canteen.

'The Mustang's ready for you, miss. Take off in five, OK?' She got to her feet, shrugged on her flying jacket, shouldered her knapsack and held out a hand to Neil. He took it and kissed it, looking up at her.

'Yes,' she said, 'let's.' He watched her go. In the bulky leather jacket with which she had only recently been issued, she looked at ease and even elegant. Her long legs were clad in tight trousers and the regulation sheepskin boots, which, when women had begun flying for the ATA, had initially been denied them. Minutes later, he saw the Mustang lift off, climb and then bank round, heading north. He visualised her at the controls, checking her route, settling into the concentration that she would maintain until she touched down two hundred miles away. 'Let's think about it,' he had suggested. And she had said, 'Yes, let's.'

'It's called a *coup de foudre*,' Alice said, when Georgina had described her first encounter with Neil Fitzsimmonds. It was a phrase that none of the other land girls would have understood.

Georgina had sprained her wrist when the under-cart of a Mosquito had collapsed under her and, being considered unfit to fly for a few days, had been sent home to recover.

'If you can ride you should be able to fly!' Lionel had protested when she persuaded him to lend her his motorbike.

'I could fly, little brother. It's a fuss about nothing! But while I'm home I want to ride over to Post Stone to visit Mrs Todd. So, keys please and stop being so horrid!'

Her bandaged wrist had hurt her when she used the throttle, taking the bike, cross-country, from her parents' acreage to the Post Stone farms, through warm air that was thick with the scent of drying hay. The high banks of the lanes were spiked with the clashing colours of early summer flowers. Campion, bluebell, milkwort, buttercup and foxglove studded brilliant green foliage, which shimmered like silk and almost met over her head as the bike hurtled through it.

Alice, sensing that Georgina wanted to confide in her, had led her through to the privacy of her sitting room.

Since Christmas, when Georgina had announced to her parents that she was, to some extent at any rate, renouncing pacifism and intended to fly for the ATA, her relationship with her family, while not difficult, was not as easy as it had been when they had been united by their common opposition to war. In consequence, she found herself more inclined to confide in Alice than in her mother on the complex subject of her feelings for Neil Fitzsimmonds.

'You mean like eyes across a crowded room?' Georgina said, confirming her understanding of the phrase. Alice nodded.

'It means like a thunderclap.'

'I know what it means,' Georgina said, 'and it was like that. Just like that. Quite ridiculous! And very odd. I felt as if I already knew him. And as though everything was decided. About us liking each other, I mean. It was a most peculiar feeling.' She sat for a moment, examining her feelings. 'Did you have a *coup de foudre*, Mrs Todd, when you first met your husband?'

Alice recalled the evening when, at a students' ball in Cambridge, she had been introduced to James Todd and he had, very formally, escorted her in to dinner on his arm. She remembered experiencing a sensation, which had not entirely pleased her, of being somehow taken over by the good-looking, well-mannered young man James had then been.

'It's so long ago, Georgie, and such a lot has happened since. I don't know. Maybe I did. A bit.'

Georgina laughed and Alice asked her what she found amusing.

'I don't think you can have "a bit" of a *coup de foudre*, Mrs Todd. It's an "all or nothing" thing, isn't it?' She hesitated and her face clouded. 'I don't think I had one with Christopher. In fact, I disliked him at first. He was so much the pushy fighter pilot. It was only later, when he went through that awful time and cracked up and everything, that I felt... I don't really know what I felt. I do sort of love him though...'

'But not the way you love this Neil person?' Georgina caught, or thought she caught, a touch of disapproval in Alice's voice and evaded the warden's question by asking one of her own.

'Did I say I loved him?'

'No,' Alice replied, 'you didn't. But all this *coup de foudre* business?'

'I think what it is...' Georgina said, trying to make sense of her feelings, 'is that the war distorts things so. Fitzy said the same thing—'

'Fitzy?'

'It's what we call Neil. Almost everybody in the ATA has a nickname. We were talking about how impossible it seems to get to know each other properly because,' she hesitated, 'because of all the pressures.'

'What pressures?'

'It has to do with not knowing what's going to happen to people. How long you've got with them. It scares you into grabbing what you can get of them in case...well...in case something happens and you...

193

you miss them. I think I'd rather hate to miss Fitzy, Mrs Todd.'

Alice had let the ensuing silence extend itself, knowing Georgina well enough to understand that if she wanted to continue she would do so when she was ready and without prompting.

'We – Fitzy and I – don't want to plunge into anything,' she continued, 'but we want to spend some time together. Really together, before either of us gets posted somewhere where we won't see each other any more.' She paused, gazing into her empty cup. 'I'm almost twenty, Mrs Todd. I think I'm old enough to take a lover, aren't I?' She searched the warden's face and when she thought she saw a flicker of suppressed amusement, added, 'You're laughing at me!'

Alice threw back her head, laughed briefly, and then, smiling, apologised. She herself had been raised by a mother whose monarch had been Queen Victoria, and the values of family and fidelity had been firmly instilled into her. But her own experiences over the past two years, together with those she had witnessed amongst the girls in her care, had widened her values and softened her judgement.

'Of course you're old enough, Georgie, and quite possibly wise enough, too.' She looked into the solemn face and the level, grey eyes which, in fact revealed very little beyond Georgina's obvious health and intelligence. 'But I'd hate you to be unhappy. I'm not old enough to be your mother but if I was I'm pretty sure I'd trust you not to get hurt – or to hurt anyone else for that matter.'

'But Christopher... Is he hurt, d'you think?'

'How long is it since you've seen him?'

'Ages. Six months at least. Lionel and I rode up to the woodsman's hut at Christmas. Christopher looked incredibly well and he was very sweet. But I could tell he still wants things on his terms. He doesn't approve of my flying. He can't understand how I can bear to have anything to do with the war. He seems to be saying, "You know how I feel and you know where I am if you want me."'

'But you don't want him,' Alice said. 'Not now, at any rate.' Georgina stared at the floor. There was a pause before she met the warden's eyes.

'No,' she said, adding, almost apologetically, 'I want Fitzy now.' Before Alice could comment she continued. 'The idea is that we go to the cottage.'

'What cottage?'

Georgina described to Alice the small cottage the Webster family owned on the North Devon coast.

'Li and I used to be taken there for summer holidays when we were kids. We adored it. It's totally isolated on a wild, pebbly beach. Oil lamps and driftwood fires and everything. I thought I'd take Fitzy there... He doesn't know yet. Perhaps the idea won't appeal to him.' Alice resisted the temptation to say that she thought it most unlikely that the idea of a weekend with Georgina in such idyllic surroundings would not appeal to him and confined herself to making Georgina promise never to do anything she did not want to do.

'Of course I won't!' Georgina responded in surprise.

'No,' Alice agreed, smiling, 'of course you won't! And when is all this going to happen?'

'Heaven knows! We've both put in for leave. Whether we'll get it and whether the dates will coincide is in the lap of the gods!'

An urgent tap on the closed door to Alice's room interrupted them.

'Gwennan's put the prong of an 'ay fork clean through 'er foot,' Rose announced. 'Mr Jack's brung her back in the truck and she's to go to Ledburton straight off so the doctor can give 'er an injection for the lockjaw. One of us is to go with 'er, Mr Bayliss says. Shall I go or will you?'

It was on 9th July, the day that Caen was finally captured by the Allies, who began at once to make better headway into France, that Reuben was found and Hester's macabre conviction proved to be accurate.

His body was discovered in shallow water some miles along the coast from the place on Omaha Beach where his unit had disembarked. This, together with evidence provided by the wound that killed him, indicated that he had been struck by shrapnel as he waded ashore and had barely set foot on French soil.

This news – that part of it that was considered suitable for her to hear – had little effect on Hester, who, they all now realised, had been grieving for Reuben since D-Day. She continued to move through the routine of her life, her face blank and her body still showing no sign of her four-month pregnancy.

A letter came from Reuben's parents assuring her that despite their loss she would be warmly welcomed into their family and that her baby would be raised alongside its cousins. A United States army widow's pension began to arrive and Hester was visited by the chaplain, who had married her to Reuben six months previously. He told her that as her case was now prioritised, she should prepare for her imminent departure for Bismarck, North Dakota.

Reuben's mother, whose name was Bette, wrote to her daughter-in-law, enclosing half a dozen snapshots of the Westerfelt family, 'so you can get to know us, dear.' Hester spread the photographs on her bedspread and stared at the unfamiliar faces. A woman who had been Reuben's mother. A man who had been his father. Two young men, one of whom looked eerily like a younger version of Reuben, but was not Reuben.

Hester's parents had been informed of their son-in-law's death but had failed to contact their daughter. The land girls were outraged by this.

'Call themselves Christians!' Marion had fumed over cocoa, one night.

'But they aren't Christians, see?' Gwennan snapped. 'They're these Pentecostal things! Not proper Christians at all!' Alice warned them to keep their voices down in case Hester overheard them.

'She knows, though, Mrs Todd,' Gwennan continued, more quietly. 'She knows what they think of her. Cast off, that's what she's been, poor kid!'

'I don't think Hes wants to go to America,' Mabel said hesitantly, and Winnie and Marion turned on her in astonishment.

'What? Not want to go and live in America with Reuben's folk! 'Course she does!'

'Anyhow, what would you know, Mabel?' Gwennan snarled. Mabel blushed and stammered, unable to articulate her opinion in the face of such scorn.

'Why d'you say that, Mabel?' Alice asked more gently.

''Cos of how she looks when she thinks about it,' Mabel mumbled.

'And how do you know when she's thinking about it?'

'You can tell,' Mabel said, 'by 'er face.'

'Daft as a brush, you are, Mabel Hodges!' Gwennan said dismissively.

'Well, I reckon she's got no choice,' Rose announced firmly, her hard Devonian voice cutting through the murmured comments of the girls, most of whom seemed unconvinced by Mabel's theory. 'She's got nowhere else to go and, fond as I am of the poor child, I haven't the room in my cottage, not when my Dave comes home, I haven't.' Rose was well aware of possible complications if Dave, still at least half in love with Hester, was to return from France to find a young widow, available, yes, but pregnant with another man's child. Next thing Dave'd be saddled with bringing up Reuben's baby! Not that Rose had anything against Reuben, of course. But it was not what she had in mind for Dave. Not what she had in mind at all. 'And the sooner she goes the better, if you ask me. So she's nicely settled in America by the time the baby comes.' Rose's tone suggested that the subject was now closed.

When, one afternoon, a cart arrived at the farmhouse gate and a gaunt man descended, dressed in black and wearing on his head something that resembled the stove-pipe hats of the 1890s, Alice guessed at once that he was Hester's father.

'I be 'ere to see my daughter,' he announced when Alice approached the porch to meet him. It was a hot day and the doors at each end of the cross-passage were standing open, allowing what breeze there was to move through the building.

Jonas Tucker was a tall, emaciated man, whose crumpled clothes hung on him, giving him the appearance of a scarecrow. Baleful eyes were burning in a face that was lined and furrowed into a mask of disapproval. His skin had a curious greyish tinge to it and was darkened by several days' growth of beard. He had removed his hat and as he stood with it clutched in his huge, bony hands, he seemed to quake with a barely controlled anger.

Alice knew of Hester's background and her strict upbringing at the hands of her father, a minister in a small religious sect based in Cornwall and known as the Pentecostal Brotherhood. She had once briefly encountered Ezekial, Hester's young brother, when, visiting his sister, he had caught her wearing a borrowed frock and reported to her father that she had loosened her hair and was being led into temptation by the land girls.

Alice was immediately shocked by the appearance and bearing of this man and her initial instinct was to protect Hester from him. But she knew she could not deny him access to his daughter and led him into the empty recreation room, told him she would fetch Hester and warned him that he would find her in a fragile state because of her pregnancy and her grief over her husband's death.

'Her wretchedness is deserved,' he said suddenly and so harshly that Alice gasped in surprise. 'She has disobeyed the laws of her Church,' he continued, his face contorted with anger, 'and betrayed her family. She has sinned against Almighty God and must bear his wrath. This is the word of the Lord. Now, fetch my daughter to me.'

Had Alice not already implied that Hester was somewhere close at hand she could have lied, telling the man that he was too late and that his daughter was already on her way to America. With little time to consider what to do, she decided to pretend to go to fetch Hester but instead of delivering her to her father, to ask Rose to conceal her somewhere and tell him his daughter could not be found. But Hester had seen the arrival of the cart from the window of Rose's cottage and knew who was waiting for her in the farmhouse. She had crossed the yard and at that moment appeared silently in the doorway of the recreation room. Sensing that she was there, Jonas Tucker turned slowly to face her.

'Leave us,' he said to Alice. But Alice stood her ground, placing herself between the man and his daughter and was relieved to catch a glimpse of Rose behind Hester, in the gloom of the cross-passage.

'So this is how it is,' Jonas Tucker said, aware of the presence of the two women. 'Well, daughter. I reckon you 'eard what I just said but I will repeat it for you!' He raised his voice, adopting the strident tone he used when addressing the small, cowering congregation in the dank chapel where he preached. 'I told 'ee that you'm cursed! And because you'm cursed your 'usband was cursed and the child ye be carryin' be cursed along with all those who do consort with 'ee! Thou art in cohorts with Lucifer himself and shall be consigned to the everlasting fires of Hell!' The quiet air shuddered and both Rose and Alice were momentarily stunned by his outburst. Then, as if at a given signal, both women moved. Rose, reaching round the open door, caught Hester by the wrist and dragged her out into the cross-passage. Like a rag doll, pulled almost off her feet, her free arm flailing, her eyes still locked onto her father's, Hester was drawn from the room while Alice took a step closer to Jonas and jabbed a forefinger into his chest.

Afterwards, she recalled feeling the hard bone of his sternum against her hand and hearing Rose slam and lock the door to the kitchen.

'If you are not out of this building in one minute I'll have you thrown out!' she heard herself say. 'Mrs Crocker is fetching the farmhands! Now, do as I say!' There were no farmhands at Lower Post Stone Farm that day and, even had there been, the maimed Ferdie and the aging Jack would not have had much effect on Jonas had he resisted them. In her own ears, Alice's voice sounded thin, but for his own reasons, Jonas, having succeeded in causing the damage he had intended, chose to obey her.

'Aye!' he shouted. 'The likes of you aluss 'as lackeys to defend you! But the good Lord knows where virtue lies and it bain't under this roof, that's for certain sure!'

'Jack!' Alice shouted, bluffing. 'Mr Vallance! In here, please! Quickly!' Jonas turned, appeared to lose his balance, collided with the door jamb and, muttering curses, stumbled through the cross-passage and out into the blinding daylight. Here he appeared to trip, and Alice was surprised to see him sprawl, headlong, onto the cobbled path. He scrambled to his feet, turned to face the farmhouse and hurled a final curse, spittle and blood from a cut lip running down his quivering chin.

Hester sat on her bed in Rose's cottage and, despite the ministrations of both women, didn't speak for several hours. They brought her first strong tea and then beef broth but she would not drink. Eventually she spoke.

'I'm all right,' she said, becoming aware of their concern for her. 'I know all that, see. He didn't need to come here to say it to me. 'Cos I know it. 'Bout being cursed an' all.'

'You bain't cursed, Hester!' Rose protested. 'What would you be cursed for? You'm a good girl what's never done no harm to no one! You was a good wife to your Reuben and you'll make a good mother to his child.' But Hester shook her head.

''Tis too late for us, Rose. Reuben's already paid the price. Next it will be me and then the little one.' She looked from one uncomprehending face to the other and then she said, 'I think I'll go to sleep now.' Alice and Rose watched as she took off her clothes, pulled her nightshirt on over her head and got into her bed.

'But 'tis on'y five o'clock, Hester,' Rose protested, knowing that Hester was barely hearing her, 'and you 'bain't 'ad no supper, my lover!' But the girl had turned onto her side and closed her eyes.

'She'm not like the rest of us, that one,' Rose said, as she and Alice crossed the yard and went into the farmhouse. 'She knows things, that girl. And it bain't healthy.'

# Chapter Seven

While morale at Lower Post Stone Farm had been sobered by Reuben's death, another situation, caused by the Allies invasion of France, had threatened to suppress the girls' spirits. Marion and Winnie in particular were dismayed when the thousands of young servicemen who had been training for the invasion and had, during that time, paid constant and welcome attention to them, were suddenly gone, shipped or flown across the channel to do what they had been prepared for. There was, however, a surprising amount of coming and going between the South of England and the North of France, and this proved to be enough to keep up the flow of nylons, chewing gum and chocolate with which, by selling it on to other girls, Marion and Winnie subsidised their incomes, so that the savings in their Post Office book continued, albeit at a slower rate, to grow.

Encouraging news of the war was arriving every day. Roger Bayliss and Alice raised their glasses to each other when the Russian army broke through the Mannerheim Line and captured Minsk, and Margery Brewster arrived a couple of weeks later with a bottle of gin and an unshakeable determination to celebrate the news that the Americans had taken Guam from the Japanese. The hostel rang with cheers when, in mid-July – when the Post Stone girls were busy with the second cutting of hay – it was announced that an attempt had been made on Hitler's life.

"Ow come they never finished 'im off, though?' Mabel wailed. 'Whatever was they thinkin' of?'

On the following Friday evening, Edward John, home from his weekly boarding school, brought with him a note from his headmaster.

'Whatever possessed you?' his mother demanded, the headmaster's letter shaking in her hand. Edward John had used his penknife to inscribe the name HITLER into the gleaming surface of the Bechstein piano which dominated the school's music room. Now, faced with his mother's anger, he was initially surprised by it.

'Because I hate Hitler, of course,' he explained. 'Don't you hate him?'

'Yes, I do! But what has that to do with the school piano?'

'It's a Bechstein!' he said, as though the answer to her question was obvious. 'It's a German piano!'

'Oh, Edward John...' Alice sighed. She could see the logic of his action and understood that it had been a misguided protest rather than the act of vandalism it had initially appeared to be. 'So would you like to see all the musical instruments and all the books and all the paintings and the sculptures – many of which are scattered all over the world to places where they are valued and loved – destroyed, just because they happen to come from Germany? And what about the plays and the operas and the music? Beethoven was a German, for heaven's sake!' For a moment she thought he was going to defend himself, so she pressed on. 'I'm ashamed of you, Edward John! Whatever you think of the Germans you have absolutely no right to damage other people's property. You will write a letter of apology to your headmaster and when we know the cost of repairing the piano you shall pay for it out of your pocket money.'

It was Edward John's Uncle Richard who met the bill. In his letter to Alice, in which he enclosed a cheque for five pounds, he seemed more inclined to sympathise with his nephew than to admonish him. *These last few years*, he wrote, *have possibly had more effect on him than you think. He's a sensitive lad, Alice, and, if I may say so without incurring your wrath, I think you should go easy on him.* Alice had bristled slightly but after some thought decided that Richard, for all his lack of experience with young children, was probably right.

'You wouldn't think,' Rose said a few days later, with the cup of strong, sweet tea that Alice had made for her, between her shaking hands, 'that a lad in the Catering Corps would get wounded, would you? And here's me thinking he was safe, peelin' spuds in some army kitchen or other and there's he with a lump of shrapnel in 'is leg!'

In fact, Rose's Dave, driving supplies to a field canteen in Normandy, had been, and not for the first time, closer to enemy action than many of the battalions of foot soldiers it was his job to feed.

The lorry he was driving along an isolated country road had been strafed by a Messerschmitt and his passenger, a young conscript who had arrived only that morning from a training camp in Hampshire, had died instantly.

Dave, in shock and bleeding heavily, had continued for several miles before arriving, with the dead boy slumped beside him, at a US army checkpoint.

''E was took to a field hospital first off,' his mother told Alice, having been given all the facts by Roger Bayliss, who had telephoned a spokesman for Dave's unit. 'And then they brung him home 'cos he has to have an operation, see, for to get out the shrapnel.' She showed Alice the piece of paper with the address of an army hospital near Portsmouth. 'I've got a cousin lives down that way so I shall go stay with her and visit Dave. You'll be all right with Hester to help you. Jack's fetching me to the station first thing in the morning. I'm going to do some cooking now, so I can take Dave plenty of nourishin' food on account of I don't reckon they'll be feedin' him proper in that hospital.'

Alice was amused by Rose's announcement. Hester, frail and listless, would not be much help with the cooking during Rose's absence from the farmhouse kitchen. But Rose was not asking for permission to go, she was simply telling Alice what was going to happen and Alice was not inclined to stand between an anxious mother and her ewe lamb, even if the lamb was a strapping young man whose wound, according to Roger Bayliss's information, was not considered serious.

'Absolutely fine, Rose,' she said. 'You go and get yourself ready. Hester and I will manage.'

'I shall make pasties,' Rose declared, 'and Mr Bayliss says I'm to pick as many strawberries as I want from his vegetable patch and to fill a canteen with cream 'cos there's nothing my Dave likes better than a bowl of strawberries an' cream!' Then her face crumpled suddenly and tears spilt down her weathered cheeks. "'E could of bin killed, Alice! 'E could ever so easily of bin killed!'

Dave Crocker was sitting comfortably in his hospital bed when his mother found him. There were nineteen stitches in his thigh. Rose had been right when she had believed he could easily have died. The shard of shrapnel, when the surgeon had removed it, had been dangerously close to the femoral artery.

She fed him the pasties she'd brought for him and then produced a platter of scones, baked that morning by her cousin. Roger Bayliss's strawberries had suffered during the long train journey so Rose had boiled them into jam. The scones, piled with the jam and crowned with Devonshire cream, were passed round the ward.

'Those boys just loved 'em!' Rose told Alice proudly when, after three days, she returned to the farm. 'Wolfed 'em down, they did! Said as they'd never tasted nothing so good in all their lives and when the war's over they're all comin' down to Demshur for some more! And Dave's doing that well he'll be walkin' in a day or so and then he'll be sent home to convalesce or some such word. Anyway, he'll be at home for a bit... So I shan't have room for young Hester no more on account of my Dave'll be needin' 'is bedroom, see. Maybe she could move back into the farmhouse? The little room

Georgina used to sleep in be empty, bain't it?'

Rose was well aware that the tiny room above the porch, into which Georgina had once retreated rather than share a bedroom with Marion and Winnie, had been unoccupied since she had left the hostel six months previously. Rose also knew that the accommodation at Lower Post Stone Farm was designated specifically for the use of Women's Land Army personnel.

Alice would, she said, discuss with Mr Bayliss and Margery Brewster what could be done.

Officially, because she was no longer in the Land Army, Hester was not entitled to be housed at the hostel but, in the circumstances and as it was unlikely to be long before her turn came to be shipped to America, she was permitted to move herself and her few possessions from Rose's cottage into what had been Georgina's room.

'It shouldn't be allowed,' Gwennan carped, predictably. 'This place is getting more like a nursing home than a Land Army hostel! Pregnant women and wounded soldiers – whatever next?'

'Preg-nant wo-men! Preg-nant wo-men!' Annie chanted, accurately imitating Gwennan's strong, Welsh accent. The other girls joined in the teasing.

'Is she preg-nant, Taff? Indeed-to-goodness! Is she preg-nant!'

* * *

Three days later and leaning heavily on a crutch, Dave Crocker arrived home. His mother had told him, during her hospital visit, of Reuben's death and about Hester's strange conviction, which had subsequently proved to be true, that he had been killed on D-Day and would be found in the sea. It was not until her son was safely home that she described to him the visit Hester's father had paid to the farm and the evil things he had said to his grieving daughter.

Dave sat for some time, absorbing these facts.

'She's got no one, then,' he said at last.

'She's got 'er 'usband's family!' Rose countered sharply, seeing where this was leading and not liking it.

'But they'm strangers to 'er, Mum. They don't know nothin' about 'er, nor she them.'

'But they want 'er, Dave. And they want their grandchild.'

'But what do *she* want, eh? 'As anyone asked 'er what *she* wants? She can't go home to her folks so she's to be packed off to strangers! They might well want the child, Mum, but would they want Hester? She's got no choice. Not that she knows of, anyhow. But she has got a choice, see. And I'm gonna tell her what it is. I'm gonna ask 'er, Mum!'

'And what is it then, this "choice"?' Rose asked him, knowing the answer.

Dave had always been popular with girls. At school

they'd given him their sweets and later cheered him, eyeing his broad shoulders and short powerful legs, as he lumbered up and down the football pitch, playing for the village team. He'd even walked out with a couple of them before his call-up papers had arrived. But he had never looked at any of them the way his mother had seen him look at Hester Tucker when he had first set his eyes on her. All the other land girls were there that day and some were more fetching than Hester, but she had been the one who caught and held Dave's attention. He had sought her out at the snowbound Christmas party and danced exclusively with her, unaware that it was Reuben she was waiting for. Now, married, widowed, pregnant and without the protection of her family, the girl he wanted was about to be sent to strangers.

Rose knew her son. Since he had been at home, recovering from his injury, she'd seen the single-minded devotion in his face when he spoke of Hester or caught a glimpse of her across the yard.

Dave had considered the implications of raising another man's child but Reuben had seemed to be a decent lad. A young soldier who had died fighting in a war he could easily have avoided and who had picked Hester, loved her and married her. Dave's code of ethics was a simple one which, had he been asked to, he would have found difficult to put into words. What he felt was almost an affinity with Reuben.

Hester had loved him. But Reuben was no longer there to be loved, or to love her or to help her raise the child whose life he had begun.

'You know what it is, Mum,' he said, looking at his mother's closed face and trying to engage the hard eyes that were avoiding his. 'You know what I'm gonna ask 'er.'

There was a cider-apple orchard across the lane from the farmhouse. Hester was sitting on the trunk of an ancient tree that had come down in a gale a few years previously. She had been gazing into space but when she saw a movement and recognised the figure making its way between the trees as Dave, her eyes followed his progress towards her.

He had discarded his crutch but walked carefully, favouring his injured leg. He stopped, twelve feet from her and waited for her to speak.

''Ow be your leg, then, Dave?' she asked him quietly, continuing before he could answer. ''Tis because of me you was wounded, see.'

'Because of you? How was it because of you?'

'Because everything bad as happens around me be my fault. And the closer folk are to me the worse it be for them.' He approached her, dropped onto his knees, sat back on his heels and winced as the skin on his scarred leg tightened. He reached for her hands but she pulled away. 'No, Dave. Don't touch me!'

'You got some infectious disease, then, 'ave you,

Hester?' He spoke lightly, attempting to tease her.

'In a manner of speakin', yes, I 'ave.'

''Course you 'aven't!' He searched her face, half smiling, still hoping to see her expression soften and lose its tension, but it did not. He sighed and, after a moment, continued. 'This 'as got some'at to do with that rubbish your dad were on about when he come to see you, right?'

''T weren't rubbish, Dave!' She spoke slowly, spacing her words. 'First 't was Reuben, see. Then you. Next 't will be the baby! I knows it!' He couldn't reach her and her manner was scaring him now.

He tried to talk to her. To convince her that the things her father had said to her were nothing more than lies designed to frighten her and that she must see them for what they were and put them out of her mind. But she closed her eyes and shook her head. Then he told her that he loved her and wanted to marry her and help her bring up Reuben's child. But she got to her feet and started back towards the farmhouse. When he followed her she turned abruptly to face him.

'No! No, Dave. Don't follow me. You mustn't follow me!' He stood watching her as she made her way through the orchard, crossed the narrow lane, walked up the path and merged into the heavy shadow of the porch.

'He's got a lot to answer for, that Jonas Tucker!'

Rose said, later that night, watching Dave toy with the helping of suet pudding, which she had contrived to have left over from the land girls' supper and had carried carefully across the yard for her son.

'But how can she believe him?' he asked, still incredulous at Hester's outburst.

'She were born and raised to it, Dave. Don't forget that, boy. Seventeen years she'd had of it by the time she come 'ere. You didn't see 'er in those early days. She barely spoke. 'Er face was scrubbed and 'er hair was dragged back into a bun. Black stockings she wore and no make-up! Months it took, for 'er to learn to trust us 'ere. But it seems 'er father still had a hold on 'er and losing Reuben like that and then you almost dyin'…'

'Did you tell her that? That I almost died? I was on'y wounded, Mum! A bit of shrapnel in me leg was all! You helped to put the fear of God into her, you did!' He pushed away the untouched plate, left the kitchen and limped upstairs to his bedroom.

Rose sat for a while, staring at the uneaten pudding. She hadn't meant to add to Hester's misery. But if it had led her to reveal to Dave the extent of the damage done to her, then perhaps, Rose thought, overcoming a slight sensation of guilt, it was for the best.

Next morning, when Hester failed to come down to the hostel kitchen at breakfast time, Mabel was sent up to the tiny room above the porch to wake her. Then, after a moment they heard Mabel's bare feet thudding down the stairs and she burst, breathlessly, into the kitchen.

'She's not in her room, Mrs Todd! The bed's made up, neat as ninepence, but 'er bags 'as gone!'

Margery Brewster applied to her superiors for a special allowance of petrol in order to drive the fifty-odd miles to the isolated North Devon smallholding tenanted by Hester's father.

'Someone must find out where she is,' she declared, emphatically, to Roger Bayliss. 'I realise that, strictly speaking, she is no longer our responsibility but I personally feel morally obliged to make sure she arrived home safely. We don't even know she intended to go home! She could be anywhere!'

Margery returned to Lower Post Stone Farm mid-afternoon and, over a cup of tea, described to Alice the bleak clutter of outbuildings, disused farming equipment, pig-pens, rotting hen-coops and rusting sheds that stood around the neglected cottage that housed the Tucker family.

'She was picking raspberries on a patch of land on the far side of the property,' Margery said, 'so I made my way over to her and asked her how she was. She was polite enough and told me she was quite well, thank you. She enquired after my health and yours. I told her you were concerned because no one knew where she'd gone. She said she was sorry you'd been worried but that she'd thought it best to come home. I asked her when she expected to leave for America but she just shook her head and went on picking the raspberries. She kept glancing, nervously, I thought, at the cottage. Then a woman, presumably her mother, came out of the door and called her in. She said she had to go and ran – yes, Alice, ran – back to the house and in through the door, which was immediately closed behind her. Someone lowered the blinds in the downstairs windows and there I was, standing in the yard with two emaciated cats rubbing round my ankles and half a dozen scrawny hens scratching in the dirt. I felt...I know it's silly of me, but I felt quite...threatened! I didn't waste much time getting into my car and driving away from the place, I can tell you! It was...well it was horrible, Alice!'

'Poor Hester!' Alice sighed.

'Yes. Poor Hester. I wonder if she will go to America.'

'Could her parents stop her, d'you think?'

'I don't suppose they could physically stop her, but...'

'They could influence her. Which is more than any of us can do now... Oh dear... Perhaps that was part of the trouble. That we did influence her. The girls taught her how to make the best of herself and how to dance. They probably changed the way she thought about things.'

'You're not suggesting they led her astray?'

'Not exactly. But their standards are very different from her's and totally opposed to those imposed on her by her parents.'

'Which were the right ones, you think?'

'No, I don't think that. But the glimpse of freedom she had when she was with us doesn't seem to have made her very happy, does it?'

'Nonsense, Alice! She was the happiest girl in the world these last twelve months! Remember the way she blossomed in the spring. And then she met Reuben and married him and, whatever else happens, she'll soon have his child to care for... She'll survive – people do. There isn't a drop more tea in that pot, is there?'

During the previous summer, when Eleanor Fullerton, then aged fifteen, had absconded from her boarding school, adopted the name Nora Fuller and arrived at the hostel during supper one evening wearing a 'borrowed' Land Army uniform, she had succeeded in convincing Alice that she was an authorised addition to the work force.

After several days her cover had been blown and she was removed by her embarrassed and angry headmistress and driven away, protesting vigorously and promising to return to the farm as soon as she was allowed to. Now, almost a year older but still too young to be accepted into the Land Army, she had persuaded her parents, as a reward for high marks in her exams, to let her spend her six-week school holiday working on the Post Stone farms.

'You must be potty, Nora or Eleanor or whatever you call yourself!' Marion exclaimed when she arrived, delighted to be back and eager to be absorbed into the chaotic life at the hostel, which seemed to appeal to her so much more than the sterile routine of her boarding school. 'Fancy choosing to live in this dump and work like a slave for next to nothin' when you don't have to!'

Eleanor's holiday assignment, which she had promised to send home, regularly, by post, was to be a five-page essay describing each week of her life on the farm. The small room over the porch that had once been Georgina's and, more recently, Hester's, now became hers.

Edward John was delighted to have Eleanor back again. The two of them had, during Eleanor's previous stay, become close friends, playing in the evenings with his Meccano set or challenging each other to games of Monopoly. But a year proved to have been a longer time for Eleanor than it had been for Edward John, who remained, in her eyes, a little boy while she had metamorphosed from schoolgirl into young woman.

'Don't you like Monopoly any more?' he asked her plaintively when, for the third time, she declined his invitation to play.

'Not much,' she said, heading for the recreation room where a Glenn Miller record was being played at full volume on the wind-up gramophone. 'You used to,' Edward John reminded her, shouting over the music.

'But that was last year! I was only fifteen then,' she said in the tone of voice that he recognised at once as the one grown-ups use when addressing small children.

'Can't you play Monopoly when you're sixteen?'

'Of course you can, silly!' Eleanor said loftily. 'But you don't want to!'

Eleanor had matured considerably in the twelve months since her brief stay at Lower Post Stone Farm. Now she was rounded where, before, she had been straight, soft where she had been hard. Her jawline was firmer, her cheekbones more defined and her movements had become fluid and feminine.

'She'm a corker, that one!' Ferdie had been heard to sigh, under his breath. Then he raised his voice, adding, as Eleanor heaved a forkful of hay up onto a cart, 'That's it, my beauty! Up and over! Up and over, that's the way!'

'She's barely sixteen, Ferdie Vallance,' Gwennan reminded him sharply, watching his eyes wander appreciatively from the crown of Eleanor's dark head, past the cut-off dungarees, to the tanned and slender thighs and calves. 'And don't you forget it!' Gwennan moved away muttering about Ferdie being 'drawn to that girl like iron filings to a magnet!'

Mabel often caught her lover with his eyes on Eleanor but she was not jealous. She knew that however much he might be attracted to her, Eleanor would never give him a second glance. So she smiled and teased him.

'She's lovely, in't she, that Nora?' she cooed, reverting to the name Eleanor had given herself on her first, brief visit. 'Fancy her, do you, Ferdie love? Reckon you've got a chance with 'er, do ya?'

'What? That one? Me?' Ferdie would enquire innocently. 'Not I! All skin and bone, she be!' He would wink at Mabel and reach down to pinch the ample buttocks that he knew were his and his alone.

Gwennan, who relished any opportunity to see evil in a situation, whether it existed or not, became preoccupied by Ferdie's fascination with Eleanor and watched him closely whenever he was anywhere near her. Stirring sugar into a late night cup of cocoa one night, she spoke to Alice about it.

'He leers at her, Mrs Todd. It shouldn't be allowed. I don't reckon she should be here in the first place. She's too young to be living in a hostel with men like him prowling round her!'

'She's almost seventeen! Only a few months younger than Hester and Annie were when they first came here.' Gwennan tossed her head dismissively and reached for the sugar bowl. 'No more sugar,' Alice said, moving the bowl out of reach of Gwennan's spoon. 'That's all we have left until next week's rations arrive.'

'It's disgusting!' Gwennan whined to Winnie and Marion the next day, as Ferdie offered to help Eleanor off a cart from which she had been unloading beet.

'It's OK, Mr Vallance,' Eleanor had assured him cheerfully, jumping down, 'I can manage, thanks!'

'Just look at him!' Gwennan persisted, glaring at Ferdie as he limped off. 'Drooling he is! Drooling!'

'Jealous, Taff?' Marion sniggered and Winnie, under her breath, added that Gwennan's attitude confirmed, if confirmation was needed, that she was 'a miserable old cow'.


'D'you ever hear from that Kinski fellow?' Gwennan asked Marion, one hot midday when she, Marion and Winnie, having eaten their lunchtime sandwiches, were sprawling half asleep in the shade of a hayrick.

'Nope,' Marion said drowsily, 'I never did… What's it got to do with you, anyhow?' Instead of answering the question, Gwennan asked another.

'He never answered your letter, then?'

'What you on about, Taff? I never sent no letter to Sergeant Kinski!'

'You did so!' the Welsh girl snapped. 'It was on the dresser when I put a postcard to my auntie out ready for the postman.'

Because the nearest pillar box was a good mile from the hostel, the postman obliged its inmates by not only delivering their mail to the farmhouse door, together with the day's supply of bread, but by collecting any letters the girls had written and taking them to the post office in Ledburton for them.

'I never did!' Marion said, sitting up, glaring at Gwennan and irritably picking bits of thistle out of her hair.

'You calling me a liar, then?' the Welsh girl demanded. 'I saw it! A couple of months ago, it were. Large as life on the dresser, tucked half out of sight and addressed to Sergeant M Kinski and then there was a lot of numbers like you 'as to put when you're writing to someone in the forces. I couldn't help seeing,' she added with an unconvincing attempt at innocence, adding, emphatically, 'so don't you dare deny it!' She swatted something that was crawling on her leg. 'Ugh! There's earwigs in this straw...' she whined, getting clumsily to her feet and slouching off.

Marion frowned. After a moment she turned to Winnie.

'You done it, Win, din'cha? You wrote to bloomin' Marvin!'

'I might of.' Winnie glanced nervously at her friend.

'What d'you mean, "might of"? Either you did or you didn't!'

'All right, then. I did.'

'Whatever for?' They were sitting now, cross-legged in the straw, facing each other, Winnie's face flushed with embarrassment, Marion's tense and accusative.

''Cos 'e asked you to write to him!'

'And when I didn't, *you* did? Without telling me? Making it look like I'd written to him?' Her hard eyes were fixed accusingly on her friend's face.

'Anyhow, what does it matter?' Winnie said defensively, getting to her feet. ''Cos he never answered, did he!'

'No. He never did.'

'And d'you know why?'

'How should I know why?'

'I'll tell you why, Marion! 'Cos he's most likely dead, that's why! Omaha Beach was where his unit went ashore on D-Day. Same as Reuben. Not many of 'em as landed there made it. That's prob'ly why he never wrote back. Never thought of that, did you?'

'How could I think of it when I never even knew you'd wrote to him?' Marion demanded. In the silence that followed they heard Jack shouting for the girls to get back to work after their lunch break. Marion got to her feet. 'Wish I had now,' she sighed, as they trudged across the field to the sheaves of barley that lay, ready to be lifted off the stubble and arranged in neat rows of stooks, where the hot sun and warm wind would dry them. 'Wouldn't have done no harm, would it really, for him to 'ave had me picture, if he'd wanted it. To keep him company, like. When he was...if he'd got wounded or anything.'

'He did have it, Marion.' Winnie had stopped in her tracks. Marion, a few paces ahead of her, turned back to face her.

'You what?' she demanded.

'That snap we took of you in your bathers. I put it in the letter.'

'You never!'

'Yeah, I did...' They stood, both picturing Sergeant Kinski, wounded, probably dying, his eyes on the snapshot of Marion, posed in the sunshine on a boulder in the shallow river.

'Did 'e get it, d'you reckon?' Marion asked, almost inaudibly.

'We'll never know, will we?' Winnie said. 'Not if he got killed, we won't. Or even if he didn't—'

'I hope he didn't, Win...'

'Come on, you two!' Jack was bellowing at them. 'There be work to do 'ere! Bain't a bloomin' picnic, you know!'

They joined the other girls and began work, stooping and lifting the sheaves, stooping and lifting, stooping and lifting, propping them, one against the other, the grains drooping gracefully at the top, the shiny stalks concealing thistles, scratching the bare legs below their rolled up dungarees. Sweaty skin that had dried while they had rested in the shade, began to prickle and itch.

'Oooh, 'ow I do 'ate 'arvestin'!' Gwennan moaned.

'I don't reckon I've got another drop of sweat left in my entire body!' Annie sighed. She had a letter in her pocket from Hector Conway. He was going to fetch her on Saturday afternoon and drive her into Exeter for tea.

A nearby barracks, recently vacated by the American soldiers who had trained there, now housed a group of Italian prisoners of war, whose labour was available to farmers in the Ledburton area. With a heavy arable crop ready for harvesting, they were in great demand and were to be seen, always with an armed guard, working in groups of a dozen or so, sometimes near but never among the Land Army girls.

Like the girls, they were usually transported by lorry to and from their various work sites but sometimes they were marched past fields in which the Post Stone girls were at work, hoeing the long rows of young brassicas or stooking the drying oats. Occasionally the Italians caught sight of the girls fetching in the milking herd or bringing sheep down from the thinning grass on The Tops to the lower pastures, which, even after the dry weather of late July, were still lush and green. When this happened the girls would pause, straighten their backs, shade their eyes and stare, for the men were beautiful.

'Ever so friendly, they are!' Mabel announced happily over supper on the day when a party of the Italians had been escorted past the gate of a field in which the girls were lifting a crop of early potatoes. 'And some of 'em's that 'andsome!'

'There's one fella who's a dead-ringer for Stewart Granger,' Winnie announced, with her mouth full.

'An' one's a bit like Gregory Peck!'

'On'y not so tall, though,' Marion added, forking up baked beans.

'Well, none of 'em's what you'd call tall, are they?'

''Cos they got short legs. All Ities 'as got short legs.'

'Lovely muscles, though!' Eva flexed a bicep and the girls laughed and whistled.

'Ooh, yeah! Lovely muscles!'

'And 'ow would you know that, miss?' Rose demanded, her face tight with disapproval.

''Cos they 'ad their shirts off, Mrs Crocker. That's how!'

'It were ever so hot, see!'

'Their skin was all brown and shiny with sweat!' Winnie licked her lips lasciviously and the girls giggled.

'That's enough of that kind of talk, thank you!' Rose's voice was sharp. 'In case you 'aven't noticed, they've an armed guard watchin' over 'em and 'e bain't there for nothing, you know! Those men was fighting our boys till they got took prisoner. They're our enemies! And don't you forget it!'

'That's not quite true, Rose,' Alice told her. 'Italy surrendered to the Allies last September. But I know what you mean and you girls need to remember that the Italians are here under certain conditions and you should treat them accordingly.'

'We on'y waves to 'em, Mrs Todd,' said Mabel. 'Mustn't we even wave to 'em, then? I reckon they're lonely, all this way from their loved ones an' their homes...'

'Don't talk such rubbish, Mabel,' Rose blustered. 'It was one of them as put shrapnel in my Dave's leg! And you wants to wave to 'em?'

'No, Rose,' Alice interjected gently. 'It was a German pilot that injured Dave... It had nothing to do with the Italian army. But it's probably best, Mabel, if you don't wave, there's a dear.'

'But why not, Mrs Todd?' Annie wanted to know. 'Surely there's no 'arm in a wave, is there?'

'Not in itself,' Alice patiently explained. 'But if you appeared to be inviting...well...friendship, it might be misunderstood, mightn't it?' Already there had been some instances of local women becoming involved with the POWs and Roger Bayliss had warned Alice to keep an eye out for any such complications where the Post Stone girls were concerned.

'What's wrong with friendship?' Annie wanted to know.

'Nothing, in normal circumstances, Annie. But where you have men who, until recently, were our enemies and who are being kept under guard, who don't understand our ways or even speak our language, gestures, such as waving or calling out – or anything – could be misunderstood and lead to...to difficulties.' She searched the faces of her girls. 'D'you understand what I mean?'

'Well, if they don't they're even more stupid than I thought they was!' Rose snapped.

On a warm, thundery evening, Eleanor, late with her letter home, decided to take it to the pillar box on the lane to Ledburton rather than leave in on the dresser for the postman to collect the next day. She took the overgrown footpath which ran through neglected woodland from the farm down to the lane where a disused barn stood, the Victorian letter box set into its crumbling stonework.

The evening was still and heavy with the threat of an approaching storm, and thunder was rumbling in the extreme distance as Eleanor moved quietly down the path, the letter, addressed to her parents, in her hand. By the time she reached the lane and had slipped the envelope into the postbox, she was conscious of the thick cloud that was rapidly reducing what was left of the daylight and realised that she would be lucky to reach the farm before the storm broke.

The trees arching over the path were in full leaf, obscuring what light there was, and as Eleanor quickened her pace she heard, or thought she heard, footsteps. Someone, or something, was moving parallel to her and slightly behind her. She stopped. The footsteps continued, moving fast. Whoever it was would soon draw level with her. She heard him – she was sure now, by the weight of the footsteps, that it was a man – trip and fall heavily. He cried out and cursed unintelligibly before continuing on, obviously in pain, blundering through the tangled saplings.

Eleanor had at least half a mile to go before the path reached the open ground below the farmhouse. She stopped again and stood still, trying to control her nerves. She told herself she was stupid to feel scared. Who could possibly be there? Who, if anyone was there, would want to frighten or hurt her? But there was someone! And why was that person struggling through the undergrowth instead of using the path, the short cut, which was as well known to all the locals as it was to the land girls themselves?

The person, moving painfully now, seemed to be gaining on her. He was breathing hard, as was she, and like her, was stumbling in the half-light, stepping on twigs that snapped noisily underfoot. Sudden gusts of wind, preceding the storm, rustled the foliage overhead.

Beside her, to her right, the woodland rose sharply and curved upwards, away from the path. If she went that way her keen sense of direction told her that she would emerge from the trees a good quarter of a mile closer to the farmhouse than the path she was following. The undergrowth on the rising ground was thick with brambles and dense with tall timbers, but her desire to veer away from whoever it was who seemed to be stalking her overrode her concern and she turned sharply right, then began to climb.

It was only a few hundred yards but the going proved to be more difficult than she had anticipated. The fading light made it hard to negotiate the tangled undergrowth, which snagged her clothes and scratched her skin. There were unexpected outcrops of rock and places where the incline was almost vertical, forcing her to scramble up through slippery blocks of mossy limestone. She grazed her knees and blood ran from her lacerated shins.

She emerged from the wood into what seemed to be the violent centre of the storm and stumbled on, blinded by lightening and deafened by thunderclaps that seemed so close to her that she could sense their dangerous energy. The farmhouse was an indistinct shape obscured by rain so torrential that it formed a wall of water which seemed likely to drown her. Choking, she lowered her head and pushed onwards, slipping and staggering over the last hundred yards, and was close to hysteria when she burst into the kitchen, where Alice and the girls had gathered, drawn together by the violence of the storm and their growing concern for the girl who was out in it. For a moment they stood gaping while rainwater poured off Eleanor.

First, they draped her quickly in a blanket and Eva ran to fetch a towel to dry her dripping hair. Then, while Annie cleaned her wounds, Eleanor breathlessly sobbed out the facts of her experience to Alice and the girls, who clustered anxiously round her.

'I heard someone, Mrs Todd! Sort of...moving in the undergrowth,' she gulped.

'Who was it?' Alice asked her.

'I don't know! I didn't see him!'

'Him?'

'It sounded like a man. The footsteps were heavy and he was...sort of gasping and mumbling. Once he must have tripped or something and he shouted out as though he'd fallen and hurt himself... I couldn't understand what he said. It was a word I've never heard before. It sounded like..."Kazzo"?'

'So you never actually saw him?'

'No! He stayed in the trees. But he seemed to be keeping level with me. It was horrible! I was scared! I didn't realise that climbing up through the wood was going to be so difficult but I couldn't go back to the path in case he was there. The thunder and the wind was making such a row I couldn't tell whether he was behind me or not. Ouch! That hurt, Annie!'

'Sorry, but you've got a thorn stuck in your knee... Here it comes!'

'Ow!'

'Sorry!'

'But he didn't catch you, Eleanor? He didn't touch you?'

'No, Mrs Todd.' Eleanor shuddered. The towel had slipped off her hair, which was hanging in dark corkscrews down her back, water dripping from the end of each curl. 'Nobody touched me.'

'I've filled the bath, Alice,' Rose announced, calm in the face of the crisis. 'A warm tub'll do her a power of good. Come on, my dear, I've got nicely aired towels and a clean nightie all ready for you!' Eleanor was about to follow Rose out of the kitchen when Gwennan came briskly into it.

'Did you say you was on the old footpath that

leads through to the lane when you was followed?' she asked, and when Eleanor confirmed this, continued, 'Then I saw who it was!' Gwennan was relishing her moment. 'I saw someone from my bedroom window, Mrs Todd. And I recognised him!'

Gwennan had everyone's attention now and in unison they clamoured for details, demanding to know who it was she had seen, while Alice attempted to subdue them. The Welsh girl timed her announcement to perfection, letting her words fall dramatically into the silence the warden had imposed. 'It was Ferdie Vallance,' she said shrilly. 'That's who!'

There was a gasp of astonishment.

'Never!' Mabel yelled. 'It were never Ferdie! Why would my Ferdie do that? You're a liar, Gwennan Pringle, that's what you are! A wicked liar!' She clenched her fists and with a howl of anger, launched herself at Gwennan, who flinched and stepped smartly aside while Winnie and Marion caught Mabel by the arms, sat her down at the table and held her there, squirming and swearing.

'You watch your language, miss!' Rose commanded. 'I won't 'ave words like that spoke in my kitchen!'

'It's not your kitchen!' Mabel muttered. 'It's Mrs Todd's!'

'No, it's not! It's Mr Bayliss's, so there!' Gwennan chipped in, punctilious even in the excitement of the moment.

'Stop bickering, you two and listen to me, please!' Alice, mustering all the authority she had acquired since she had found herself in charge of these girls and this place, turned to Gwennan.

'I want you to think very carefully about this, Gwennan,' she said. 'What you have said has serious implications and may involve the police.'

'And so it should, Mrs Todd!' Gwennan answered crisply. 'You should be telephoning 'em now, this minute!'

At the mention of the word 'police', Mabel burst into noisy tears, Gwennan's strident voice rising over them.

'I've seen the way that man looks at Eleanor – we all have! – his eyes is all over her! He can't hardly keep his hands off of her!'

'But 'e was on'y lookin'!' Mabel wailed. 'He never would of touched 'er!'

'Hang on...how could you have seen him from your window, Taff?' Annie asked. 'It's rainin' stair rods!' She peered out of the low window. 'You can't hardly see your hand in front of your face out there.'

'You calling me a liar, then?' Gwennan snarled back at her.

Leaving the girls, Alice and Gwennan went up the stairs and into Gwennan's bedroom, where Alice stooped down and peered out through the small, low window. At first she could see almost nothing. The landscape was lost in the drifting rain and fading daylight. Then, as her eyes adjusted to the poor light, Alice could just make out the place where the footpath emerged from the trees. It was several hundred yards away and as Annie had suggested, heavily shrouded in murky rain – but it *was* just visible.

'It's darker now than it were when I saw 'im,' Gwennan said defensively. 'But you must admit, I could of!'

They returned to the kitchen where Alice had to admit that, in her opinion and despite the poor visibility, it was possible that Gwennan could have seen someone emerge from the wood.

'That's not to say who it was, though, is it?' Mabel shrieked.

'No,' Alice agreed, 'but whoever it was…' Before she could continue Gwennan's sharp voice filled the kitchen.

'There's no "whoever" about it, Mrs Todd!' Gwennan interrupted. 'Ferdie Vallance was who I saw! Ferdie Vallance! And d'you know why I am so certain it was him?' She paused dramatically, her eyes meeting and challenging the eyes of everyone in the kitchen, from the shivering Eleanor, past the blubbering Mabel, the astonished Elsie, Eva and Nancy and the disapproving Rose, to the intrigued Marion and Winnie and on, round the crowded room, to the concerned and perplexed Annie and then to

Alice herself. 'I'll tell you why,' Gwennan said. 'It's because he was limping, that's why! Rolling from side to side and dragging his left foot! And there's only one man round these parts as walks like that!'

They had all been convinced that Gwennan was at best embellishing the truth or at worst lying. No one could believe that Ferdie would have stalked Eleanor, however much he admired her, or even lusted after her. He was, they all instinctively believed, a simple but honourable man.

In the total silence that followed Gwennan's words, Alice quietly suggested that Eleanor should go and have her bath. She went, with Rose, out of the kitchen and up the stairs.

While the girls watched, stunned into silence, Mabel whimpering miserably, Gwennan sat self-righteously at the table and boldly engaged the eyes of anyone who dared to meet hers. Alice pushed her feet into her rubber boots, took an umbrella from the porch and made her way through the downpour across the yard to the barn where the hostel telephone was housed.

'What shall I do?' she asked Roger, who had been finishing his evening meal when his housekeeper came to tell him that Mrs Todd was on the line. 'It's a serious accusation and I don't think she's lying. Eleanor is scratched and bruised but was not molested in any way, thank goodness... But what do we do about Ferdie?'

'I'll come down,' Roger told her. 'Be with you in ten minutes.'

They led Gwennan through to Alice's sitting room and sat her in one of the two small armchairs, Alice opposite her, while Roger paced up and down the length of the room. He warned Gwennan that she had made a very serious allegation which could have far-reaching consequences for Mr Vallance and that she must be absolutely certain that what she had told them was the truth. Then he questioned her, very calmly and precisely, about what she claimed to have seen, and asked her to repeat her evidence for identifying the man as Ferdie Vallance.

'It was his limp,' she said sullenly. 'It was the funny way he walks because of being injured by your tractor when he was a lad.' Roger remembered the incident fifteen years previously when Ferdie, in his mid-teens had been trapped for two hours and Christopher, then only ten years old, had crawled under the overturned tractor and given him brandy to deaden the pain until he could be freed.

Roger completed his interrogation, thanked Gwennan for answering his questions and told her she could go.

'Will you be calling the police in now, then, Mr Bayliss?' Gwennan's tone seemed to suggest that she would not tolerate much delay on his part.

'Just leave us, please, Gwennan,' Alice said. She

opened the door, watched Gwennan go through it and invited Roger to sit down. They sat for a while in silence.

'Well...' Roger said. 'I suppose I'd better report this.' He got to his feet. 'I know the chief inspector in Exeter. I'll give him a call and find out how we should proceed.'

'Shouldn't you speak to Ferdie first?' Alice asked him. 'He might have some explanation for why he was there.'

'It's hard to imagine what! He was two miles from his cottage. It was almost dark. A thunderstorm was about to break and he knows that footpath, Alice! Must have used it a thousand times. Why would he be struggling through the undergrowth beside it and not walking along it, as he has done all his life? And according to your girls, he was, understandably, rather smitten by Eleanor.'

'It's one thing being smitten, Roger, and quite another to... Oh, I don't know. I was just trying to think of some innocent reason why he might have been there. It's not that I don't trust Gwennan – surely she wouldn't invent anything so outrageous – but she's always very quick to see the worst in people... What's that?'

From Alice's window they saw, through the half-light, the wavering beam of a bicycle lamp.

The policeman, helmeted and draped in a waterproof

cape, dismounted, leant his machine against the gate post and, head down, lumbered through the torrential rain towards the porch.

The girls had begun to disperse from the kitchen and were gathering instead in the recreation room, intending to expand on the unexpected drama that was unfolding and, some would have said, deliciously breaking the monotony of life at the hostel. And here, they realised, as Rose opened the door to a police constable, came the next thrilling instalment.

The policeman stood awkwardly in the cross-passage, dripping rainwater onto the slate floor.

'Constable Twentyman!' Roger said, making his way through the girls. 'What can we do for you?' Twentyman tilted his head and eased off his helmet.

'Just to let everyone here know that we got 'im, sir!'

'Got who, Twentyman?'

'The POW, sir!' The constable looked round at the astonished faces. 'But p'raps you didn't know, sir. We've 'ad trouble getting round to all the farms, what with the storm. One of the Italians, sir, made a break for it a couple of hours ago. Seems he got a "Dear John" from his girl in Naples. Anyhow, they picked him up just down the lane, from 'ere. Reckon he'd lost himself. He couldn't of got far on account of he'd busted his ankle! Limping along the lane, he was! He's bin took off to hospital, poor fellow. Now, if you'll excuse me, sir? Only I've got a few more calls to make. Just to put everyone's mind at rest, you see. 'Night, ladies.'

Constable Twentyman ducked under the low lintel and, settling his helmet back on his head, loped through the rain to his bike. He cycled unsteadily off, avoiding the brimming potholes, the dim beam of his lamp blurred by the downpour.

Alice assembled the girls. Roger Bayliss, fixing his eyes on Gwennan Pringle, lectured them about the dangers of jumping to conclusions and making unsubstantiated accusations.

'I guess we were all as guilty as each other,' he said thoughtfully, as he and Alice, alone in her sitting room, sipped sherry. She nodded.

'Poor Ferdie!' she said. 'He would have been mortified!'

'And that wretched what's-her-name…?'

'Gwennan. But she didn't lie, Roger. She *did* see a man down there and he *was* limping.'

'So she assumed it was Vallance—'

'And so did we! Just as Eleanor assumed that whoever was in the wood was about to molest her, when he probably didn't even know she was there. Thank goodness he was caught and everything was explained.'

'He wouldn't have got far with a Pott's fracture! Poor lad, loses his girl and then smashes his ankle.

Just not his day, was it?' As they laughed, partly with relief that the outcome of the incident was less serious than it might have been, they heard a tap on Alice's door.

Eleanor, in her dressing gown, hesitated when she saw Roger and suggested she should come back when Alice was alone. 'Only there's something you should know, you see,' she said.

Roger excused himself and Eleanor sat down nervously in the chair opposite the warden. Her hands and forearms were badly scratched and an abrasion on one cheek was turning from pink to a delicate mauve. Alice asked her how she was feeling and she said she felt stupid.

'Anyone would have done the same,' Alice assured her. 'It's horrid when you think you're being followed. And you didn't accuse anyone of anything, so...'

'No, I didn't. But I did do something stupid, Mrs Todd. It's to do with what you said the other day, about not waving to the Italians.'

'Did you wave to them?'

'Well, not exactly wave.' Eleanor was looking seriously embarrassed now and neither of them spoke for a moment.

'Well...what did you do?'

'Jack had sent me down to the water meadow to oil the hinges on the gate because they kept locking up. I was crossing the bridge and a kingfisher flew

243

under the central arch and it looked so lovely, Mrs Todd, that I sat on the bridge and waited to see if it would come back, but it didn't. And then I heard the Italians coming. They were marching along and singing that "feniculi-fenicular" song, you know the one.' Alice said she did. 'Well, they were going in the same direction as I was – at least as far as the barn where the footpath starts – so I thought I'd better stay where I was until they'd gone past.'

'That sounds a sensible decision.'

'Well, yes. But when they saw me they started whistling and calling out. I don't know what they said because it was in Italian. The guard shouted at them. He said "Get your eyes down and your filthy minds off!" which I thought was pretty horrible. They made rude signs at him behind his back and laughed. Well, you could hardly blame them!'

'Did you laugh too, Eleanor?'

'I might have done... I shouldn't have done, should I? Then the guard stopped to roll a cigarette while they all went past me... But one of them stooped to tie his boot lace, or he may have just pretended to, anyway, he sort of dropped back and came over to me. He said "bellissima" or something and kissed his fingers as though he was tasting something nice and then he put the tips of his fingers on my knee and...and smiled. It was so sweet, Mrs Todd! You couldn't possibly have minded!' Alice was not so sure about this but she confined herself to asking what happened next. 'Oh, it was awful! The guard turned round and saw us and came over, shouting. He was terribly angry. He hit the Italian, quite hard, with the butt of his rifle and called him a randy dago bastard! Then he kicked him in the shins and jabbed the barrel of the gun into his ribs, shoving him back towards the other prisoners, who were all shouting and whistling. I felt so sorry for him. He turned round to look at me and blew me a kiss. He looked so sad.'

'Eleanor, you didn't...you didn't blow a kiss back, did you?'

'No, Mrs Todd! I almost did. But I didn't. D'you think he was the one who ran away? And if he was, d'you think it was my fault he did? Because he's in terrible trouble now. Not only because of his ankle but because he's broken the rules that POWs have to obey and Gwennan says he could get locked up for it!'

Alice told her they would probably never know whether or not the prisoner who had escaped had been the one who had spoken to her or whether, had he been, her behaviour had provoked him into making a bid for freedom.

'He'd had a letter,' Alice told her, 'from his girl. Breaking off their engagement. They think that's what had upset him.'

245

'So it wasn't me?' Eleanor said, brightening visibly.

'No,' Alice said, 'I shouldn't think it was you.'

'Well, I certainly shan't wave to them any more! Or even look at them!'

'I think you should go to bed now, Eleanor.'

'Yes, Mrs Todd.'

Eleanor's enchantment with life at Lower Post Stone Farm ended that night. Her parents arrived to collect her a few days later and drove away, delighted that their scheme had worked. By indulging her passion for the land she had seen the folly of it and was now eager to return to their particular fold. She was subsequently presented at court and narrowly missed becoming debutante of her year. Her parents experienced no further worries on her account.

# Chapter Eight

It was in July that Annie received the results of her second Ministry of Agriculture exam. The buff envelope caught her eye as she entered the kitchen but she took her place at the supper table without claiming it. It was Gwennan who spotted it and drew her attention to it.

'There's a letter on the dresser for you, Annie. See? Looks like it's from the Min of Ag! Scared to open it, are you?'

'I'm sure she needn't be!' Alice said evenly. 'You passed your last exam easily enough, didn't you Annie?' Alice, having carefully sliced a plum duff into equal portions, was placing them on the girls' plates, where Rose neatly doused them with generous helpings of custard.

'Yeah, but this last one was on Farm Machinery, Mrs Todd. Tractors and drills and threshing machines and that. Jack was going to give me some help on the vehicle maintenance section but he never...' She eyed the envelope nervously. 'Reckon I know what it'll say.'

'Go on, Annie! Open it!' Mabel reached the letter down from the dresser and laid it on the table beside Annie's plate.

'Come on, lass,' Marion urged her, spooning up custard. 'Get it over with!'

Annie slit the envelope and drew out the printed notification. There was a hush as she read it. Then she waved the printed page triumphantly above her head.

'Yes! I passed! Wait 'til I tell Georgie! She always said as I could do it!'

'Let's see!' Gwennan demanded waspishly, as though she needed proof of Annie's success. 'Credit, it says...' She handed the certificate back to Annie and returned her attention to what was left of her pudding. 'But what's the point of it?'

'You what?' Marion exclaimed, a loaded spoon halfway to her mouth.

'I said, what's the point? A girl like Annie's never going to get much of a job, is she? Not with her background! What's a few certificates, when all's said and done? Useless they are. Except to hang on the wall if you want to show off!'

'You're a miserable cow, Taff! D'you know that!'
Annie's retaliation was loud.

'Keep your temper, Annie, please,' Alice said.

'Well, I'm sick of it, Mrs Todd! Carp, carp,
carp! That's all she ever does! That and make false
accusations!'

'I do not!'

'You do! You're a spiteful, mischief-making...'

'That's enough!' Alice felt as though she were
refereeing a boxing match. 'If you've finished your
meal, Gwennan, I suggest you go to your room. Now,
please!'

Gwennan's chair scraped back across the slate
floor.

'Righto!' she snapped, her spoon clattering into her
empty plate. 'I'll go! I know when I'm not wanted
and who the favourites are here!' From the doorway
she threatened, not for the first time, to resign. 'I
could lodge a formal complaint! I could tell them
this place is a shambles and refuse to work here no
more!'

'Hooray!' Mabel shouted, waving her own spoon
in the air.

'Don't let us keep you, Taff!' Eva called, her mouth
full of pudding.

'Good riddance to bad rubbish!' Winnie chanted
venomously, but as Marion opened her mouth to join
in, Alice's voice cut the air.

'Stop this, all of you!' Alice was quite surprised by the authoritative tone she had managed to produce. 'Finish your puddings and try to act like grown women and not a bunch of badly behaved children!' The girls, even Marion and Winnie, who, before doing as they were told, giggled in token defiance because no one, not even the warden, was going to tell them when they could or couldn't speak, obeyed Alice and finished their food in silence.

'My certificates *are* worth having, Mrs Todd,' Annie said when supper was over and she and the warden were alone in the kitchen.

'Of course they are!'

'Now I got them I could get a proper farming job, you know. I could apply to be an assistant manager or a forewoman. There's good work for people with qualifications...if I want it.'

'And do you want it, Annie?'

'I dunno. I never meant to stay in the country for the rest of me life. I on'y come 'ere 'cos it's different.'

'My gran's coming to visit!' Mabel announced. 'She's stoppin' at the Malsters Frid'y, Sat'd'y and Sund'y nights! I've swapped me milkin' rota with Elsie so's I'll 'ave all day Sund'y off!'

'And is she bringin' little Arfur, wiv 'er?' Eva enquired. Being a newcomer to the farm she had not yet met the toddler who, officially, was Mabel's brother but was, Eva had been interested to learn, in fact her son.

'You bet!' Mabel beamed.

Arthur, who was now more independent, irrepressible and fleet of foot than he had been on his previous visit to the farm, had, by the Saturday lunchtime, fallen into the horses' drinking trough, been stung by a bee, torn his trousers on a nail, broken three hens eggs, tried to eat pig swill, slipped off the back of the most docile of the dairy herd and landed, head first, in a bucket of milk.

Cries of 'Arfur! Come here!', 'Don't do that, Arfur!', 'Leave that alone!', 'Get down!', 'Get up!', 'Get off!', echoed round the yard and in and out of one or other of the barns.

On the Sunday afternoon a calf was unexpectedly born and while Mabel and Ferdie were involved in the difficult delivery, Arthur went missing. Alice and Edward John, invited by Roger Bayliss to afternoon tea at Higher Post Stone Farm, heard Mabel's frantic cries as she searched the yard for the little boy and went, with their host, to help to find him.

'Come 'ere this instant, you little brat,' Ferdie bellowed. 'I'll tan your 'ide proper when I gets my 'ands on you!'

'Don't shout at 'im, Ferdie!' his mother pleaded. 'You'll scare 'im!'

'I'll give him "scared"!' Ferdie muttered darkly, putting his shoulder against the stubborn door of an outhouse and searching its dark interior. 'Where be to, you little varmint?'

It was Edward John who located Arthur. He had crawled into the bull's pen and was sitting, sucking his thumb, under the manger that ran the length of one side of it, while Sherman – a massive Devon Red, already sire of many excellent heifers and bullocks and named by Christopher Bayliss after the American General who routed the Confederate troops and whose name was subsequently given to a tank – regarded him suspiciously, swaying his head in increasing irritation and pawing at the straw with huge, uncompromising hooves. Seeing Edward John, Arthur removed his thumb and announced, shakily, that he didn't like the gee-gee.

'No, I don't much, either,' Edward John told him. 'You just keep quiet, Arthur, and don't move.' He instructed Alice to attract Sherman's attention by offering him a handful of fresh hay. 'I shall crawl round and try to pull Arthur through the gap where he got in.'

Alice did as she was told and held the hay out to the bull, and although he made no move to eat it, he extended his massive neck towards her and blew his warm, fragrant breath in her direction, meeting her eyes in a way that she found slightly disconcerting.

'That's right, Mum! Now he's watching you and I'm going to...' Moving carefully, so that he did not startle the bull, Edward John lowered himself slowly into the straw and reached through the heavy timber framing of the pen.

'You take care, Edward John,' Ferdie warned, under his breath. 'He'm a nasty-tempered bugger, that one!'

Getting a firm grip on Arthur's jumper, Edward John hauled him quickly out. Arthur protested noisily and Sherman swung round, lowered his head, and ripped his horns through the straw that covered the floor of his stall.

Mabel seized her son and shook him hard, telling him he was a wicked child, before bursting into noisy tears, the pair of them howling in unison.

Roger Bayliss, who had arrived in time to witness the last seconds of the rescue, shook Edward John's hand and warmly congratulated him.

'Well done, that boy!' he said. 'Very well done indeed!'

When James Todd wrote to Alice suggesting that their son should spend part of his summer holidays with him and his new wife, Alice was uncertain of his motivation. Did he miss the boy? Was this invitation designed to repair the damaged relationship between father and son? Was James requesting the boy's company merely out of a sense of duty, or was this request nothing less than a thinly disguised attempt to impose his will on his ex-wife?

Whichever it was, Edward John firmly refused to go. When Alice explained that she didn't want him to lose touch with his father he asked her why not. A question she found it hard to answer.

'He is your father, Edward John, and I expect he misses you.'

'He should have thought of that before he left us,' Edward John stated sullenly. 'Tell him I won't go.'

Alice wrote to James, tactfully explaining that Edward John was very happy on the farm and planned to spend his summer holidays helping out where he could by working in the harvest fields, and that she felt that this was a sensible, healthy and patriotic thing for a young boy to want to do. She suggested that perhaps he could visit his father in the Christmas holidays instead. James Todd wrote back and said no. He had booked rooms at a seaside boarding house in Norfolk and on the following Saturday, Edward John was to be put on the morning train to Paddington where he would be met.

'He's flatly refusing to go!' Alice confided to Roger Bayliss. 'What do I do? What would you do if it was Christopher?' Roger considered this and then said that he had heard that children of divorced parents sometimes played off one against the other.

'Having lost his mother,' he added vaguely, 'Christopher had no opportunity to do that, of course... I really can't advise you, Alice. I don't feel competent to make a judgement. Sorry to let you down!'

'But if you were in James's position? How would you feel, d'you think, if your son didn't want to spend time with you and clearly, well, disapproved of you? Would you persist in seeing him and try to win him over? Or would you leave him be for a while and let him adjust to the new status quo – I mean, in Edward John's case, to his stepmother, the coming child and the fact that he feels his father has...rather let us down? What would you do?' Roger looked disconcerted. He shook his head as though he was trying to clear it.

'D'you know, Alice, I'm really no good at these complicated issues. It's been so long since I had to deal with anything like this that I seem to have somehow lost the knack!'

Alice looked at him. It occurred to her that perhaps he never had possessed 'the knack', as he called it. Certainly he had, since Alice had known him, demonstrated very little emotional involvement in his own son's troubles, allowing him to go through the trauma of his breakdown and subsequent dismissal from the RAF without the impulsive attempts to support him which, Alice had thought at the time, would have come naturally to most fathers.

Roger had, it was true, made Christopher as comfortable as was possible in the woodsman's cottage where he had chosen to live in self-imposed exile, although, to Alice, Roger's actions, where Christopher was concerned, always appeared to stem from a sense of duty rather than from parental affection. Perhaps this was all he should be expected to do, or was capable of doing. But it seemed to Alice not to be enough. He was looking at her.

'Have I...have I disappointed you?' he asked, and was relieved when she laughed and shook her head.

'I think I shall insist that he goes,' she said after further thought. 'It's only for two weeks. The experience can't do him any harm and he may even enjoy it.'

Edward John, on the days leading up to his departure, made it clear to Alice that he had no intention of enjoying his enforced holiday and parted coolly from her on the station platform.

Four hours later, the clamour of the bell mounted on the wall of the barn that housed the telephone, filled the yard.

'Where is he?' James Todd demanded angrily. 'We were supposed to meet under the clock, but he's not there!'

'Go and look for him!' Alice shouted into the receiver. 'He must be there! I put him on the train myself!' She stood in the gloom of the barn, her pulse racing. Rose crossed the yard and suggested that Alice should go back into the farmhouse and have a nice, steadying cup of tea while she waited for news, but Alice refused and stood, rigid, on the stone step at the entrance to the barn, ready to snatch the receiver from its cradle as soon as the bell rang. Five minutes became ten and then twenty before the silence was broken.

'He was on the train,' James said, sounding as nervous now as Alice herself felt. 'The guard remembers seeing him. But we've searched the station and there's no sign of him and we're about to involve the police... Are you there, Alice?' James asked, when there seemed to be nothing but silence at the end of the telephone line.

'I shouldn't have made him go,' she said desperately. 'He didn't want to and I insisted!' It was James's turn to be silent. Then he told her he was going to hang up and join the search. He would telephone her as soon as there was any news at all.

Rose, a great believer in the soothing and sustaining power of tea, brought a cup of it across the yard to Alice, sat her down on the stone step and encouraged her to drink it while she waited for James's next call.

''E'll be all right!' Rose soothed. ''E's no fool, that boy! 'E knows how to watch out for 'imself! Prob'ly he just got the place they were supposed to meet mixed up, you know what kids are! 'E'll be standin' waitin' somewhere, with 'is little suitcase beside 'im, good as gold, you'll see!'

After twenty more minutes, Alice began to pace up and down the yard, clenching and unclenching her fists and deaf to all Rose's attempts to allay her fears. When the telephone bell rang both women were equally startled.

Alice seized the receiver.

'James!' she shouted, 'what's happened?' Rose saw a look of astonishment spread across Alice's face. 'Who...?' she asked. Then she asked again who the caller was and then said 'Ruth?' Rose watched as Alice listened. Ruth, she knew, was Alice's friend, the woman she had been staying with when she'd almost been killed by a doodlebug. 'With you?' Alice was demanding. 'What's he doing with...? In a what? A taxi? Oh my God, Ruth! Thank heaven!' Alice was suddenly overcome with laughter and was briefly unable to stop. 'No, no' she managed, gulping back the inappropriate sound. 'I'm not laughing because it's funny! No! Of course it isn't a bit funny! Yes! Very naughty indeed! Tell him I am extremely angry with him and I'll telephone you as soon as I've contacted James and put him out of his misery!' She cut the call and turned to Rose. 'He's all right! He arrived ten minutes ago at Ruth's, in a taxi! She said he reminded her that she is his godmother and asked her to invite him to stay with her because he doesn't want to go on holiday with his father! That is so naughty! What am I going to do with him, Rose?'

Rose was smiling with relief. 'A good wallopin' is what 'e deserves, puttin' you through that! But I doubt 'e'll get one, 'cos 'tis my belief, though you'd never admit it, that you're rather pleased with him!'

'Operator?' Alice was saying into the telephone receiver, 'could you very kindly put me through to the stationmaster at Paddington? That's right. Paddington Station in London... Yes, it is an emergency, a small boy has been lost. Thank you. Yes, I'll hold.'

If they were honest, everyone, from Roger Bayliss through Margery Brewster to the land girls themselves, who knew of Edward John's reluctance to spend time with the man of whom, because of their loyalty to his ex-wife, they disapproved, applauded Edward John's act of defiance.

James Todd, when Alice managed to reach him by telephone, had been in the stationmaster's office giving a full description of his missing son to a young police constable. Humiliated and angered by the boy's behaviour, he suggested, when the situation had been explained to him, that Ruth should put Edward John on the next train back to Ledburton. He told Alice, curtly, that he himself was leaving immediately for his holiday in Norfolk.

Aware that Edward John was regarded as something of a hero, Alice asked the girls not to show any sign of approval of what he had done.

'It was discourteous of him and very embarrassing and worrying for his father,' she told them.

'I reckon 'e showed a lot of spunk!' Marion muttered and Winnie agreed. 'Fancy 'im gettin' in a taxi and goin' halfway across London all by 'imself! And 'e's on'y a tiddler!'

'If 'e was mine I'd be that proud of 'im!' Mabel said warmly to Alice, 'after the way 'is father treated you!'

'If you ask me,' Gwennan announced, although no one had asked her, her clipped accent cutting the air and her manner sententious, even by her standards, 'Mrs Todd's quite right to be worried. What he done was deceitful and if he was my son I'd punish him severely!'

'I'll bet you would, Taff!' Annie said. 'Beat 'im to within an inch of 'is life and enjoy every minute of it!' The girls laughed derisively at Gwennan until Alice told them sharply to stop.

'Gwennan is right,' she said. 'It was very wrong of him and he will be punished. But I'd ask you all to leave it to me and not to discuss it with him, all right?'

Roger Bayliss, who took Alice to the station to meet her son, lectured the boy quietly as they drove back to the farm.

'I don't suppose you had any idea how worried your mother was,' he said, taking the car smoothly through the familiar lanes. 'I don't believe that if you had thought about it carefully you would have acted as you did. Your father, too, was most concerned. Your behaviour was both churlish and thoughtless, Edward John. I had expected rather more of you than that.'

To his eleven-year-old mind, Edward John's plan had seemed to be a good one. It was true that he hadn't appreciated the effect his virtual disappearance from the face of the earth would have on his parents. He believed that as soon as he arrived at his godmother's home she would telephone his mother to tell her where he was and, as he did not value his father's feelings, he failed to consider them. It had not occurred to him that Ruth might have been away from home when he rang her doorbell and he had failed to take into account the hour it would take him to find a cab and cross London in it. An hour during which his father, after a fruitless search of Paddington Station, had given Alice the alarming news that her son was missing.

The light was fading as Roger brought his car to a halt at the farmhouse gate. It had been a long day. Edward John was tired, hungry and ashamed. However hard he tried to prevent them, the hot tears that had welled up in his eyes began to spill down his cheeks.

'I honestly don't think you've got anything to worry about there,' Roger murmured to Alice as he left her at the gate.

Edward John wiped his eyes on his sleeve, spooned up the thick vegetable broth that Rose had saved for him and then went, contritely, to bed. The next morning Alice told her son what his punishment was to be.

'For a week you will not go up to the higher farm and if you leave this building you will stay where I can see you. You will write a letter to your father apologising to him for your very bad behaviour and to your godmother to say how sorry you are for involving her in an embarrassing family matter.'

'I thought that was what godmothers were for!'

He was challenging her. Alice met his quizzical eyes with a cold stare and told him that if he was going to answer back he could spend the morning in her sitting room and think about his poor conduct until he was ready to apologise properly for it.

Edward John wrote his letters – *Sorry, Father*; *Sorry, Aunt Ruth* – printed the addresses onto their envelopes and, while the land girls were assembling hungrily in the kitchen for their suppers that night, stood them on the dresser, ready for the postman.

'What a good boy!' Marion whispered, winking heavily at him and nudging Winnie.

On the following morning the BBC announced that

Paris had been liberated and that French and Allied troops were marching triumphantly up the Champs Élysées. That evening Roger and Alice were invited to celebrate the good news over drinks with some acquaintances of his.

'Why have you got on your best frock?' Edward John asked his mother when, after supervising the girls' supper, she prepared herself.

'It's not "best" exactly...' She was aware of her son's eyes, registering every detail of her appearance as she leant towards the oval mirror above the mantelpiece to check her hair and her lipstick.

'You haven't done your hair like that for ages.'

'No.'

'You look pretty.'

'Thank you.'

'Someone might want to marry you.'

'Oh...?' She smiled. 'I shouldn't think so.'

'But you could, couldn't you? Marry someone, I mean. Now that you and Father are divorced.'

'In theory, yes, I could. But I don't plan to.'

She was dressed in cornflower blue linen. The frock, which she had hardly worn since the war had so radically changed her life, still fitted perfectly, despite the intervening years. Edward John watched as she smoothed the skirt over her hips and settled the narrow leather belt at her waist.

'People do though,' her son said, thoughtfully

regarding her. She was ready to go. At any moment Roger would arrive to drive her to the party.

'I shan't be late, darling,' she said. 'Get ready for bed at about eight, right?' Her son nodded and offered her his cheek to kiss. 'Lights out at half past nine. Promise?'

'All right... Mum? Why did Marion wink at me when I put my "sorry" letters on the dresser?'

'Did she? I've no idea why.'

'And what's an old heave-ho?' Alice looked at him in surprise. 'Winnie said, rather quietly, so you wouldn't hear her, "Well done, our kid! Giving your dad the old heave-ho!"' He pronounced the words precisely, clearly mystified by them.

'Did she? I really don't know what she meant by that. I think she was probably not minding her own business. I have told you before that sometimes the girls say things they shouldn't and that it's best to ignore them.'

'Is it because they were badly brought up?' he asked innocently. Alice sat down beside him and looked into his face. How she loved him.

'Not necessarily "badly", darling. But differently. They're dear girls and we respect them, don't we? But that doesn't mean we have to behave exactly as they do.'

'Do we behave better than they do?' he asked. Alice saw the golden opportunity and seized it.

'Not always, Edward John. I doubt whether any of them would have upset their parents as much as you upset yours yesterday!' She heard Roger's car arriving at the farmhouse gate. 'Think about it, sweetheart.'

As Edward John watched Roger hold open the car door for his mother, it occurred to him that if she ever did remarry, Mr Bayliss would make an acceptable new husband for her. But people were supposed to be in love when they got married and he wasn't sure whether his mother and Mr Bayliss were in love, although they were always very nice to each other and laughed a lot when they were together. Perhaps the being in love bit wasn't so important at their age. He decided to read *Swallows and Amazons* and maybe not switch off the light until he heard the sound of Mr Bayliss's car, bringing his mother back to the farm.

It was towards the end of September that Gwennan Pringle committed an act that she later came to regret. What she did was a direct result, possibly little more than a knee-jerk reaction, to something that happened to her and which not only delivered a cold clench of fear but provoked a violent surge of anger against her destiny and at the unfairness of life. She was overwhelmed by a sense of injustice. Why should she be the victim of a cruel fate while others, whom she felt were less deserving than she of good fortune, seemed to be enjoying it in abundance?

What had happened to her was that, one night, as she dried herself after washing in bathwater already pink and soapy from Marion and Winnie's use of it, she glanced at her reflection in the steamy mirror. The sight of her taut and angular body was, of course, familiar to her. What was unfamiliar was the slightly puckered appearance of her left nipple. It was the same puckering that her sister Olwen had displayed to Gwennan two years previously, and which had been an early symptom of the cancer that had recently killed her.

Gwennan had rubbed her nipple vigorously with her rough, damp towel until it grew pink and appeared almost normal. Then she turned away from the mirror and the sight of the suspect breast, promising herself that she would never again look at it or touch it. That was how she chose to deal with it. By denying not only what she had seen but the knowledge of what was going to happen to her. To her anger, her sense of outrage at the unfairness of it all and the jealousy that washed over her, she reacted differently.

Unlike the other land girls, who shared their troubles with each other, sometimes with the warden and even, occasionally, with Margery Brewster, Gwennan's clenched and defensive personality prevented this and, following her frightening experience in the bathroom, she distanced herself more than ever from the rowdy camaraderie of the hostel. She pursed her lips, narrowed her eyes, applied herself diligently to her work and if she felt exhausted at the end of a particularly heavy day, she attributed the sensation to over-exertion rather than as a symptom of failing health.

Since her sister's death, Gwennan rarely received any letters, but on the Saturday after her frightening discovery and while she was still numb with shock, she intercepted the postman and carried the handful of envelopes into the empty kitchen, examining each as she went.

There was a picture postcard of Harlech Castle for Miss Hannah Maria Sorokova from Hector Conway, who was in Wales on some War Artists' Scheme work. A buff envelope, clearly from the US military, would require forwarding to Hester Westerfelt at her parents' smallholding in North Devon. A third letter, the name of its sender, Sergeant M Kinski, printed on its reverse side, was addressed to Miss Marion Grice.

The arrival of this token, perhaps only of flirtatious friendship but possibly of much more, overwhelmed Gwennan. Why should Annie and Marion be lucky while she herself was not only ignored and unloved but also doomed to an early and cruel death? Witnessing the light-hearted adventures of her fellows seemed to her to be like having salt rubbed into her wounds. In every direction she saw friendship, excitement and optimism, and in some cases, love itself, all of it excluding her. But these girls were no better than she! Some were less moral, less honest and less hard-working! But there they were: Mabel, fat and happy with her Ferdie; Annie with her Ministry of Agriculture exams successfully behind her and clearly enjoying the attentions of Hector, who was not only well-educated but who owned a motor car. Georgina, deployed importantly by the Air Transport Auxiliary, seemed cool and confident when she visited the farm during her infrequent days of leave. Both Eva and Nancy had boyfriends and even the rat-catchers had had each other and, in Gwennan's opinion, an undeserved, even unseemly, happiness together. The warden, too, though recently divorced, seemed fortunate in her friends and Mr Bayliss was, Gwennan considered, quite inappropriately attentive to her. What had any of them done to deserve happiness when she, Gwennan, was the one with the highest standards of morality? Yet she had no one. She had never had anyone. And now she had this disease. It was too unfair. As it seemed that no one and nothing would level the score on her behalf, she would have to do it for herself. She would redistribute some of her own bad luck. For a start, the letter from Marvin to Marion would somehow go astray so that both of them would be deprived of that much happiness at least. But even then, on that Saturday morning, when the letter addressed to Marion had slipped so easily from the shelf down to lie amongst the cobwebs between the kitchen dresser and the wainscot, Gwennan felt a pang of guilt that weighed her down and made her feel more tired, more isolated and more miserable than ever. Over the following weeks, her conscience would wake her in the night. 'But,' one half of her mind would say to the other, 'she hadn't heard from him for months. Since well before D-Day. She most likely thinks he's dead and if she doesn't hear from him she'll be none the wiser. And anyhow, she doesn't deserve him. Or any bloke, come to that. She went with anyone who fancied her before she met the sergeant as well as after! Writing to her, indeed! He should know what sort of girl she is! See if he'd write to her then!' And so she justified her spiteful deed.

The evenings and the mornings grew darker as first autumn and then winter took hold of the land. Rain filled the ditches and the cart ruts, clouding the streams and saturating the fleeces of the sheep. The river seethed and churned, breached its banks and spilt across the water meadows until the floor of the valley became a shallow, marshy lake.

The land girls returned to the hostel each night wet and muddy, their fingers and noses pink from the cold. With the worst of the weather ahead of them and the diversion of Christmas still many weeks away, their morale was at a low ebb and they quarrelled amongst themselves and complained, even more than was usual, about their conditions.

One wild night, Nancy, known for her forgetfulness, returned to the dark porch to fetch the pair of damp socks she had left inside her boots and which she needed to dry, ready for the next morning.

'Mrs Todd!' she called from the cross-passage, 'there's something funny out there!'

Alice peered at the shape that was wedged into a shadowy corner of the porch and as far as was possible from the rain that was being driven in by the wind. At first the object appeared, to Alice, to be a large, badly wrapped parcel. There was sacking draped over the top, then came a piece of stained canvas and below that the folds of a dark, heavy fabric trailed down, almost to the ground. Then she saw that a clenched and bony fist was gripping the two edges of the canvas, holding them together, and that a pair of saturated, oversized boots protruded from the fabric where it dripped onto the cobbles. Alice leant closer, Rose at her elbow.

'Who are you?' she asked. 'What do you want?'

A face pushed forward between the edges of the sack. It was an old face, lined with age and so grimed with dirt that the skin resembled weathered stone. Straggles of stiff, grey hair protruded from the sacking, framing a handsome bone structure and a pair of bright, deep-set eyes. The smile, which revealed gaps between discoloured teeth, illuminated the face and was so infectious that Alice and even the wary Rose found themselves responding to it.

'Marlie, my dears! That's who I be. But don't you mind me. I'll do just fine here, so I will.' She snuggled her undefined shape further into the corner of the porch and closed her eyes. The accent, which Alice recognised as Northern Irish, reminded her of a gardener she and James had employed just before the outbreak of war.

'What you goin' to do with 'er?' Rose whispered, leaning round Alice to stare at the extraordinary damp bundle.

'Well, we can't leave her out here! She'll die of something!'

'You let her inside,' Rose declared, 'and we'll *all* die of something!'

Opening her eyes, scanning the faces of the two women leaning over her and concluding, immediately and correctly, that Alice would prove to be the softer touch, Marlie focused her attention on her, bestowing on her another huge, toothless smile and ignoring Rose, who continued to fret about fleas, carbuncles and bedbugs.

'A cuppa tay'd be acceptable, if you're askin',' Marlie

announced. 'With a dash of the creater in it, p'raps? For to warm an old woman's heart?'

'What's the "creater"?' Rose demanded suspiciously.

'I think it's whiskey,' Alice told her, and Rose said some people had a blooming cheek and wondered whatever next.

Alice began easing the piece of canvas from the old woman's bowed shoulders. 'We'd better leave your... outer thing...in the porch, I think.' She took Marlie's cold hands in hers and heaved her gently to her feet, drew her along the cross-passage and through into the warm kitchen, moved a chair closer to the range, sat her down and watched her steam.

Marlie declined to remove her boots, which, she assured them, had been given to her only days before by a soldier and kept her feet bone dry. The unravelling shawls and buttonless cardigans were barely damp but the hemline of her skirt, which appeared to be made of an old blanket, was heavy with rainwater.

Rose produced a mug of tea and Marlie nodded encouragingly as several spoonfuls of sugar were stirred into it, wrapped her bony hands round it and sipped noisily. As there was no whiskey, Alice donated a dash of sherry from the bottle she kept in her room and from which she occasionally offered a glass to Roger Bayliss or, sometimes, to Margery Brewster, if she seemed out of sorts when she visited the farm.

The land girls, clustering in the doorway,

described, for those behind them and who could not see past them, the events that were unfolding in the kitchen.

'They've took off some of her clothes and hung 'em up to dry!'

'Rose 'as give 'er a cup of tea!'

'Five sugars, she's had!'

'She's that soaked there's steam comin' off of her skirt!'

'Rose 'as fetched 'er a plate of leftovers!'

'Crikey! She don't half tuck in!'

'Are you on your way to somewhere?' Alice asked Marlie, conscious of the looming question of what was to be done with her. It was already past eight o'clock and the night was pitch dark. She could hardly turn the old woman out into the rain. But as Marlie grew warm and her clothing began to dry, a smell spread from her which made Mabel, whose own particular blend of body odours had so offended her hostel mates, seem positively fragrant.

'Pherff!' Mabel whispered. 'She don't half...' She stopped in mid-sentence and had the grace to blush.

'Look who's talkin'!' Winnie giggled. Mabel was mortified.

'I'm not that bad any more!' she protested, turning to Alice for support while the rest of the girls, though not unkindly, enjoyed her embarrassment and broke into laughter when Alice herself smiled before assuring

Mabel that, no, she was not that bad any more.

The old woman, now warmed, fed and drying, seemed to be drifting towards sleep.

'Marlie!' Alice said, hoping to prevent this. 'Much as I'd like to, I can't offer you a bed here. This is a Land Army hostel, you see, run by the Ministry of Agriculture. The rules are very strict about...' Marlie was shaking her head and laughing gently.

'Don't upset yourself, my dear!' she said. 'You've done me proud, so you have!' She began to heave herself to her feet, found standing difficult and subsided again onto her chair. 'If you have a bit of a barn somewhere that'd keep off the wet, then the good Lord will bless you for your kindness. If not, I reckon I'll find me a bit of shelter somewhere along the way, so I will!'

Watching the old woman had made the land girls keenly aware of the youth and strength which, they realised, almost guiltily and with the possible exception of Gwennan, they took very much for granted. Within the last hour or so most of them had washed off the day's mud in a hot bath, even if the water in it had been shared. They had filled their bellies with food that was satisfying and wholesome, the clothes they were wearing were dry and the beds in which, later that night, they would sleep, were clean and warm.

Complaints about the cold, about the rain, the snow, the summer heat, the low wages, the monotonous food, the hostel rules, the lack of privacy, the dearth of entertainment, the unreliable plumbing, the overtime, the mud, the earwigs, the exhaustion and the homesickness – all filled the hostel on a regular basis, morning noon and night, seven days a week. There was usually one girl or another with a grudge or a sore throat or a blister or a painful period. Someone who had lost something or broken something. Who felt insulted, neglected, cheated, thwarted or, in one way or another, deprived of her rights. So they would grouse and mutter, squabble, whine, bully, snub, insult and sometimes rage. But here was this woman, whose name was Marlie, who was grimed and wet, reeking and old, but who would be grateful to be allowed to sleep in a barn.

As they stared thoughtfully at her, wondering how she came to be how and where she was, homeless and filthy on a dark, wet night, Marlie seemed to read their minds.

'It's me brothers,' she volunteered suddenly, and in response to the dozen pairs of eyes which were focused on her, continued, 'It's me baby brothers, so it is. The two of them came across from Derry when the war began for to find work. Liverpool they went to. "Marlie," they said, "we'll go ahead and get work and a place to live, then you'll catch the boat and come over to us." Promised to meet me on the dock, so they did! The older boys had already gone, see.

New York they went to and then Chicago but where they are now, only the good Lord knows!'

Rose had refilled Marlie's cup with tea. She drank noisily and then pulled a face. 'Could you be a little kinder regarding the sugar, d'you suppose?' she asked Rose, who, with something less that good grace, dipped her spoon three more times into the sugar bowl.

'And did they? Your brothers?' Annie asked. 'Did they meet you on the dock?' Marlie shook her head.

'No, they did not! I took meself to the address they'd given me, so I did, and what did I find?' She looked from one fascinated face to the next, at the girls gathered round the table to the girls in the doorway and the girls peering in from the cross-passage, and at Alice's face and at Rose's. 'I found a bombed house, so I did! No roof! Just rubble inside it. Only the four walls standing, so they were!'

'And no sign at all of your brothers?' Gwennan asked, her gaunt face sober and almost sympathetic.

'And no sign at all of me brothers.' Marlie sighed, shaking her head. 'No Donal and no Liam.'

'Had they been killed?' Winnie asked.

'Oh, no!' Marlie said emphatically. 'Not killed! Not they! Not our Donal! Not Liam! No, no, no! They'd have just took 'emselves off to somewhere safe! That's what they'd have done, so they would! But can I find the pair of them? No, I cannot! They could hardly leave a forwarding address on a pile of rubble, now, could they? Been looking for the pair of them ever since, so I have! Years it must be now! I tried the places where Irish folk goes for the work. Big cities, they were. But not a sign of them! "D'you know of a Donal?" I'd ask, "D'you know of a Liam?" But no one did. I went to lots of towns, so I did. Can't remember the names of 'em but there was always a next one and a next one, so there was.' Her eyes seemed to be focused on some vague and distant future. Some time and place where her tiredness would overcome her. Where it would all stop.

'There's Exeter down the road from 'ere,' Winnie suggested helpfully.

'And then Plymouth,' Marion added, pointing vaguely westwards.

'Is that right?' Marlie asked, rousing slightly. 'Maybe I'll try them next, then. I'll track 'em down, those brothers of mine, so I will, that's for sure! And when I find 'em, what a time we'll have! We'll crack open a bottle of good Irish whiskey, Donal and Liam and I, so we will, so we will...'

Rose shone the torch and Alice took Marlie's arm and steadied her across the yard. They let her into the barn, spread a thick layer of straw in one of the empty stalls and covered the old lady with a horse blanket.

In the morning Mabel carried a bowl of porridge across the yard but returned with it, minutes later, to the kitchen.

'She's not there, Mrs Todd. Reckon she gone lookin' for them brothers of 'ers.' Alice was unsurprised by this and, it had to be said, slightly relieved. Roger Bayliss discouraged vagrants and Gypsies on the grounds that their presence in the neighbourhood always seemed to coincide with pilferings and poachings. As well as this they were considered by the Ministry of Defence to be a security risk, and since the start of the war there had been instances when men – and even women – masquerading as tramps, had been convicted of spying for foreign intelligence.

'Oh, I do hope she finds 'em!' Mabel said. 'D'you think she will, Mrs Todd?'

''Course she won't!' Gwennan said flatly, and although her view was not one anybody wanted share, it was plain to most of them that the old woman's quest, given her age and circumstances, was unlikely to prove successful.

'She's gone a bit potty, I reckon,' Gwennan added, watching disapprovingly as Mabel appropriated and rapidly devoured the porridge that had been intended for Marlie. 'And anyhow, they're most likely dead if their lodgings was bombed.'

'Always the optimist, eh, Taff!' Marion sneered. But they all knew Gwennan was almost certainly right, and in the brief silence before the horn of Fred's truck summoned them out into the cold morning, they pictured Marlie plodding off, accosting strangers and asking them, 'Have you seen Donal? Have you seen Liam?'

No one at the Post Stone farms ever knew that, a fortnight later, the body of an old woman was found stranded on a sand bar in the Exe Estuary. The condition of the corpse and the lack of any form of identification or evidence of foul play discouraged the local police from pursuing their inquires. A verdict of accidental death was recorded and the case was closed.

# Chapter Nine

One afternoon, when a south-westerly gale was driving veils of rain across the valley, Alice heard the sound of a motorbike arriving at the farmhouse gate and guessed that the figure, concealed in bulky waterproofs, was Georgina's and that the bike and the garments were borrowed from her brother, Lionel. She stood in the porch, stripping off the heavy oilskins.

'Go through to my sitting room,' Alice said, 'I'll bring us some tea.' But when Georgina followed her into the kitchen and sat down at the table, she turned to her and asked, 'Are you all right, Georgie? You look a bit...I don't know...wan.' Alice spooned tea into the battered enamel teapot. 'I thought it was this week that you and your...what's his name?'

'Fitzy.'

'Yes. Fitzy...' Alice stopped speaking and searched Georgina's face. 'Didn't it...work out?'

'Well...no.'

'Was his leave cancelled?' Alice knew that Georgina and Neil Fitzsimmonds had difficulty in getting leave at the same time and that their idea had been, as soon as it could be arranged, to make their planned visit to her parents' cottage on the North Devon coast.

'It wasn't that,' Georgina said, accepting the cup of tea Alice had poured for her. 'He's on leave this week, the same as I am, but we didn't go to the cottage. I told Fitzy I couldn't. I don't really understand why. It's not that I don't like him. I do. I find him very... attractive...but...I think I enjoy his company most when we're with a bunch of fliers. He's great fun, he dances like Fred Astaire and he looks absolutely stunning...but...'

Alice was strongly tempted to say, 'But he is not Christopher Bayliss?' but decided against it at this point and bit her tongue.

'Was he very disappointed?' she asked instead.

'He was a bit,' Georgina said, sipping the hot tea.

Alice had always considered Georgina to be the best-looking of her land girls. Strands of dark hair, which had escaped from the borrowed leather helmet and goggles and had been plastered to her face by the wind and rain, were drying in the warmth of the kitchen, while her cheeks, still flushed by the rough weather, were a rosy contrast to her high, pale forehead and solemn eyes. She looked, Alice thought, more beautiful than she had ever seen her.

'What?' Georgina asked suddenly, and Alice, realising that she had been staring, shook her head and smiled.

'Nothing,' she said, 'I was just thinking...' Again, she was tempted to bring up the subject of Christopher Bayliss and again she checked herself. 'I was just thinking how very pretty you are.'

'Apart from looking wan!' Georgina laughed.

'Yes,' Alice said. 'Apart from that!'

There was a longish silence before Georgina spoke and Alice was certain, from the intensity of her eyes, that she was about to broach a subject that was important to her. But as she gathered herself to speak, the back door was flung suddenly open and Rose, with rubber boots on her feet and a dripping umbrella in her hands, burst into the kitchen.

'Just look at it!' she blustered, without acknowledging Georgina. 'Rainin' cats and dogs, almost dark and 'e's still not back!'

'Who isn't?' Alice asked, forgetting that Rose's Dave was home on leave and had gone off somewhere on his bicycle.

'Dave! My Dave, that's who! Said he was popping into Ledburton for a quick pint at lunchtime, but that were hours ago! I reckon I knows where 'e'm to! Over to Hester's folks' place, that's where! And d'you know what for?' Alice and Georgina shook their heads. "Cos my guess is as 'er baby will 'ave come by now! That's what for! Why can't he keep out of it? Why did 'e 'ave to go getting mixed up with that Pentecostal lot? Nothing but trouble, they are! Why can't 'e find 'iself a nice sensible sort of a girl?'

'Because he loves Hester?' Georgina ventured.

Rose turned on her furiously.

'But *she* don't love 'im, Georgina! She was Reuben's girl and now she's Reuben's widow and her baby's Reuben's child. And anyhow, what do you know about anything! Runnin' round after Christopher Bayliss all that time 'e were sick and then walkin' out on 'im!' She peered, frowning, through the window into the deepening twilight. Then a surge of relief transformed her face. 'Oh! The light's just gone on in me cottage! Me son's home! Thank the Lord!' She had the grace to look slightly embarrassed as she made for the door, her umbrella already half open. 'I'll just make sure 'e's all right and I'll be straight back to help with supper, Alice!' and she was gone.

Alice and Georgina sat for a while in silence. 'I didn't exactly walk out on Chris, did I?' Georgina asked, without really expecting or wanting an answer.

'Not exactly,' Alice said.

* * *

283

When Dave Crocker had cycled away from Lower Post Stone Farm that morning and headed north-west across Dartmoor, the wind had been rising, dragging low cloud across the tors. Toiling, despite a tightening in his scarred leg, up the steep inclines of the moor and freewheeling gratefully downhill, he made good time and found himself, by midday, at the gate to Jonas Tucker's near derelict five acres.

By then rain was not far off and the high ground was already obscured by cloud. On a washing line, half a dozen nappies flapped in the damp wind and as he stood wondering how he should approach the forlorn cottage which was the Tuckers' home, Hester, carrying a wicker basket, rounded the corner of the building, hurried towards the line and began to unpeg the nappies. When Dave called her name she turned to face him and then glanced nervously at an upstairs window.

The wind had risen and was driving the rain before it. Hester stood, facing Dave, with her back to the wind while it smacked into his face.

'You'm getting soaked,' she murmured uneasily. 'You shouldn't be here.'

'Your baby's come, then,' he said, taking the basket from her and holding it while she put the rest of the nappies into it. She nodded. 'Be it a boy?' She shook her head.

'A girl,' she said. 'Three weeks old, she be now.

I calls her Thurza.' She looked up at the window again. 'You'd best go, Dave. My father 'as took sick. If 'e sees you 'ere 't will make 'im worse. I be the one who's brought this on 'im, see. My wickedness is what's made 'im ill. I must go in.'

'This be nonsense, Hester! 'Ow could you 'ave brung it on 'im? What's up with 'im, any'ow?'

'He has the fallin' down disease and can't walk proper no more. It started when I strayed from the path of righteousness! I have brought a pestilence on my family, like I told you in the orchard that day!'

They heard the rattle of the sash window before Jonas Tucker's voice reached them.

'Get inside the 'ouse, daughter!' he bellowed through the noise of wind and rain. 'Get indoors afore some other evil do befall us!' Jonas slammed the window down and stood with his hands, one on each side of it, pressed against the frame, his face inches from the pane. He was dressed in a striped nightshirt and his grey hair straggled to his shoulders.

'He means Thurza!' Hester whimpered. 'He means she'll be next! First Reuben killed! Then you wounded. Then Father struck down! Next it'll be my baby or my brother, Zeke, if I don't do proper penance for my sins!' She pulled the basket from Dave's hands and hurried towards the house. In the window, Jonas Tucker raised a fist and shook it at Dave before turning, lurching unsteadily away from the window and merging into the gloom of the room behind him.

'She's 'ad her baby, then, Reuben's wife?' Rose asked her son when she found him sitting, his jacket and corded trousers dark with rainwater, in front of her fire. When he did not answer her she told him he'd best get out of his wet clothes before he caught his death, took his coat from him and watched him drop the sodden trousers onto the floor and shuffle up the stairs in his long johns.

'I never thought as I'd be pleased when Dave's leave was over,' Rose confided in Alice the next morning, 'But 'e's bin that low since 'e went over to Hester's place!' She sat, her jaw set and her eyes gazing hopelessly into space. 'I can't see no end to this, Alice! 'E won't give up on 'er and she won't give up on that religion of hers!'

'What if she did, Rose? Would you be happy for Dave to take her on and be a father to Reuben's child?'

'It bain't so simple as that though, be it? Hester would be a nice enough girl if she'd been brought up reg'lar, with ordinary folk for parents. But with her head full of this nonsense... Oh, I don't know! When she was here with us she seemed normal enough, after she'd settled in, like, didn't she! And when she and

Reuben got wed and all. Nice, happy little couple, they made. But since that poor lad got killed and all this hocus-pocus about Hester being cursed started up... I don't know what to think of her and I wouldn't wish any of that on a son of mine! Would you?'

At the first opportunity, Alice discussed the situation with Margery Brewster. They sat in Alice's sitting room, one on either side of the fire. In response to Margery's repeated glances at the decanter, Alice poured her a small sherry.

'From what Dave told his mother, Jonas Tucker is obviously ill,' Alice said. 'Physically and quite possibly mentally as well. In the circumstances, he probably can't provide adequately for his family and his psychological state could make him dangerous, couldn't it? I don't think its safe for Hester or the baby to be there in that hovel, do you, Margery? Can't the Americans ship her out to her in-laws or something? Anywhere would be safer and healthier for her and the baby than where she is now!'

'They can't make her to go if she doesn't want to, Alice. And apparently she doesn't! She won't even draw Reuben's pension! They sent his regimental chaplain to see her and she asked him to leave her to make her peace with her Lord or something. They can't force her to do anything against her will.' Margery sipped the sherry appreciatively. 'Poor Dave is terribly upset and Rose was in tears about the whole situation. If the problem was simply with Jonas Tucker I believe Dave would be prepared to go up there and bring the silly girl back here with him. But it's Hester herself who is determined to stay there and she seems to really believe what her father has instilled into her, about her whole family reaping the consequences of her supposed transgressions! It's positively medieval!' Margery smiled winsomely and held out her glass. Alice refilled it. 'It would be amusing if it wasn't so tragic!' she sighed. 'But it proves you can't remove seventeen years of brainwashing in six months!'

'It ain't fair!' Mabel protested, during one of the series of protracted discussions she and Ferdie now found unavoidable and which focused, unproductively, on the subject of their future after the arrival of the coming baby.

Ferdie had blandly accepted the fact of Mabel's pregnancy. Like any of the other creatures with whom they shared the farm, their union was going to result in the arrival of young. The practicalities and even the responsibilities of parenthood hardly concerned Ferdie as month succeeded month and Mabel's condition remained their secret. To those familiar with her shape, always concealed by loose and bulky clothing, her pregnancy remained, even at this late stage, surprisingly undetected by those who lived and worked with her. When Gwennan accused her of getting fatter, Mabel simply replied that she was, as her mother and grandmother had been before her, a big eater.

Nevertheless it was she, rather than Ferdie, who was most concerned about their future.

'There's bloomin' Hester gettin' money from the Yanks for her baby while us'll get bugger-all for ours!'

'It's 'cos she be a widder-woman, Mabe, with no 'usband to fend for her nor her little 'un!' Ferdie seemed to Mabel to be inclined to sentimentalise Hester's situation, perceiving her as the young, defenceless victim, while Mabel was assumed to be tough and savvy enough to look out for herself and, presumably, for her offspring too.

'But I've got no 'usband, neither, Ferdie Vallance, in case you 'adn't noticed! And who's gonna look out for *me* and *my* baby, eh? And then there's little Arfur! Gran says the V2s is worse than them V1s was! At least you could hear the doodlebugs comin'! But there's no warning with these new ones and the craters is that big you could fit a double-decker bus in 'em, Gran says!' Ferdie hung his head.

'I does me best, Mabe. I dunno what more a bloke can do!' She leant across the table that was strewn with debris from their latest meal and ran a greasy finger over the stubble on Ferdie's unwashed cheek.

'I knows you does, lover. I knows you does.' They

smiled and soothed themselves with second helpings of spotted dick.

Somewhere in Mabel's simple mind lurked a vague notion that when her baby arrived everything would fall into place for her and Ferdie. For one thing, pressure would be put on them to marry. The other farmhands, Jack and Fred, had wives. Women who, for decades now, had been neatly installed in two of the three labourers' cottages, the third of which, since the death of first one, then the other of Ferdie's parents, had been occupied solely by him. What could be more right and proper than for Mabel to become his wife and move in with him? Surely Mrs Todd, Mrs Brewster and Mr Bayliss would, between them, see to all of that? Then, the only thing necessary to make life perfect for Mabel would be the absorption into her new family of her unacknowledged son.

So it was that, doggedly and diligently, during the weeks leading up to Christmas and to the inevitable moment when her child would make its first appearance in the world of the Post Stone farms, Mabel continued to work as hard as her increasingly bulky body would allow, her back aching, her bladder leaking, her distended belly coming between her and the cow she was milking.

'She looks just like Mrs Tiggy-Winkle!' Edward John said, remembering a childhood favourite and watching Mabel trot, rotund and amiable, across the yard. 'If you laid her on her side at the top of a hill, she'd roll all the way down!'

Margery Brewster planned her seasonal drinks party for the day before Christmas Eve, a day that happened to coincide with the first severe gale of the winter.

A violent west wind, carrying with it squalls of heavy rain, roared across the south-west peninsula, flooding villages, uprooting trees and marooning stock. The land girls, who had spent the afternoon driving the sheep up onto higher ground and moving the bullocks from a byre that was liable to flooding into the large barn at Lower Post Stone Farm, together with the cartload of swedes that would keep them fed until the water levels fell, returned to the hostel, soaked to their skins as the gale reached its peak and darkness began to fall.

On the heights of the forested land, within the thick walls of the woodsman's cottage, Christopher Bayliss, sitting at a table that was strewn with books, looked up from the volume that had been absorbing his attention and listened as a particularly violent gust racked the surrounding trees. He heard a splintering crack, as, somewhere in the twilight, a heavy branch split from a tree and crashed to the ground. He pulled on his weatherproof jacket and, taking his torch, went out into the noisy twilight to inspect the damage.

The sky in the west was just light enough for him to make out the shapes of low cloud streaking across the moor, while the woodland surrounding him was in almost total darkness. The shattered branch lay harmlessly fifty yards or so from him, the torn limb a stark white in the beam of his torch. An outhouse door had broken its catch and was banging in the wind. He secured it and began making his way back towards the cottage.

It was then that he saw, wavering towards him, a headlight, its beam moving erratically up the track and through trees that glistened eerily as the light swept across their streaming trunks. He caught the unmistakable sound of an engine and realised that the approaching vehicle was a motorbike.

It was obvious to him that the rider was having trouble negotiating the treacherous surface of the track, parts of which had already been washed out by the torrential rain, leaving rocks and the roots of trees exposed.

As the bike reached the top of the incline, Christopher caught, through the uproar of the gale, the unmistakable, groaning creak that signals the imminent fall of a doomed tree.

The ancient ash, which Christopher had recently discovered to be riddled with honey-fungus and had scheduled for felling, was being overwhelmed by a wind that had forestalled his axe. He caught the succession of splintering, shattering sounds as the massive trunk twisted and juddered. Then, for a long moment, the ash appeared to freeze and to hang, motionless, as though choosing the direction in which it would fall. At the precise moment when the tree began its descent, the trunk at first almost stationary while the upper branches moved, with increasing momentum, through the arc that would deliver them violently to the ground, Christopher saw the motorbike slew suddenly sideways off the track, the light from the blazing headlight becoming lost as it was engulfed in undergrowth.

The tree struck the ground immediately in front of Christopher and the tangle of fractured timber lay between him, the bike and its rider.

He fought his way through the smashed branches to the place where the machine lay on its side, embedded in the forest floor. The motorcyclist, protected by goggles and a leather helmet, had rolled free of the bike and was sitting on the ground beside it, apparently unhurt and extending to Christopher a heavily gloved hand.

'What the hell d'you think you're doing here?' he demanded furiously, relieved not to be faced with a mutilated corpse and pulling the rider upright as he spoke. 'Quite apart from risking your neck on a night like this, you're trespassing!' The motorcyclist pulled off the goggles and the leather helmet. For a moment Christopher didn't recognise the face that was laughing up at him, or the fall of dark hair that was shining in the torchlight.

'That was the best double take I've ever seen in my life!' Georgina, shouting over a noisy gust of wind, was laughing at the look of astonishment which had replaced the anger in Christopher's face. 'Hello, Chris!' she said. 'Yes! It's me!'

His expression, as he recovered from his surprise and took in her unexpected arrival and the manner of it, was not quite what she had anticipated. Although he was smiling down at her and was saying all the right things – about being glad to see her and relieved that she was unhurt – there was something about his eyes that was obvious to her, even in the moving torchlight. An evasiveness, almost a defensiveness, that reminded her suddenly of his father.

'It's my brother's,' she said, reaching down and struggling to pull the motorbike upright. 'You've seen it before. When he brought me up here last Christmas. Don't you remember? He'll kill me if I've damaged it!' Between them they righted the heavy machine and propped it on its stand. Georgina took the torch from Christopher, made a hurried examination of the bike, breathed a sigh of relief when her inspection confirmed that no obvious harm had been done to it and switched off the ignition. With the headlight extinguished, they were in almost total darkness.

'Aren't you going to ask me in?' She spoke easily enough but she felt the beginning of a sense of unease. He took her by the arm to steady her across the uneven ground, focusing the beam of his torch carefully onto its treacherous surface.

Inside the small, low-ceilinged space, he helped her out of the borrowed wet-weather gear, sat her beside his fire, uncorked a bottle of Chateau Neuf du Pape, poured her a glass and wished her a merry Christmas. She touched the rim of her wineglass against his and sipped thoughtfully, taking stock of his appearance.

He seemed different. Almost a year, she realised suddenly, had passed since she had seen him. Since then the slow recovery from his breakdown had continued. He looked fit and appeared to be stronger and more robust than she remembered, and very different from the stressed and exhausted creature he had been when she first met him, only weeks before the catastrophe that had put an end to his career in the RAF.

He seemed relaxed and sat watching her appreciatively. She had pulled off her muddy boots and was sitting on his sagging, sheepskin covered sofa, wearing slacks and a turtle-necked sweater, both of which were the same soft, blue-grey colour. The firelight illuminated her smooth skin and was reflected in her eyes. Her dark, damp hair framed her face and merged into the shadows. After they had exchanged a few pleasantries a silence fell between them.

'Perhaps I shouldn't have come,' she said finally, engaging his eyes and surprising him.

'Why ever not?'

'Because... I don't know,' she was sitting on the edge of the sofa, her glass in both her hands. 'But... I'd somehow got the impression you wanted me to.'

'I do want you to. What makes you think I don't?' She shook her head, half smiling.

'I don't know.' There was another pause 'You seem...sort of...complete, Chris. As though you don't need...interruptions.'

She had noticed that the table under the window was loaded with books of various shapes and sizes. There were piles of handwritten notes and a scatter of loose foolscap pages. She got to her feet and, carrying her wineglass, went to the table and examined the titles on the spines of the books. 'You're studying something!' she said, flicking through the pages of a thick textbook.

'Arboriculture,' he told her, watching her. 'The history and cultivation of trees. I'm not too bad on the practical side but I needed to mug up on the technical stuff if I'm to have any chance of qualifying for a job I'm after.'

'Very impressive!' Georgina said, realising that the tone of their conversation had reverted to the brittle, predictable exchanges of their early acquaintance, when their backgrounds had resulted in a relationship that neither had enjoyed but which had been irrevocably changed by his breakdown and her reaction to it. Before she could explore this situation, he spoke again. He had realised, he explained, while he had been living and working alone in the forest, that life had to go on after his crack-up.

'I had hoped, at one point, as you know, that it might have involved you. The "life going on" bit I mean. But...well, it didn't, did it? I mean, you went your way and I, after a while, found a way of my own and now I'm heading in that direction.'

She studied him for some time and then, embarrassed, returned to the sofa, arranged herself more comfortably than before and sipped her drink. She nearly told him how fine the wine was but didn't want their conversation to slide into chit-chat about the obvious delights of her favourite red.

'It's odd,' she said eventually. 'It's as if you have been three different people since I've known you.'

'Three?' he asked. He seemed, to her, to be only politely interested.

'Yes. The first was before your crack-up, when you were very stressed and so clever at hiding it that it was hard to see past the performance – the RAF hero and all that. The second was when you were sick. You were completely different then and I rather liked you.' He laughed and asked her whether that was because he had made her feel like Florence

Nightingale. She smiled, shook her head and then became serious again.

'You were...I don't know...you were sort of...'

'Needy,' he told her. 'You felt protective.'

'Not only.'

'No. Not only. You also felt sorry for me. And a bloke doesn't like it when his girl feels sorry for him.' Georgina shrugged. She was too honest to deny her feelings or the logic of his reaction to them.

'You were going through a bad time,' she said, and again they sat in silence while a gust of wind moved noisily up the valley and through the trees surrounding the cottage.

'Look, Georgie,' he began gently. 'I've been up here for over a year now, quietly getting myself back together in the only way I know how, while you,' he smiled at her, 'must have been having one hell of a time!'

'The ATA, you mean? Well, yes. It has been amazing. Incredible, really, when I think about it. Which, in fact, I seldom have time to do!' She was conscious of prattling on. 'I would never have considered myself capable of half the things I've done. I've met some fantastic people, and...'

'Georgie!' he interrupted her, 'You don't have to tell me! I know! I've done it! I know what fliers are like. All that gung-ho camaraderie. And the fear. The gut-wrenching fear. I know, more or less, what

298

happens to people in wartime.' He paused, smiling, she thought, slightly indulgently, at her. 'Believe me I do know how things have been for you this last twelve months.' He refilled his glass and drank fast. A first and possibly the only sign that his nerves were not quite as steady as she had thought. She would have preferred it if he had used the word 'guessed' instead of 'know'.

'Yes, of course you know what it's like. I didn't mean to suggest that you didn't. Sorry!' She wondered why she was apologising. Of course he didn't know precisely how it had been for her. Certainly not all of it. How could he? Nevertheless the tension between them seemed to have eased slightly. Christopher heaved himself up out of his deep armchair and lobbed a couple of pieces of wood onto his fire, dropped back into the chair, offered her a cigarette and, when she refused, lit one for himself.

'You'll have had experiences,' he said, flicking his spent match into the fire. 'And I don't only mean professional ones. I know what goes on. How the situation everyone is in intensifies feelings. Emotions get sharpened. Inhibitions get overridden. It's all part of what the war does to people. So, no doubt you will have had some "adventures".' He suddenly smiled. 'Don't feel guilty! I'm not the least bit jealous! Honestly!'

'As it happens you have no cause to be.' She

spoke quietly, staring into her half-empty wineglass. 'But you're right about the opportunities. There were lots of those.' He was looking at her with a new intensity, his cigarette burning down towards his fingers. 'The women I am working with are amazing. So professional. All, in their various ways, attractive, some beautiful. There was plenty of attention, if you wanted it. I noticed that the younger ones, whether or not they were married or even only spoken for, fell into two groups. Some of them were what my mother would call "free with themselves". One or two had long-term and very passionate affairs, usually with fliers. Others...didn't. I was one of those. I did, once, get very close to someone. We were going to spend a leave together. But, in the end, although I did have strong feelings for him at the time, I decided against it.' He was watching her closely.

'Why?'

'For a long time I didn't know! I still can't explain it. I felt... I don't know...as though there was something blocking my view of things. Something getting between me and...this guy. Something. Or someone.' She sat for a moment. 'Then,' she said, almost inaudibly, 'a few weeks ago, I realised what it was that was getting in the way. So you see, that was why...' She stopped and sat looking at him.

He had changed, she realised, over the months they had been apart. Of course he had. She had been a fool not to appreciate that in her absence and as the months passed, he would heal, physically and mentally. He had become, she understood suddenly, a third version of himself – the recovered Christopher. Like the first, he found her attractive. Unlike the second, he had thrown off the needy, forlorn, dependent version of himself, from whom, after she had played her part in his initial recovery, filling the gap left by his distant and disengaged father, she had withdrawn, disappointing him by forsaking the pacifism she herself had taught him and involving herself in a war he deplored. Now, a year older and although not too young to explore their own feelings, they were still too young to reveal their findings to each other or even, perhaps, to dare to try to define them for themselves. Possibly it was fear of damage that made them cautious, protecting themselves from exposure and not fully comprehending what was at stake. Unaware of how easily a faulty decision at this age can scar a lifetime.

Georgina, following her own path and focused on it, had not properly considered Christopher, unrealistically expecting him to remain in the curious, suspended state in which his breakdown had left him and in which, she had assumed, his feelings for her would not alter. 'You know where to find me,' he had said almost a year ago, and yes, here he was, geographically in the same place but not emotionally, she understood now, with a sense of shock. He had been in love with her. Her withdrawal from his life, when she turned her back on pacifism just as he was adopting it, had hurt him. But he had recovered from her. He had taught himself to live without her. She had stupidly expected him to be waiting to welcome her back. To hold out his arms to her and take her to bed.

She was ready for him now. Over the last months she had begun to understand herself and she knew what she wanted and who it was she wanted. But Christopher wasn't holding out his arms, nor did his expression suggest the reaction of a young lover to the immediate prospect of the consummation of his feelings for a girl with whom he had been in love for over a year.

She could have told him, almost without thinking and certainly without considering the consequences, that he was what had stood between her and the affair with Fitzy. Instead, she stood up and was about to shove her arms into the sleeves of Lionel's waterproof jacket when Christopher got quickly to his feet and took it from her.

'No, Georgie. Don't go. I need to explain to you what's happened to me. Where I've got to and what I have become. Sit down.' She sat, staring gravely at him.

'I feel so stupid,' she said.

'Why? You're not stupid! You couldn't possibly know the effect this past year has had on me! Perhaps I am this third person. The third version of myself that you were just talking about. Not the first version, the exhausted mess, strutting about, trying to be normal until I simply couldn't fly any more and everything fell apart. And not the second, the raving lunatic that you visited in the nut-house, or the recovering "walking-wounded" Christopher that I was a year ago...'

'And felt sorry for?'

'And felt sorry for, bless you.' He took her hand, kissed it briefly and gave it back. 'Bless you, Georgie, for doing that and being there! No one else was. My father couldn't cope with it, poor chap. He was, and still is, as embarrassed as hell about what happened to me. All that "lacking moral fortitude" stuff and going AWOL and getting discharged – it crucified him! He can't look me in the eye, Georgie! My own father! And you, darling, darling girl, were "sorry" for me! No. Don't apologise for that! It was a logical and a very sweet reaction. But not one that develops into a healthy love affair, right?' She could not contradict him.

'So...what now?' She asked him. 'What do you mean by "what I have become"? Are you going to stay up here in the forest and live like a hermit? Or become a priest? A missionary, perhaps? In darkest Africa?' They were laughing now.

'No. I'm going to emigrate,' he said, and saw her smile fade and her eyes widen in astonishment. 'I've got more studying to do and a thesis to write but, if things go according to plan, in a few months' time I'll be qualified for this job I've applied for. It's in New Zealand. Working for their Forestry Commission.' There was a long pause while Georgina stood, transfixed, her face blank, her lips slightly parted.

'Whoops!' Christopher smiled. 'Now who's doing the big double take?' She managed to laugh with him as he refilled her glass. He watched her take two gulps of the wine. Then she sat down on the sofa and stared into the fire.

'Well, that's wonderful!' she said eventually, conscious of trying to sound relaxed and positive, even slightly detached. 'I'd just...never thought...about you...not being here, somehow. And New Zealand couldn't be further away, could it, from all of us? All the people who have made you feel... How have we made you feel, Chris? And who, other than me, is involved?' She considered for a while. 'Your father is, of course. I could never understand the way he reacted when you...when you...'

'Cracked up?'

'Yes. And nor could Alice.'

'Alice?'

'Yes, Alice. She was very concerned about you and...and about him.'

'Was she? How very kind of her! But why about him?'

'She's fond of him, Chris. Possibly more than she realises, I think. Oh, please don't tell her I said that!'

'I mustn't tell *her* what *you* think *she* thinks of my father...?'

'The thing is – well, one of the things – is that although she is fond of him she feels that his treatment of you, when you...when you really needed him...was so awful that she, well...rather hated him! Everyone at the hostel did!' Christopher was almost laughing at her.

'That was extraordinarily supportive of you all! I had no idea how much effect my disaster was having!'

'Of course you hadn't. But they saw you, Chris, when the military police arrested you. They saw the state you were in! And they saw your father turn away, yes, literally turn away! No one could understand it. It was why I came to visit you in the hospital.'

'Because he refused to?'

'Right. Until the day he brought your discharge papers to you.'

'I remember,' he said. 'You came to see me that day, too, didn't you?' She nodded and then watched as he sat still, his mind digesting what she had told him.

'At the beginning,' Georgina said, 'Alice defended him. She was always certain there had to be a reason for him to behave as he did. But, as the months passed and you stayed up here, alone, and he stayed down there, alone, I think she felt there must be something lacking in him. Which I think is sad because...' She let the sentence hang. She could see that his mind was exploring another tangent.

'Yeah...well, my relationship with Pa has always been a bit dodgy,' he said. 'It started when we lost my mother. I think I reminded him of her too much – she and I were very alike, physically. Seeing me about the place made it harder for him to come to terms with her absence than if I hadn't been there. Which, a lot of the time, I wasn't, actually, what with boarding school and then flying school and then the RAF... Oh, he was very generous, all that sort of thing, but...it probably disappointed him when farming didn't appeal to me. Anyhow we were never what you'd call close. And then came the big one! I cracked up, went AWOL and ended up in a madhouse! I wasn't exactly every father's idea of the perfect offspring! Sons don't come much more disappointing than me!'

'Alice thinks there's more to it than that,' Georgina said.

'More? Heaven forfend, Georgie!'

'And you keep using the word "disappointment", Chris! Why? It's not "disappointing" when your son experiences what you went through. Alice thinks something must have caused your father to react as he did. As though there has to be some...some excuse for it.'

'And what do you think, Georgie?'

'I think it was unforgivable. And it still is unforgivable! And he deserves to lose you.' Christopher laughed. She was thinking that she, too, deserved to lose him.

'Well, it's true that it's largely because of him that I want to get away from here. I don't think I can face spending the rest of my life avoiding eyes that are so full of reproach.' He reached forward and flicked his cigarette stub into the fire. 'You never told me what it was that "got between you" and your affair with this flier fellow.'

For a moment she looked at him. Then she lowered her eyes and shook her head.

'Christ!' he said suddenly. 'It wasn't anything to do with me, was it?' She wasn't sure whether he would have been pleased if she had admitted that it had been because of him that she had withdrawn from her arrangement with Fitzy. Maybe, for Christopher, it would have complicated things. Muddied the waters of his apparently clear-cut decision to emigrate. He looked sharply at her, trying to read her, and then, sensing that his intensity was disconcerting her, busied himself refilling their glasses.

It would be so easy, Georgina realised, to admit that he was right and that her arrival at the cottage demonstrated her willingness to continue and further their relationship. In this scenario he would have been overwhelmed with happy surprise. He would have kissed her, they would have gone to bed and in the morning, over bacon and eggs, they would have discussed the future and he would have said, 'Come to New Zealand with me!' as though that would have been the easiest, happiest and simplest thing imaginable. Which, of course, they would both have known it was not.

A violent gust of wind howled through the trees and struck the solid old building. The door and the tiny windows rattled and creaked under the onslaught.

''Struth!' Christopher said 'I think you're stuck here for the night, Miss Webster! Oh, I'm not suggesting any impropriety! I have a bed in the room through that door and this sofa, I'm sure you will agree, is much more comfortable than it looks. So...no strings... Right?' They both knew there were strings. What they were uncertain of was how strong the strings were and where they would lead them. He got to his feet.

'And now I'm going to feed you! There's ham, cheese and pickle... Or a slice of Eileen's excellent game pie... The choice is yours.'

\* \* \*

Rose pulled the tray of mince pies from her oven and slid them onto the kitchen table where Dave, who had arrived home for Christmas an hour previously, was sitting, idly leafing through the local paper.

'These pies be for Mrs Brewster's party!' his mother announced, ''Er wanted for me to bake her some of my extra special ones. She give me the butter, a pound of sultanas, half a bottle of port and ten shillings for me trouble, 'cos she's too posh for to make 'em 'erself, I reckon. Or too tiddly!'

'Still knocking the gin back, be she?' Dave enquired listlessly.

'Reeks of it, she do! I'm never sure whether Alice don't notice it or just pretends not to, out of the kindness of 'er 'eart!' She was arranging the pies carefully in a basket. 'D'you remember Albertine?' she asked her son, glancing sharply at him in order to catch his reaction to the name.

'Albert who?'

'No, Dave! Albertine. Albertine Yeo. Eileen's niece. She were in your class at school. Lovely girl she's grown into. A real hourglass figure, she's got! She's gonna to be the parlourmaid at Mrs Brewsters' party. All dressed up in a black satin frock with white frills and a cap with ribbons, she'll be!' When there was no noticeable reaction from Dave, his mother sighed heavily and slammed her oven door. How long, she wondered, was this pining for Hester Tucker going to last?

The postman seldom had occasion to call at the Tuckers' smallholding but one morning a parcel was delivered into Hester's hands. It was about the size of a shoe box and was addressed to Miss Thurza Westerfelt.

'Who be there, Hester?' her father's thin voice called from the upstairs room in which his illness now confined him.

'Nothing, Father. Just a package from the seed merchant.' She bit her lip, for she had lied.

Thurza lay in her crib, waving her arms, and when Hester leant over her, greeted her mother with a amiable, toothless smile.

'Looks like you've got a Christmas present!' Hester said, stripping off the brown paper wrapping and lifting the lid of the cardboard box.

Until last year's Christmas, which Hester had spent at the Post Stone hostel, she had never, because the Pentecostal Brotherhood disapproved of such frivolity, given or received a Christmas present.

The rag doll had hair made of loops of yellow wool. Its eyes were bright blue glass beads and the rosebud mouth was outlined in crimson thread. Its dress was made of pink gingham and the long, floppy legs were sheathed in white stockinette with shoes embroidered onto the ends of them in black wool.

Hester held the doll out to her daughter who, young as she was, reached for it and pulled it down towards her mouth. 'No, Thurza!' Hester said, laughing. 'You mu'n't eat the dolly!'

Under the doll was a sheet of paper on which Dave Crocker had printed the words, *Dear Thurza, this is for your Christmas. Tell your Mama that I loves her truly and I always will do. Tell her I am here whenever she wants to come to us or I will fetch her anytime. She only needs to say the word.* Signed *D Crocker. Corporal*. Then he had written, *Her loving Dave* and added the date, which had been 10th December 1944.

Behind her, Hester's mother came silently down the stairs in her black stockinged feet, taking her daughter by surprise.

'What have you there?' she asked. 'Your father is expecting nothing from the seed merchant.' It was too late to hide the doll and Hester did not resist when her mother took it from her, turned and went soundlessly back up the stairs.

She stood, Dave's letter in her hand, until she heard her mother returning. Seconds before the woman re-entered the room Hester crumpled Dave's letter and threw it into the low fire that was smouldering in the grate.

'He says you'm to burn the doll,' her mother said, 'and if you will not do it, I must.' When Hester did not move, her mother carried the doll to the grate and laid it across the smoking wood. 'And now the letter,' she demanded. She had seen the letter in Hester's hand and assumed that she was concealing it. 'In your pocket, I suppose. Give it to me, Hester.' At that moment the sheet of paper on which Dave had printed his message and which until then had been curling and slowly turning black in the fireplace, suddenly ignited, yellow flames engulfing it and licking round the doll.

''Tis already burning, Mother,' Hester said.

Her mother, mistrusting her, peered into the flames until she was convinced that what Hester had said was true. Then she stared, her face as bleak as a bone, at her daughter, before turning away from her and creeping back up the stairs.

The Brewsters' party was in full swing when Alice and Roger arrived. Supper at the hostel had been delayed by the fact that the rain-soaked girls had taken longer than usual to get dry and warm before devouring the shepherd's pie Alice and Rose had prepared for them.

The path from the farmhouse porch to the gate where Roger's car stood had been awash after the heavy downpour, so rather than remove her evening shoes and put on rubber boots, Alice allowed Roger to carry her to the car and deposit her into it without her feet touching the muddy ground and with Rose and Annie smiling and nudging one another in the cross-passage.

For the occasion of her party, Margery had borrowed from Roger Bayliss not only his housekeeper, the reliable and competent Eileen, but her niece, Albertine. Eileen had produced platters of what she called her 'savouries', which the girl, her maid's uniform rather tight across her chest and around her thighs, was offering to the guests while Gordon Brewster, beaming at his door, greeted the familiar faces. Margery herself, already flushed and perspiring, was presiding over the punch bowl when Alice and Roger presented themselves.

'Punch!' she roared, and then lowered her voice to a stage whisper. 'Looks innocent enough but it has the kick of a mule, I promise you! It's based on an old family recipe handed down from Gordon's mama! But it seemed a bit lacking when I tasted it, so I beefed it up with a couple of bottles of brandy that Gordon didn't know I had! In they went, when the dear soul's back was turned!' She gave each of them a glass, filled two more and sailed off, slightly unsteadily, through a sea of guests, to meet and greet some new arrivals. Later, when several people were clearly feeling the effects of more alcohol than they were used to, Eileen and Albertine came through from the kitchen with plates of Christmas cake, cut into neat cubes, the dried fruit, candied peel and sugar for the marzipan and the icing, all having been carefully hoarded throughout the year.

In common with their fellow guests, both Alice and Roger felt mellow, relaxed and warm. Tomorrow was Christmas Eve. By evening most of the land girls would have left for their homes, Edward John had already arrived from his school, the news of the war was good, victory was in sight and the ambience in the Brewster house that evening was benign and optimistic. At nine o'clock the guests charged their glasses and wished one another a merry Christmas. Margery, Alice decided, was very sweet, Gordon, her husband, delightfully Dickensian as he stood, blushing, under the mistletoe.

'Roger,' Alice heard herself say, 'if I asked you to do something, would you agree to, without asking what it was?'

'Agree to...?' he asked, bemused. 'Without...?'

'You have to trust me!' Alice said. 'Don't you trust me?' For a moment he hesitated and then, with a feeling of immense pleasure, realised that, yes, he did trust her.

'Yes,' he said. 'Yes, I do! All right, what's the deal?'

'It's Christopher,' she said, leaning forward and

taking the lapel of his jacket between her finger and thumb so that, whatever happened next, she would have hold of him.

'Christopher?' he echoed blankly, his face clouding, unable to imagine anything that Alice could possibly ask of him that would involve his son.

'I cannot bear to think of him up there in the forest, all by himself in that isolated hovel for a second Christmas! Last year was a different matter. He had chosen to be alone while he recovered from his breakdown and I understood that you felt you had to humour him. But this year – no! Absolutely not! He is becoming a hermit! He need only stay for twenty-four hours or so but *I* insist that *you* insist that *he* spends Christmas Day at Higher Post Stone Farm and eats dinner with you, me and Edward John! I know I've already accepted your invitation but, if it doesn't include your own son, I shall withdraw that acceptance and Edward John and I will not, after all, join you! There! What do you say?' She was trying very hard not to laugh but he looked so affronted and shocked that however hard she fought to control it, the laughter kept erupting.

'Are you drunk, Alice?' he asked her, lowering his voice, glancing round at the other guests and hoping that none of them had noticed her extraordinary outburst.

'Possibly,' she admitted, 'and if I am I really do

apologise! Perhaps you should have a word with our hostess about the punch! Nevertheless, Roger, you agreed to do as I ask and what I ask is that you and I drive up to the woodsman's cottage, pick up Christopher and bring him home!'

'Now? Alice, are you insane? It's blowing a force eight gale out there and pouring with rain!'

'No,' she announced coolly, 'look.' Outside the window the sky had cleared and stars were visible.

'The track'll be washed out!'

'Then we'll use the farm truck.'

'But...your frock!'

'You can lend me your duffle coat and a pair of rubber boots. Come on! Say goodnight to Margery and Gordon!'

As they left the party and drove to Higher Post Stone Farm, Roger was laughing too.

'This is absurd, Alice!'

'I know! But isn't it fun?'

'What if he won't come with us?'

'Leave that to me. I can be formidably persuasive when the need arises!'

'So I've noticed!'

They found a warm coat for Alice and a pair of rubber boots that more or less fitted her. He led her out to the truck, helped her up into the cab and drove carefully out of the yard.

Although the rain had stopped, the lanes through

the valley were awash and the ditches overflowing. There were several places where Roger, swearing under his breath, had to negotiate shallow, fast-moving floodwater. Then, as the land rose and the engine laboured up the steep incline and into the forest, the state of the surface of the track became a problem, causing the truck to lurch wildly, lose traction and slew from side to side.

Roger, Alice noticed, now seemed to be enjoying himself. Perhaps it was the pleasure of meeting her challenge, of being as good as his word, a man capable of dealing, without flinching, with the darkness, the cumbersome vehicle and the treacherous terrain. She glanced at him, his profile was just visible in the greenish glow from the dashboard lights. She liked what she saw, reached across and patted the back of his hand as he gripped the wheel, gritted his teeth and controlled a dangerous slide on a patch of slippery clay.

They were almost there. The lights from the cottage windows, low as they were, were just visible, glimmering through the trees.

'Must have a word with that boy about his blackout!' Roger muttered, negotiating a final bend before the hillside levelled out.

It was here that they came upon the fallen tree, its upper branches effectively blocking the track. Roger swore under his breath.

'Looks as though we'll have to walk the last few hundred yards. Think you can manage that? It'll be pretty heavy going?' Alice thought she could and got down from the cab of the truck. It was then that she caught sight of the motorbike and at once recognised it as the one Georgina often borrowed from her brother.

'Looks as though Christopher has a visitor!' Roger said, shining his torch onto the mud spattered bike. 'Just shows how we misjudge people, Alice my dear! Here's you feeling sorry for the solitary boy and here's he, entertaining! Come on, then!' he said, putting his hand under her elbow. 'As we've come this far, lets go and give 'em a surprise!' But Alice took Roger's hand and guided the beam of the torch back onto the motorbike. She couldn't precisely recall the figures and letters of Lionel's number plate but the machine looked very familiar. Then she saw, protruding from the pannier, a glimpse of a rain-soaked scarf. A scarf which, she was absolutely certain, belonged to Georgina.

'I think not,' she said, firmly.

While she herself was delighted that Christopher and Georgina were together in such romantic and intimate circumstances, she wasn't certain what his father's reaction would be. Would his conventional, Victorian morals be affronted? Was he likely to be unimpressed by Georgina's behaviour, especially, as seemed likely to Alice, she might now be a potential daughter-in-law? 'No,' she repeated, leading Roger back to the truck, opening the door on the passenger's side and climbing up into the cab. 'I don't think we should barge in on them, Roger. Not tonight.' He pulled a face.

'Very well,' he sighed, unsure whether he was amused by Alice's change of mind, baffled, regarding the reason for it, or very slightly irritated by it. Like Professor Higgins in the Shaw play – he'd forgotten its name – he never could understand the workings of a woman's mind.

He had to reverse most of the way down the track which twisted his neck in an uncomfortable way and convinced Alice that now was definitely not the time to confess that she knew the identity of Christopher's visitor.

# Chapter Ten

Alice, embarrassed by what must have appeared to Roger to be incomprehensible behaviour on her part, felt guilty and was, without realising it, especially attentive and charming to him when they sat sipping milky Horlicks on either side of the warm Aga in his kitchen. She had changed out of the borrowed coat and boots and they found themselves giggling irresponsibly at the expense of their fellow guests at the Brewsters' party and at the surprising effect Margery's punch had had on some of them.

'I would never have thought the vicar's sister would prove to be such a brilliant exponent of the Charleston,' Roger said, conjuring the image of the usually staid woman who had, that evening revealed an unexpected side to her character. 'I had always thought of her as strait-laced and a bit dour...'

'Or that Margery could deliver Juliet's speech so movingly!'

'She almost brought tears to my eyes. I wonder how many other talents are concealed under bushels in this parish. It's amazing what a drop of alcohol can do!'

'On a slightly negative note,' Alice said more seriously, 'I am rather concerned about Margery's drinking, Roger.'

'She does put it away a bit,' he said easily, relaxed and warmed in his own kitchen, with Alice's presence pleasing him. 'Only on special occasions though, eh?' Alice thought better of telling him that when the registrar made her regular visits to the hostel, there was frequently a telltale whiff of gin on her breath.

Roger was enjoying looking at Alice, whose appearance, as a result of their foray up into the windswept forest, was slightly dishevelled. The touch of make-up she had applied before the party still highlighted her eyes and cheeks, while her hair, less confined than usual, was framing her face in a way that delighted Roger so much that he drew breath, intending to ask her, then and there, whether she would consider marrying him.

He planned strengthening his case by telling her that, in his opinion, Edward John was growing into a fine boy and that it would be his privilege to help prepare him for adulthood. He would confess to her that, for months now, he had thought of very little but how happy it would make him if she accepted his proposal. He was, in fact, so occupied by this silent rehearsal of his declaration that he was almost unaware that Alice was speaking to him. 'Sorry,' he apologised. 'Didn't quite catch that.'

'I was just saying,' she smiled, 'that I had a Christmas card today from the man Ruth introduced me to. You remember? The architect who is threatening to put me in touch with some contacts of his who will, he believes, employ me as a design consultant? Apparently they have some impressive new projects in the early stages of development. It won't be for ages, of course – certainly not until the war is over – but it's very much on the cards... Roger?'

'What?'

'Are you listening?'

'Certainly am!' He spoke brightly, disguising, he thought, his huge disappointment. She was planning to leave Ledburton. He was going to lose her.

'Only you look...' she hesitated, 'suddenly rather tired. Perhaps you should take me home?' He got to his feet, smiling gamely.

'Yes,' he said. 'Perhaps I should.'

To Alice's surprise, Rose was waiting up for her, filling her time by cutting neat crosses into the bases of the Brussels sprouts ready for Christmas dinner.

'The telephone kept on ringing, Alice,' she said. 'At first I didn't answer it but then I thought p'raps I'd better, in case anything 'as 'appened.'

'And has it?'

'In a manner of speaking, yes. It were Georgina's father. Seems she went out on 'er brother's bike and she bain't come 'ome. Leastways she 'adn't done when 'e telephoned. 'E wondered if she was 'ere 'cos 'e knows as she rides over to see you sometimes.' Rose was watching Alice's face.

'I'll go and 'phone him,' Alice said, locating her address book and torch, pulling on her rubber boots and preparing to cross the yard to the telephone. 'What...?' she asked, aware that Rose was staring at her.

'I reckon you knows where Georgina be!' Rose declared. ''Ow come you know, Alice? I mean to say, I can guess where she be, but I can tell by your face, that you *know*!'

Rose had to wait for Alice to return from the barn before she could satisfy her curiosity.

'What did you say to 'im?' she demanded. Alice sat down at the table.

'What would you have done, Rose, if...'

'If what?'

'If you knew where Georgina was but you also knew she would be in trouble if her father knew.'

323

'My goodness!' Rose was flushing with excitement. 'You think she be with Master Christopher, don't you?' She had never rid herself of the habit of referring to Christopher as she had done when he was a small boy.

'I'm certain she is! Her brother's motorbike was on the track near the woodsman's cottage. There were lights in the window and smoke coming from the chimney...'

'And what was *you* doing there?' Rose, who usually knew, more or less precisely, where everyone in the Ledburton area was – and why – had never been so baffled or intrigued in her life.

'Mr Bayliss and I drove up—'

'You and...? Drove? Up there? In this weather?'

'In the truck, Rose, yes. The rain had stopped. And the worst of the wind—'

'But, in the name of heaven, why would you do that?'

'It's complicated.'

'Certainly is!' Rose was enjoying herself. It wasn't often that she felt smarter than Alice. 'So it bain't only your girls as gets into scrapes round 'ere then, be it?' she purred.

'It was during the Brewsters' party,' Alice explained, 'that I suddenly felt concerned about Christopher being alone over Christmas. It seemed to me to be the perfect time to attempt a reunion – a sort of reconciliation between father and son! But I suspected that what with Mr Bayliss being how *he* is and Christopher being how *he* is—'

'I knows what you mean. Dead stubborn, the pair of 'em!'

Alice hesitated. She had always resisted discussing their employer's shortcomings with Rose. 'Well, yes,' she conceded, 'so I decided that if it was going to happen at all, I was going to have to make it happen. It was probably Margery's punch,' she added vaguely.

'What was?'

'It clouded my judgement. Gave me Dutch courage.'

'There was gin in it, then!'

'Brandy, actually,' Alice admitted ruefully. 'And lots of it!' Rose was thrilled. Her boss, her employer and probably most of the other guests at the Brewsters' party, all drunk as lords!

'So the two of you drove up to the forest and there they was, eh? Georgina and Christopher! Bet they was pleased to see you! Whatever did they say when you two turned up?'

'We didn't.' Rose stared at Alice in disbelief.

'You mean...you snuck off? Just got back in the truck and...' Rose's pleasure was complete. She shook her head, buried her face in her apron and laughed as Alice had never heard her laugh before. 'I can just see

the two of you creepin' away! Like a pair of naughty...'
She stopped abruptly. Alice looked so stricken with
embarrassment and concern that it seemed to Rose to
be unkind to be enjoying the story so hugely. 'No real
'arm done though, lovey, eh?' she said, collecting herself.
'I reckon Mr Bayliss should be proud of 'is boy! 'Avin'
it away with a lovely girl like Georgina!'

'The thing is, he doesn't know it was Georgina!
He wanted to knock on the door but I wouldn't
let him! All he knows is that it's someone with a
motorbike. He probably thinks it's an old school
friend of Christopher's, or an RAF colleague.'

'So how come you're so sure it was 'er? It might
of bin 'er brother Lionel, mighten it?' Or anyone with
a motorcycle, come to that?'

'No. It was definitely Lionel's bike, and Georgina's
scarf – that royal blue cashmere one she was given
for her birthday – was hanging out of the pannier,
Rose. It had to be her!' There was a pause while Rose
applied her shrewd mind to the whole, fascinating
scenario. After some moments of thought she asked
Alice what she had said to Georgina's father.

'What could I say?'

'You could of told 'im the truth... But you didn't,
did you?'

'Not quite.'

'Well, what did you tell the poor man?'

'That a tree was blocking a lane and Georgina

had been forced, by the storm, to take shelter with friends but that she was quite safe and I was certain she would return home as soon as she possibly could. Well, most of it was true!' Rose, unconvinced, shook her head reproachfully.

'And what did he say to that?' she asked. 'Didn't he want to know where this fallen tree's to and who his precious daughter be with?'

'Yes. I expect he did. But—'

'But? But what?'

'But I pretended the line had gone dead. I kept saying "Sorry, I can't hear you," and then I hung up. I left the receiver off the hook so that if he telephones again he'll think the lines have come down in the gale.' She looked at Rose's self-righteous face. 'Oh, I know, Rose! It was dreadful of me! What would you have done?'

'Lord knows! But then I bain't so quick and clever as what you are, Alice!' They sat in silence for a while before Rose added magnanimously, 'I reckon, all things considered, you done right. And now you'd best just sit tight and keep mum!'

'But supposing that when Georgina gets home her parents tell her they spoke to me on the phone! Georgina will know I'd lied! And she'll know I knew where she had been! Oh, heavens! It's true, isn't it, what they say about weaving a tangled web when we practice to deceive!'

'Grandma Crocker allus said as you needed to be sharp as a tack if you was goin' to lie and get away with it. But Georgina bain't stupid, Alice. She'll think of something.'

The early morning of Christmas Eve was mild and windy. The girls were to work until midday, when the lorry would deliver them to Ledburton Halt to catch trains to their various hometowns.

'I get to Paddington at four o'clock, Mrs Todd,' Annie had announced at supper a few days previously. 'Hector's meeting me and I'm taking him home to meet my mum and dad.'

'What? That posh bloke?' Marion queried, with her mouth full of fish pie, which, as a result of a disappointing delivery from the fishmonger, contained less fish and more potato than usual.

'Yeah. Why not?' Annie answered, colouring slightly.

''Cos you know what happens with you and posh blokes!' Gwennan smirked, remembering Annie's brief and painful affair with Georgina's brother.

'Hector's not stuck up like Lionel!' Annie protested. 'And anyhow, my Grandad Sorokova knows some of the Polish war artists that Hector's been working with. Hector says he's very keen to meet him, so there! I reckon he'll like my folks!'

'But will 'is folks like *you*?' Gwennan snapped

back, her barbed tongue finding its mark.

'Maybe they will and maybe they won't,' Annie said defensively, ignoring the cynical smiles of the other girls.

'Why wouldn't they like her?' Mabel demanded, holding out her plate for seconds. 'What's not to like about our Annie? She's lovely!'

'Yeah, but she's common, Mabel,' Marion explained dismissively to the plump, baffled girl. 'And 'is folks is prob'ly even posher than what 'e is. So if 'e ever takes 'er 'ome with 'im, they'll most likely give her the cold shoulder!'

The same thought had occurred to Annie. In the course of one of their early conversations Hector had told her that his father was a don in an Oxford college. She had searched for the word in the dictionary Georgina had given her and been daunted by one of the definitions, which read 'a senior member of staff at Oxford or Cambridge', which sounded, to Annie, ominously lofty.

She knew that Hector's mother had died when he and his brothers were still schoolboys and that they lived with their father in the family home together with his elderly sister. Annie had assumed that this woman acted as a surrogate mother to the Conway boys and managed the household for their father. What she did not know was that Sybilla Conway was herself an academic and that domesticity was not one of her fortes.

Over the years, Sybilla had allowed the rooms, which were always overflowing with books, manuscripts, paintings, prints and a sprawling and as yet uncatalogued collection of fossils, to descend into near chaos. Nevertheless it was a happy house where a Mrs Potter, known affectionately as Pottie, kept the four men, plus the one eccentric woman, warm and fed. Pottie dealt with the laundry and did her best to keep the stacks of books under control and the floors swept. None of this was at all what Annie expected the Conway's home to be. Consequently she was, for all the wrong reasons, nervous, when Hector had suggested that one day soon, when she had some leave, he would take her there to visit them.

A repeat of last year's weather, when, on Christmas Eve, a blizzard had put paid to the land girls' plans and marooned them in the snowbound farmhouse, seemed unlikely. On that Christmas Day, Alice's almost empty larder had been miraculously replenished with lavish supplies provided by an American army training base whose personnel were also, because of the snow, in effect confined to barracks. To the astonishment of the stranded girls, twenty or so GIs had arrived at the farm on Christmas morning in a Bren gun carrier laden with cooked hams and turkeys, plum puddings, muffins, pastries and cookies. They brought crates of beer and Coca-Cola and Alice had been presented with a bottle of champagne.

The riotous party had continued all day and, unabated, had carried on into the evening. Marion had met and boogied with Marvin Kinski while Rose's Dave, on a 48-hour pass, had danced every dance with Hester Tucker, only hours before Reuben, after trudging for five hours through the snow to keep his date with her, arrived and slid onto the third finger of her left hand, a pretty ruby ring that had belonged to his grandmother.

This year, only Alice and Edward John, together with Gwennan, Elsie and Eva, who had volunteered for milking duty over Christmas, were to remain at the farm.

Mabel's grandmother and little Arthur had already travelled down from London and were installed in Ferdie's cottage. Rose would cook a capon at the hostel while Alice and Edward John were to join Roger Bayliss for Christmas dinner at the higher farm.

Ferdie had procured, possibly feloniously, a piglet for his guests. Butchered and prepared for roasting on a spit, it would rotate inches from his red-hot range while potatoes were baking to a golden brown in his oven.

'What you wrapped up like that for?' Gwennan demanded that morning, glaring at Mabel, who was balancing her considerable bulk on a creaking milking stool. 'You got on so many clothes you can hardly fit on that stool! Any minute now it'll fall to bits under the weight of you! And it's not even cold, Mabel! What's the matter with you?'

Mabel buried her face in the cow's side and said nothing. Freezing weather in early December had enabled her to continue to conceal the evidence of her now-advanced pregnancy under several layers of jackets, coats, scarves and waterproofs. But the temperature had risen over the last few days during which she had not only been far too hot but was so constricted by these layers of clothing that she could barely move. She now looked almost completely rotund and was becoming increasingly uncomfortable. She knew, instinctively and from experience, that the birth of her secret child was imminent. She bit her lip and tugged at the cow's teats.

Several times, over the past few months, Mabel and Ferdie had attempted to address their situation. Their discussions always foundered when they reached the uncompromising certainty that if Mabel confessed to being pregnant she would have been instantly dismissed from the Land Army, forcing the pair of them and the coming child to survive on Ferdie's meagre wage.

'I can't hardly live as it is,' Ferdie had told her each time she had raised the question of their immediate future. ''Ow can I feed a wife and child on what I earns?'

'But what'll we do, Ferdie?' She had been sitting beside his fire, running her calloused hands over the protrusion that overflowed her lap. 'She's not gonna stay in 'ere much longer! And that Gwennan Pringle knows there's some'at up! Any minute now she's gonna guess and she'll go to the warden and she'll say, "That Mabel Hodges be in the family way, Mrs Todd and what are you gonna do about it?" And Mrs Todd'll go to Mrs Brewster and Mrs Brewster'll go to Mr Bayliss and...'

'She?' Ferdie asked, looking sharply at the worrying bulge. 'You said "she", Mabel. Don't reckon 'tis a girl, do ee? 'T won't be no girl! Us Vallances don't 'ave girls! 'T will be a boy, my lover! A fine big boy! Or I'll want to know the reason why!' Mabel stared at him in amazement. The sex of the coming child seemed to her to have very little bearing on their difficulties.

In the woodsman's cottage, Christopher had been the first to wake. He was immediately conscious of Georgina, curled against him. They were lying on their left sides, like two spoons in a cutlery drawer. He had never imagined that on the dilapidated sofa, piled with old cushions and sheepskins, where he had so often slept alone, there would be room for two. And not only room, but that two could be so divinely accommodated by its sagging contours.

Georgina was sleeping soundly, her left arm stretched out over the edge of the sofa, her right arm folded against her chest. Christopher's arm was round her, his fingers loosely holding her right wrist. Her breathing was almost imperceptible.

The two of them fitted so perfectly together that Christopher decided that, after their months of estrangement, he could not risk losing this intoxicating closeness and would never move again. He would lie, quite still, for ever, sublimely conscious of the concave line of Georgina's ribcage from her bare shoulder to where the convex curve of her hip began. He carefully inhaled the smell of her hair and, with the tip of his tongue, tasted the skin at the nape of her neck. The sun could rise, move to its low, winter zenith, and then lose itself in the murk of a midwinter sunset and still he would not move. He dozed, blissfully, while the light through the small, uncurtained window, slowly increased.

Then she was awake. Inhaling luxuriantly and rolling onto her stomach where she lay, propped on her elbows, looking down into his face. They smiled. Their eyes met and held. Then she sighed and said she must go because her parents would be worried about her. He extricated himself from the sheepskins and, wrapping his faded dressing gown around himself, opened the fire, which, well stoked on the previous night, began to draw vigorously. The water in the filled kettle, already hot, seethed as he spooned tea into an old porcelain pot he had discovered, together with numerous ancient bottles, dumped in the yard and had kept because, although it was chipped and lidless, he liked the pansies that were painted on it.

'Tea,' he announced. 'You must at least have a hot drink before you go.' She was out of the bed and pulling on her clothes, her body lithe and luminous in the wintry morning light.

She glanced at Christopher as he fetched milk from the linhay and set cups on the table. He was naked under his dressing gown, his hair dishevelled, his face relaxed but intent on what he was doing. She felt a surge of pleasure at the prospect of a thousand future mornings when she would enjoy this image of him. Seating herself at the table, she watched him pour the tea.

'What will you tell your folks?'

'The truth.' She answered without hesitation.

'Will they be angry with us?'

'They'll probably be surprised.' She sipped carefully at the hot tea. 'But they'll have to accept it, sooner or later.'

'Accept what, exactly?'

'Us. The fact that we've got this far.'

He was tempted to ask her to define how far that was but rephrased his question.

'And will that be enough for them?'

'It will have to be. Don't rush me, Chris!' She smiled and blew him a kiss across the table.

'I'm not, honestly! I just don't want them to think—'

'What? That your intentions are dishonourable? I promise to assure them that they're not! In fact, I'm the one whose behaviour could be perceived as dishonourable, aren't I? I mean, people are always accusing me of trifling with your affections!'

'Are they? Who, for instance?'

'Well,' she hesitated, 'Rose, for one.'

'Rose? Rose Crocker?' He was astonished and could barely control his amusement.

'And Alice.'

'Ah. Alice. Her views seem to feature strongly these days! What Alice thinks about my pa and now what she thinks about you and me!'

'She's a good person, Chris. I admire her. So of course I listen to her and value her opinions. She likes you. She's always thought that you and I should, well...at least take each other seriously. In fact, I believe she thinks we love each other.'

'And don't we?'

'This tea's too hot. Put some more cold milk in it, please. I must go home!'

'Don't we, Georgie?' he persisted, half serious and gently challenging her, as he added the milk to her tea.

'Well, I do.' she said gravely, meeting his eyes. 'I really do, Chris.'

'And I do! So good old Alice got that right, bless her!'

'It's just that...' she hesitated. He waited, paying her serious attention while she sorted out her feelings. 'It's just that there have been so many versions of you since we met! You, before you cracked up. You really messed up. You recovering but still a bit...you know...' He nodded. 'And you now. Fit and fine and focused on the future...'

'And on you. But then I always was focused on you, madam, as well you know!'

'But what I mean is...you confuse me! Are there any more of you out there? And if so, will I like them?'

'You'll like one!'

'Which one?'

'He's a lovely old chap! Eighty-five if he's a day! Silver hair, all his own teeth...and he adores you! Always has. Always will! So? What d'you reckon?'

She was on her feet, laughing, reaching for the borrowed wet-weather gear, locating the goggles and helmet.

'I reckon if I don't get home pretty soon, my folks will have organised a search party and how embarrassing would *that* be?'

He held the heavy coat as she thrust her arms into

it and then turned her to face him, took her in his arms and kissed her.

They skirted the fallen tree. Christopher kick-started the motorbike and satisfied himself that it was in good order after its night in the rain. The track, although strewn with debris, was reasonably dry. He warned her to take extra care on the steep decent to the valley floor.

'Is there petrol in your truck?' Georgina asked him, astride the bike and shouting over the noise of its engine.

He nodded. 'Pa insists that it's kept topped up in case of emergencies. Why?'

'I want to introduce you to my parents. Will you come for Christmas dinner? There'll be a goose. Will you? Please? My father won't set the dogs on you, I promise!'

'In that case how can I refuse!'

He stood listening while the sound of the motorbike dwindled away down the hillside. Then he climbed onto a tree stump, filled his lungs and delivered to the forest in a robust baritone all six verses of 'God Rest Ye Merry Gentlemen'.

He made porridge, located saws and axes and by midday had cleared the branches of the fallen tree so that the track was passable and he would be able, the next day, to drive the truck to Georgina's home.

* * *

'Boss wants you two girls to take a load of straw up the lambing pens,' Jack shouted to Mabel and Annie as they hosed down the last of the milking stalls. 'Soon as you'm finished 'ere, he says. The cart be loaded ready, so look lively.'

'But I'll miss me train,' Annie wailed.

'Not if you gets your finger out, you won't!'

Lion, the heavier of the two shire horses, leant his great shoulders into the incline and heaved the cart steadily uphill towards The Tops, where the byre used for lambing stood with its back to the north wind. Annie eased the cart in, as close as possible to the entrance. Anxious to get the job done in time to catch her train, she began heaving the straw off the cart and into the byre where they were to spread it across the dry, earth floor.

'Come on!' she urged Mabel, who seemed to be making very heavy weather of the work. 'Put your back into it, Mabe, or I'll never get to London!'

It was half an hour later, as they spread the last of the straw, that Mabel's waters broke.

'Whatever is the matter?' Annie asked. 'Are you poorly or what?'

Mabel stood, hunched forward, her palms on her knees, and groaned loudly, the amniotic fluid pooling between her feet. Annie watched, aghast.

'Mabel! You've piddled yourself!'

'It's not piddle, Annie!' Mabel gasped, recovering

from the contraction. 'It's me waters 'as broke! It's me baby coming!'

When Annie stood gaping, Mabel pulled open her bulky jacket and cupped her hands around the bulge that she had managed to conceal for so long. 'What d'you think this is?' she asked, gathering herself for the next contraction and then staggering under the impact of the pain. Annie, left with no time to react to the astonishment and shock she was feeling, grasped Mabel's flailing hands in hers and supported her.

'Quick,' she said, as the contraction passed. 'Get onto the cart! We gotta get you back to the farm!' But Mabel was breathing hard and shaking her head.

'No!' she said. 'No time, Annie! Arfur come quick! This one's no different! Oh... Ow!' She doubled up again and pushed Annie away from her as though her intrusion into the sequence of pain and then no pain was a hindrance to the arrival of the child.

When the third contraction had passed she waddled into the byre and, by the time the next one began, had lowered herself carefully onto the straw, set her back to the rough, stone wall, drawn up her knees and was preparing to push, her sweating face twisting and turning puce with pain and exertion.

Apart from watching a feral cat deliver a litter of kittens in one of the farm mangers, which, compared with what was happening to Mabel, had been a comparatively simple and almost charming occasion,

Annie was unfamiliar with the process of childbirth. Mabel's situation terrified her. She could not believe that a human being could survive such an appalling experience. Mabel was obviously about to die and Annie felt totally helpless, useless and scared. She knelt down in the straw beside the gasping, writhing creature that Mabel Hodges had become.

'What do I do? Tell me what to do!' Annie beseeched her.

'Nothing!' Mabel puffed, managing a faint, breathless smile. 'Not yet! Wait! I'll tell you when!'

It was a short labour and a violent and noisy delivery but suddenly there was a small, glistening thing squirming in the straw and Mabel was reaching forward and scooping it into her arms where it screwed up its angry crimson face and gave a great yowl of protest at this sudden exposure to an inhospitable and confusing world. Mabel quickly checked that the child had the right number of arms, legs, ears and eyes and then pointed to a pair of shears hanging from a nail on the drystone wall.

'What d'you want them for?' Annie asked, feeling suddenly faint.

'To cut the cord,' Mabel told her.

'You can't use them, Mabel! They're for shearing sheep! They're rusty!'

'Just give 'em here, Annie! And a twist of that binding twine off of the straw bales. Ta.'

Annie flinched as Mabel snipped the hose-like connection between herself and her child, tied it off, wrapped the infant in her cardigan and cradled it against her huge breasts.

'How-do, Scarlet O'Hara!' she said sweetly, smiling into the hideous little face. 'How-do, Scarlet O'Hara Vallance.'

Mabel had made an agreement with Ferdie. If their child was a girl, she could choose her name. If it was a boy, as Ferdie was certain it would be, he would be christened Winston Ferdinand Horace.

'We best go back down to the farm now, Annie,' Mabel said, hauling herself to her feet. 'I'll get in the cart and you drive Lion.'

Annie, her knees wobbling so strangely that she could barely stand, managed to do as she was told. Her respect for Mabel was enormous. She settled the mother and the child on what was left of the straw, flicked Lion's reigns and began the steep, awkward descent to Higher Post Stone Farm, the cart pitching and rolling down the uneven track.

At first they travelled in silence. Then, from time to time, Annie heard Mabel give a deep groan. After a while and when the groans had become more frequent, she said, breathlessly, 'You best stop, Annie, 'cos I reckon there's another one comin'!'

The boy, a lusty twin for Scarlet O'Hara, came slithering onto the straw moments later. The shears were at the byre so they wasted no time in wrapping the little boy in Annie's jacket and encouraging Lion into a dangerous trot.

An hour later Mabel was sitting up in the double bed in the Vallance cottage with a robust, pink baby in the crook of each of her plump arms while Ferdie stood, bursting with unrealistic pride, beside her.

'She was just wonderful, our Mabel!' Annie, her colour restored, told Alice when Fred collected her and drove at breakneck speed to the station. 'She was so brave! And she knew exactly what to do! But it was awful, Mrs Todd, and I'm never, ever going to have a baby myself! Never, ever. That's for sure!' They got Annie to the station seconds before the London train pulled out.

Eileen located a cradle and a crib, together with a plethora of other useful nursery items dating from the days of Christopher's infancy, from the attics of Higher Post Stone Farm, and between them, she, Mrs Fred and Mrs Jack contrived to produce, for the fortunate infants, nappies, nighties, bootees, shawls, blankets and even a couple of knitted matinee jackets, that were only very slightly moth-eaten.

Rose, who had trudged up from the lower farm, was sure she had, packed away somewhere, not one but two Christening robes. 'The older one was Grandma Crocker's!' she announced. ''T will 'ave turned a bit yellowish after all this time, I daresay, but a soak in a drop of bleach'll bring it up lovely, you'll see!'

Two by two, before they left for Christmas with their families, the land girls had climbed the steep stairs to Ferdie's bedroom to pay their respects to the babies and their beaming parents. Alice, meanwhile, who had arrived at the higher farm just as the doctor was leaving, and having assured herself that all was well with both mother and children, allowed Roger to lead her into his sitting room, where Eileen brought them a tray of coffee and biscuits.

They sat discussing the future of the suddenly and significantly enlarged Vallance family.

'It's astonishing that no one knew!' Alice exclaimed. In hindsight, Mabel's increasing girth should have attracted more attention than it had and almost certainly would have done, had she not always been so rounded.

'We'll have to get them decently married if they're to stay here,' Roger said firmly. 'Very quietly and as soon as possible. I'll telephone the vicar.'

'But what will they live on?' Alice wanted to know, as much for her own peace of mind as anything. 'The Ministry will have Mabel out of the Land Army in no time!'

'The thing is...' Roger began, thoughtfully stroking his chin. 'My manpower situation is going to need rethinking when this caper is over. It seems likely to me that a lot of the lads who were farm labourers before they were called up won't want to return to the land. Their experiences in the forces, not to mention the various skills they'll have picked up, will have changed their outlook on life. Made them more ambitious. Whereas some of the girls – your Annie Sorokova, for an example – might well be inclined to take up careers in farming.'

'Not Mabel, though,' Alice smiled. 'I haven't noticed her studying for any Ministry of Agriculture exams!'

'No. But she's a useful and hard-working member of my workforce, Alice, and she's already virtually running the dairy. I took her over to Tom Lucas's place the other week. He's recently installed a milking machine. He showed Mabel how it works and she grasped the mechanics of it in no time! She's not stupid, that girl. Just uneducated. She took to operating that equipment like a duck to water!'

'Did she? How splendid! So...are you going to offer her a job?'

'I'm seriously considering it. With a bit more training I think she's up to it. I've done the sums. With her wages, plus Ferdie's, plus the cottage, they should manage well enough.'

'But what about the babies? The twins won't raise themselves, you know!'

'Mabel can arrange her hours round the milking schedule, and there's Eileen, Mrs Jack and Mrs Fred, don't forget. All motherly souls. They'll help out... What?' he paused, catching Alice's reaction to this. She was looking amused and mildly disapproving. 'Farm labourers' wives do this, Alice! Always have! They mind each other's babies and take their toddlers with them into the harvest fields if necessary! Get the nippers working as soon as they can walk, bless them!'

'How fortunate for you!' she was laughing at him and he felt slightly and briefly embarrassed.

'You know, Alice,' he smiled, 'you would have made a formidable suffragette!'

'Wouldn't I! Pity I got my timing wrong!' But she leant towards him and squeezed his arm. 'I think it's a great plan, Roger!' He put his own hand on top of hers and they sat that way for a moment.

He gathered himself together, preparing to enquire about her plans for a post-war career and to ask her whether she would consider marrying him. Since the consultancy work that clearly meant a lot to her might not be a full-time commitment, he hoped she would consider retaining a small flat in London for when she was required to be there, while spending the rest of her time with him at Higher Post Stone Farm. But just as he was about to speak, Eileen appeared in the doorway and asked if they'd finished with the coffee tray.

Alice got to her feet and Roger, deprived for a

second time within twenty-four hours of the moment when he had been about to make his proposal, found himself offering to drive her down to the lower farm.

'Thank you,' she said, 'but first I must go and drool over these babies.'

Edward John, fresh from a performance as Melchior in his school's nativity play, stood, astonished and smiling, at the foot of Ferdie's bed.

Both babies were sleeping soundly, one in the crook of each of Mabel's arms, which, clearly, had been designed for precisely that purpose, while Ferdie began telling Edward John how strongly young Winston resembled his own father.

'Horace, my pa were called,' he announced, not for the first time that morning, 'and a more handsome fella you couldn't wish to meet! So Horace is to be me son's third name, Edward John. First Winston, after Mr Churchill, second Ferdinand, after me, and third Horace, after me pa, see!'

'And what's the little girl's name?' Edward John enquired.

'Oh, just plain Scarlet O'Hara, she be,' Ferdie said. 'Should rightly of bin Ruby in remembrance of me ma but no, Scarlet O'Hara she is to be called, after the lady off of the pictures!'

Edward John stared at the baby girl's jelly-bean

cheeks, the fluffy halo of silky, gingerish hair, and failed to make a connection between this Scarlet O'Hara and the raven-haired, crimson-lipped beauty, dressed in a white crinoline and with a dark green velvet ribbon round her tiny waist, with whom he had recently fallen in love in the stuffy darkness of the one-and-ninepenny seats of the cinema in Exeter.

'It's just like "Away in a Manger", isn't it?' he said, turning excitedly to his mother as she entered the bedroom and joined the group of admirers at the foot of the bed. 'Except we've got a Mabel instead of a Mary and two baby Jesuses!'

The light of friendship during their darkest hour

MUDDY BOOTS
*and*
SILK STOCKINGS

JULIA
STONEHAM

*a&b*

## WWW.ALLISONANDBUSBY.COM

For more information and to place an order, visit our website
where you'll also find free tasters, exclusive discounts,
competitions and giveaways.
Be sure to sign up to our monthly newsletter to
keep up-to-date on our latest releases,
news and upcoming events.

Alternatively, call us on
020 7580 1080
to place your order.